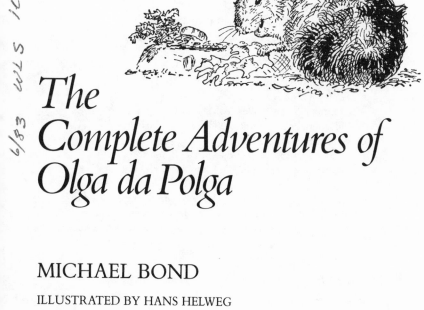

The Complete Adventures of Olga da Polga

MICHAEL BOND

ILLUSTRATED BY HANS HELWEG

DELACORTE PRESS / NEW YORK

Published by
Delacorte Press
1 Dag Hammarskjold Plaza
New York, N.Y. 10017

THE TALES OF OLGA DA POLGA, OLGA CARRIES ON,
OLGA TAKES CHARGE, and OLGA MEETS HER MATCH
were first published in Great Britain by Kestrel Books.

THE TALES OF OLGA DA POLGA:
    Text copyright © 1971 by Michael Bond
    Illustrations copyright © 1971 by Hans Helweg
OLGA CARRIES ON:
    Text copyright © 1976 by Michael Bond
    Illustrations copyright © 1976 by Hans Helweg
OLGA TAKES CHARGE:
    Text copyright © 1982 by Michael Bond
    Illustrations copyright © 1982 by Hans Helweg
OLGA MEETS HER MATCH:
    Text copyright © 1973 by Michael Bond
    Illustrations copyright © 1973 by Hans Helweg

Manufactured in the United States of America

First U.S.A. printing

Library of Congress Cataloging in Publication Data

Bond, Michael.
    The complete adventures of Olga da Polga.

    Contents: The tales of Olga da Polga — Olga meets her match —
Olga carries on — Olga takes charge.
    1. Children's stories, English. [1. Guinea pigs — Fiction. 2. Short
Stories.] I. Helweg, Hans, ill. II. Title.
PZ7.B6368Co   1983   [Fic]   82-72753
ISBN 0-440-00981-2

CONTENTS

The Tales of Olga da Polga

Olga Meets Her Match

CONTENTS

Olga Carries On

Olga Takes Charge

The Tales of Olga da Polga

CHAPTER ONE

Olga Sets Out

From the very beginning there was not the slightest doubt that Olga da Polga was the sort of guinea-pig who would go places.

There was a kind of charm about her, something in the set of her whiskers, an extra devil-may-care twirl to the rosettes in her brown and white fur, and a gleam in her eyes, which set her apart.

Even her name had an air of romance. How she had come by it was something of a mystery, and Olga herself told so many fanciful tales about moonlit nights, castles in the air, and fields awash with oats and beautiful princesses – each tale wilder than the one before – that none of the other guinea-pigs in the pet shop knew what to believe.

However, everyone agreed that it suited her right to the very tips of her fourteen toes, and if some felt that it wouldn't come amiss if Olga was taken down a whisker or two it was noticeable none of them tried to do it, though many of them talked of the dangers of going out into the world alone, and without the protection of the humans who normally looked after them.

'You can't do without the *Sawdust People*,' warned one old-stager known as Sale or Return, who'd lived in the shop for as long as anyone could remember and was always listened to with respect because he'd once been away for two whole days. 'It's a cold, hard world outside.'

But Olga would have none of it. 'You can stay here

if you like,' she would announce, standing in the middle of the feeding bowl in order to address the others. 'But one of these days *I'm* going. Wheeeee! Just you wait. As soon as I see my chance I shall be away.'

Olga was never quite sure whether she really believed her words or not, but she liked the sound of them, and secretly she also rather enjoyed the effect they had on the others.

Each night, before she settled down in the straw, she would look at her reflection in the water bowl, puffing out her cheeks and preening herself so that she would look her best if any likely looking customers came along.

And then it happened.

Quite unexpectedly, and not at all in the way Olga had always pictured it.

There were no grand farewells.

There was no battle royal.

No wild dash for freedom.

There were no cheers whatsoever.

In fact it was all over in a flash.

One morning, just as Olga was in the middle of her breakfast, a shadow fell across the cage and she looked up and saw a row of faces outside staring in at her.

There was the Sawdust Person she knew as the owner of the pet shop; a man she had never seen before; and a small girl.

It was the girl who caught Olga's gaze as she looked up from the feeding bowl, and as their eyes met a finger came through the bars.

'That's the one,' the girl said. 'The one with the cheeky look and the oats sticking to her whiskers.'

The door in the roof of the cage clanged open and a rough, hairy hand descended.

'She's yours for twenty-two and a half new pence,' said the gruff voice of the pet-shop owner, grabbing hold of Olga. 'To tell the truth I shan't be sorry to see the back of her. She's been a bit of a trouble-maker ever since she came in.'

Olga gave a squeak of outrage and alarm, and as she disappeared from view, kicking and struggling, some

of the older guinea-pigs nodded their heads wisely with an 'I told you so' expression on their faces.

But many of the younger ones looked rather envious, for when your world is only two foot square almost anything else promises to be more exciting. Some of them were put off their food for the rest of the morning.

But if the other inhabitants of the pet shop wondered what was going on when Olga da Polga suddenly disappeared from view, Olga herself was in a dreadful state.

She didn't mind standing on an open and friendly hand once in a while, but it was quite a different matter being grabbed hold of and plonked – there was no other word for it – *plonked* into a cardboard box without so much as a by-your-leave.

Straight after a large breakfast too!

Her heart was beating like a tom-tom. Her dignity was shattered, her fur ruffled beyond description.

To cap it all she felt sick.

She had also made an important discovery. Going places when you know where you are going is one thing, but when you don't know it's quite a different matter.

For a moment or two she lay where she had landed,

hardly daring to breathe. But after a while, opening first one eye and then the other, she cautiously took in her new surroundings.

It was dark, but there was a friendly smell of fresh sawdust, and through a hole just above her head there came a shaft of light and a cooling draught of fresh air.

Olga had just begun to tell herself that perhaps things weren't so bad after all when, without any warning whatsoever, the box rose into the air and began jiggling up and down in a most alarming manner.

And as it tipped first one way and then another Olga began to wish she hadn't been so boastful in the past in case it was some kind of punishment. Old Sale or Return had often gone on about the way humans behaved and how strict they could be. Olga had always thought it was sour grapes because he'd been 'returned' by one, but now she wasn't quite so sure.

There was worse to follow, for just as she was in the middle of trying to work out how many times she *had* actually boasted or told a story which wasn't exactly 'true', the jiggling stopped; there was a roar, and a strange tickling began to run through her body, starting in her toes and ending where her tail would have been had she owned one.

'Oh, dear! Oh, dear!' she wailed. 'Whatever's happening now?'

And then in a flash it came to her.

The noise, the tickling, the feeling that she was going somewhere even though she herself wasn't moving . . . it could only mean one thing.

'A motor car!' she exclaimed, jumping up and down with excitement. 'I'm in a motor car!'

Olga knew all about motor cars because she'd seen them through the pet-shop window, but never in her wildest dreams had she ever pictured herself *riding* in one.

Gathering her courage in both paws she clambered up the side of the box and by standing on tip-toe managed to peer through the hole above her head.

Of the houses and shops she'd grown up with there

was no sign. Instead, all she could see was green countryside, miles and miles of it.

Fields, hedges, trees, banks covered with luscious-looking dandelions and thick, mouth-watering grass, all flashed past with the speed of the wind.

'If this is the outside world I've heard so much about,' decided Olga, 'I think I shall like it. It's much, much better than a stuffy, crowded old pet shop.'

Then she pricked up her ears, for above the noise of the engine she caught the sound of voices. First a deep one, then another, much younger, which she recognized as belonging to the little girl who'd picked her out from among all the others.

'You'll have to look after her, Karen,' said the deep voice. 'Come rain or shine. No excuses.'

'I promise.' The second voice paused for a moment and then went on. 'I do hope she likes her new home.'

'She'd better,' came the reply. 'It cost me enough to build. What with the wood and the roofing felt, glass for the bedroom window, wire netting for the door, legs to keep her away from Noel . . .'

As the man's voice droned on Olga sank back onto the floor, hardly daring to believe her ears. 'I'm going to stay with some Sawdust People,' she breathed. 'All by myself!'

'And in a waterproof house with a bedroom,' she added dreamily, 'on *legs*.

'Why, I must be going to live in a palace. I really must!'

CHAPTER TWO

The Naming of
Olga da Polga

If Olga da Polga's new home wasn't exactly a palace it certainly seemed like it, and it was definitely the nearest she was ever likely to get to one.

After the cramped and crowded conditions in the pet shop it was like entering a different world.

The hutch was large and airy and it was divided into two halves. Both floors were neatly covered with sawdust and the rooms were separated by a wall which had a hole cut in the middle so that she could easily pass between the two.

The first half was a kind of all-purpose room; part dining-room, part play-room; with a wire-mesh door, a small ash branch in one corner so that she could keep her teeth nice and sharp, and two heavy bowls – one marked OATS and the other marked WATER.

Olga tried out both before turning her attention to the second room. This turned out to be even more exciting than the first, for it not only had a *glass window* to keep out the weather but there was a large, inviting mound of fresh-smelling hay as well.

Olga spent some time pressing the hay flat so that she would have somewhere comfortable to sleep without being too hot, and then she settled down to think things over.

Really, all things considered, life had taken a very pleasant turn.

The sun was shining. The birds were chirping. Even the noises seemed friendly; the clinkings, singing, and occasional humming sounds from somewhere inside the big house as Mr and Mrs Sawdust – which was what Olga had decided to call them – went about their work.

Every so often there was a reassuring murmur of voices outside as one or other of the family peered through the glass to make certain she was all right.

First came Mr Sawdust, then Mrs Sawdust, then some other people called 'neighbours' and they all had a friendly word or two to say to her.

Finally Karen Sawdust herself arrived with an enormous pile of grass, a bunch of dandelions, and a

large juicy carrot neatly sliced down the centre, which she placed temptingly alongside the feeding bowl.

'We're going to choose a name for you now,' she announced, as Olga stirred herself and came out of the bedroom to sample these new delicacies. 'And we have to make sure it's right because tomorrow Daddy's going to paint it over your front door. There'll be no changing it once that's done.'

Olga nibbled away, half listening, half in a world of her own.

'Daddy fancies Greta and Mummy's rather keen on

Gerda, but I'm not sure. They don't sound *special* enough to me.' Karen Sawdust put her face against the door as she turned to go. 'I do wish you could tell us what *you* would like for a name.'

'Greta? ... Gerda? ... *Painted on my front door?*' Olga's world suddenly turned upside down.

She paused, a carefully folded piece of grass half in, half out of her mouth, hardly able to believe her ears.

'But I'm Olga da Polga,' she wailed, addressing the empty air. 'I've always been Olga da Polga. I can't change now – I really can't.'

★

That night, long after darkness fell and everyone else had gone to bed, Olga was still wide awake and deep in thought.

'I suppose,' she said to herself, for what seemed like the hundredth time, 'I suppose I ought to be counting my blessings instead of grumbling. I mean . . . I have a nice new home . . . food . . . I'm among friends . . . but I *would* like to keep my own name, especially as I'm having it painted on.'

The more Olga thought about it the sadder she became, for she couldn't help remembering a remark one of the older inhabitants of the pet shop had once made. 'Always hang on to your name,' he had said. 'It may not be much, but when you're a guinea-pig it's sometimes all you have in the world.'

Olga's own name was firmly imprinted on her mind. OLGA DA POLGA.

It had taken her fancy straight away and now she had become so used to it she couldn't begin to picture having anything else. When she closed her eyes she could still see it written in large black letters on the side of an old cardboard box.

Suddenly she jumped up in excitement, her mind in a whirl. Could she? Was it possible? She felt herself trembling at the sheer audacity of the idea.

It would mean a lot of hard work. A lot of difficult, almost impossible work. And yet . . .

Getting out of her warm bed, shivering partly with the chill of the night air and partly with she knew not what, Olga made her way through into the next room.

Clutching the ash branch firmly in her mouth she set to work. Scratching and scraping, starting and stopping, she worked and she worked and she worked. Sometimes pausing to smooth the sawdust over before beginning all over again, she tried not once, but time after time and still it wouldn't come right.

Dawn was breaking before she crawled back into her bedroom at long last and sank down in the hay. Her paws were aching, her fur was covered in

sawdust, and her eyes were so tired she could hardly bear to keep them open.

'It looks plain enough to me,' she thought, gazing back at the result of her night's work, 'but then, I *know* what it's meant to be. I only hope the others understand as well.'

Gradually, as she enjoyed her well-earned rest, the air began to fill with sounds of morning. Strange, unaccustomed sounds. In place of the usual grunts and rustles of the pet shop there were dogs barking, clocks striking, the sound of bottles clinking, and somewhere in the distance the noise of a train rattling on its way. In fact, there were so many different noises Olga soon lost count of them.

And then, at long last, came the one she had been waiting for. There was a click, the clatter of a bolt being withdrawn, and a moment later a now familiar face appeared on the other side of the wire-netting.

In the pause which followed Olga could almost hear the beating of her own heart.

'Mummy! Mummy!' With a shriek of surprise the face vanished from view. 'Come quickly! Come and see!'

Olga jumped to her feet. 'Wheeeee! It's worked! It's worked! Wheeeeeee!' Squeaking with joy and pleasure at her own cleverness she ran round and round her dining-room, scattering sawdust and the result of her labours in one wild whirlwind of delight.

'Olga da Polga?' exclaimed the voice of Mrs Saw-dust. 'Written on the floor? Don't be silly ... how *could* it have been?'

A face appeared at Olga's door. '*I* can't see any-thing at all. You must have been dreaming.'

'All the same,' there was a pause, 'it *is* rather a nice name. If I were you I'd keep it.'

When they were alone again Olga looked out of her window at Karen Sawdust and Karen Sawdust looked back at her.

'Grown ups!' said Karen with a sigh. 'They *never* understand these things. Still, we know it happened, don't we?'

Olga da Polga lifted up her head proudly. 'Wheeee! she cried, in the loudest voice she could possibly manage. 'Wheeee! Wheeeeee! Wheeeeeeeee!'

And really, there was nothing more to be said.

CHAPTER THREE

Olga Takes a Bite

Olga was so worn out after her night's work that straight after breakfast she went back to bed, and she slept and she slept and she slept.

She vaguely remembered waking once to a rather strange smell, but it turned out to be Mr Sawdust doing something to the outside of her house so she promptly went back to sleep again. He'd been using what looked like a tiny tail on the end of a stick, which he kept dipping in a tin full of black stuff.

Whatever it was everyone seemed very pleased with the result, for they kept repeating her name, which was all very comforting.

Olga had no idea how long she stayed asleep after that, but it must have been quite some time, for when she finally woke, the sun, which had been on the bedroom side of her house at breakfast time, was now shining through her front door.

She stirred gently, stretched, scratched a few remaining grains of sawdust from her fur, shook herself, and then sat very still as a strange feeling came over her that she was BEING WATCHED.

She peered out of her window and then hurried to the front door, but there wasn't a soul in sight.

Taking a few nibbles from a lettuce leaf, she helped herself to an oat or two for good measure and was about to settle down again when it happened.

Glancing up for no better reason than the fact that it made a change from looking down she caught sight of a strange, upside-down face watching her from the top of the hutch. Worse still, a moment later a long, black object, like a piece of furry rope, slid into view and began swinging lazily to and fro.

Left . . . right, left . . . right, it went . . . just like the pendulum of a clock, brushing against the wire-mesh door, not more than an inch from her nose. If it hadn't been for the fact that every so often it paused, as if to show it was capable of other things, and gave a flick in the opposite direction, the motion might well have sent Olga off to sleep again.

She watched it for a moment or two longer and then came to a decision.

There was only one way of telling if both head and object belonged to the same creature and she took it.

Biding her time, she waited until it made one of its

sudden changes in direction, curling for a brief moment through one of the holes in the wire, then she made a dive.

As Olga sank her twenty teeth into the offending object it was wrenched from her grasp and a loud high sound of mingled pain and alarm echoed round the garden.

The yowling and howling that followed as both face and object disappeared from view was enough to waken the dead.

It certainly brought the Sawdust family running.

Doors banged. Voices called out. Feet clattered . . .

Olga watched with growing interest as first one member of the family and then another ran past her house.

'I don't know who or what it was,' she thought, 'but start as you mean to go on – that's what I always say.' And she went back to her oats.

'Kutchy, kutchy, kutchy . . . come on down. Kutchy, kutchy, kutchy.'

'Goodness knows what frightened him so.'

'Come on down . . . kutchy, kutchy.'

'WRETCHED ANIMAL!'

The voices began to grow more and more impatient.

Mr Sawdust hurried back past Olga's house, only to return a few minutes later, red in the face and breathing heavily, as he struggled beneath the weight of an enormous wooden object about twice as long as he was tall.

'I've had to borrow an extending ladder from next door,' he called. 'We'll never reach him otherwise.'

'An *extending ladder*!' Olga grew more and more interested. She had no idea what it meant but it sounded most exciting.

'I must do this more often,' she thought. 'It's a fine way to pass the time on a summer's evening.' And she hurried round her house taking bites out of anything that happened to get in her way.

But the others didn't seem to share Olga's enthusiasm.

Cries of 'Be careful!' and 'Mind you don't slip!' floated up from the garden.

It seemed that the object Olga had bitten was now sitting at the top of a very tall pine tree and there was even talk of fetching something called a Fire Brigade.

But to Olga's disappointment, for she had never seen a Fire Brigade before, let alone been the cause of having one fetched, just as the excitement and Mr Sawdust had both reached their highest point the object took it into its head to come down again by itself.

'Cats!' said Mr Sawdust bitterly.

There was a banging and clattering and a moment or so later he came past Olga's house again, still carrying the ladder, and looking even more red in the face than before.

'Noel, you naughty thing!' Karen Sawdust came into view carrying a very cowed and frightened looking bundle of black fur in her arms. 'I don't know what Olga will think of you. Why can't you be good like her?'

There was no knowing what Olga thought of Noel, for she appeared to be much too busy munching her oats to bother with looking up, but it was only too clear what Noel thought of Olga. As he was placed on the ground he arched his back and his fur bristled and he glared at the hutch with a 'just you wait' expression on his face.

Olga looked down at him haughtily. 'Wheeeeee!' she squeaked, from the safety of her dining-room.

'You can't frighten me. My house has legs to keep me safe from you. Mr Sawdust told me. He went to great expense.'

Noel gave a kind of hissing snort. 'Legs are meant for climbing,' he said menacingly. 'So just you wait. One of these days I'll bite your tail so hard it'll . . .'

He broke off and stared as Olga turned her back on him.

'You . . . you haven't got a tail!' he exclaimed.

'No,' said Olga primly. 'I haven't.'

'But all furry animals have tails,' said Noel.

Olga turned round again to face him. 'Guinea-pigs haven't,' she replied. 'That's what makes us different.'

She paused, a thoughtful gleam in her eye as she felt another sort of tale coming on. 'We lost them a long, long time ago,' she said with a sigh. 'If you like, I'll tell you just how it happened. It's really rather romantic.'

CHAPTER FOUR

Olga's Story

'Once upon a time,' said Olga, who if she wasn't yet
sure of what her story would be about, at least knew
how it should start. 'Once upon a time, guinea-pigs
had the most marvellous tails imaginable. Long and
thick, with fur like silky-cream. If you can picture a
great long yarn of the finest silk . . .'

'A great long yarn is right,' interrupted Noel with
a yawn. '*Do* get on with it. I don't want to hang
around here all night. I have work to do.'

'I'm only telling you all this,' said Olga coldly,
'because I don't want you to get the wrong idea. I
wouldn't like you to confuse guinea-pigs' tails, as
they were then, with any ordinary sort of tail – like a
cat's for instance.'

She paused, partly for effect, but mostly to think up what to say next.

'Have you ever heard of Peru?' she inquired hopefully. 'That's where we guinea-pigs first came from.'

'I've heard of it,' said Noel, not wishing to sound too ignorant. 'I've never *been* there.'

'Oh!' Olga looked slightly taken aback. 'Er . . . well I don't suppose for a moment you've ever heard of Barsance,' she said, using the first word that came into her head. 'It's so small no-one has *ever* heard of it.' And she glared at Noel as if to dare him to say he had.

'Barsance used to be joined on to Peru,' she continued, 'until one night when there was a terrible storm and it broke off.

'It was so small that at the time I'm talking about, which was long, long ago, there was only room for one of everything.

'There was one king who ruled over a kingdom which had only one house with one inhabitant.

'This king lived with his stepdaughter in a one-roomed castle perched on an enormous rock overlooking the village, and he was known far and wide as the most crotchety and bad-tempered old king there had ever been.

34

'But it was said by the few who'd seen his step-daughter that she was the most beautiful princess in the whole world; as beautiful as he was ugly, and as sweet as he was unkind and selfish.'

Olga stared dreamily into space as she began to be carried away by her own story. 'Her eyes . . .'

'Did she have more than one eye?' asked Noel eagerly.

'Her eyes,' said Olga firmly, 'were so beautiful that when you gazed into them it was like looking into *one* very still lake of the deepest blue you could possibly imagine.

'But they were sad eyes, for her step-father was very jealous of her beauty and never allowed anyone near the castle in case they took her away.

'Each morning when she woke she looked at herself in the mirror and gave a sigh as she thought of all the wonderful things that might have happened had she been a normal princess living in a land where there was more than one of everything.

'And then she would retire to the one tower the castle possessed and sit gazing dreamily out of the one window in the hope that one day she would be rescued.

'It wasn't a very tall tower, for it needed only one

step to reach it, but the rock on which the castle stood was sheer as a cliff and tall as a mountain, and the castle itself could only be reached across a single draw-bridge and by climbing a tunnel hollowed out inside

WELCOME
TO
BARSANCE

the rock. It was so tall that even the one eagle which inhabited the land of Barsance seldom rose above it, but spent most of its time swooping and soaring in the valley below.

'As time went by it seemed to the princess that she would never be rescued.

'And then one day a tall stranger rode into the village on horseback and inquired of the only inhabitant about the beautiful princess he'd heard tell of in distant lands.

'The man directed the stranger to the castle, but when the king saw him approach he flew into a terrible rage, and raised the drawbridge as he sent him packing. And in his temper he locked the heavy oaken doors and hurled the key far out into space so that it was lost for ever.

'The prince was beside himself with grief, for in the short time he'd been at the castle he'd caught sight of the princess sitting alone in the tower and he realized that all the things he'd heard tell of her were true. And hadn't she waved? And hadn't he caught the sound of her voice calling out to him for help?

' "Oh, if only I could rescue her," he cried. "If only I had wings so that I could fly up and take her away with me."

'He gazed up at the rock, but it was polished smooth as glass and by its side the one small rope he was able to find in the village was like a matchstick compared to the tallest pine.

'Time after time, feet slipping, fingers torn and bleeding, he tried to scale the rock, but it was no use. With a sinking heart he realized that not only would he never reach his loved one but that even if he went for help by the time he returned she might be dead, for without the key there was no getting in or out of the castle.

'Suddenly he felt he was being watched, and when he turned he found to his surprise what seemed like a million pairs of eyes staring at him across the border from Peru.

'Peru,' said Olga, for Noel's benefit, 'was full of guinea-pigs at the time for it was before we'd been discovered.

'One of these guinea-pigs stepped forward. "Tell us," he said to the prince, "what are you doing?"

'The prince sat down wearily and told his story. The guinea-pigs listened with sorrow, for they knew the princess well and thought highly of her. Unlike her step-father, who was forever driving them away and shouting at them, she always had a kind word to spare or a tasty tit-bit to drop down from her tower.

'When the prince had finished his story the guinea-pigs disappeared for a while and there was a strange rushing sound, like a gathering wind, as they whispered together. And then there were squeaks and grunts the like of which had never been heard before in the whole of Peru, let alone the kingdom of Barsance.

'At last they returned, dragging behind them a long, silky rope.

'At a signal from their leader the eagle came swooping down out of the sky, took hold of one end of the rope, and flew up to the princess waiting high above.

'With the rope securely tied round the bars it took the prince only a matter of moments to climb up to the tower and even less time than it takes to tell before he was back down again with the princess at his side.

'He lifted her on to his horse and then, as he turned to thank all those present for their trouble, he suddenly realized the great and noble sacrifice they had made in his honour. For each and every guinea-pig had given up its tail so that it might be woven into the rope which had saved the princess.

'The prince could think of no way to repay the guinea-pigs for their act of kindness, so instead he bestowed on them the highest award he could think of.

'Not simply a medal – which would be very difficult to pin on and might fall off and be lost – but a rosette to be worn on their fur and on the fur of those who came after them until the end of time.'

Olga turned round and looked at her own rosettes. 'Which is why,' she said, 'if you are a guinea-pig with a rosette it's very likely you are a direct descendant of those very same guinea-pigs who gave their tails away all those years ago.'

Olga felt so moved by her story that a lump came into her throat and for a moment or two she found it quite difficult to swallow her oats.

Noel thought for a moment. 'I don't think I'd give

up *my* tail for a princess,' he said bluntly, 'however beautiful she was.'

'Guinea-pigs happen to have generous natures,' said Olga. 'Not like cats.'

'If you're so generous,' said Noel, 'how about letting me have a piece of your grass before I go out for the night?'

But Olga was fast asleep. Telling tales could be very tiring. Especially tales about tails.

Besides, she'd had quite enough of cats for one day.

CHAPTER FIVE

Olga Makes a Friend

Olga soon settled down as one of the family. She loved her new home and it was nice to hear her name being called each morning at breakfast time.

She also made quite a number of new friends. Other guinea-pigs were brought along by their owners to say hello, not to mention several rabbits, a hamster, two budgerigars and a collection of mice.

Really, life was very pleasant.

If she had a complaint at all, and she wouldn't have dreamed of mentioning it even if she had been able to, it was that during the middle of the day her house often grew a little too warm for comfort. Often she secretly wished she could romp and dance on the lawn she was able to see through her bedroom window, for it was shaded by a large tree and looked very cool and inviting.

43

Then one morning she was wakened by a strange new sound. Saw . . . saw . . . saw. Bang . . . bang . . . bang. It was most disturbing and it showed no sign of stopping.

Suddenly, just when she thought the worst was over, the door of her cage opened and she found herself being picked up and placed inside a strange, tall, upside-down affair, half hutch, half wooden frame covered on three sides by wire netting.

No sooner had she settled down to inspect her new surroundings than someone took hold of the contraption and turned it over.

Olga had to scramble like mad in order to keep her footing and when she finally recovered she found herself staring out at a kind of long, bottomless cage.

'Really!' she thought. 'Whatever next? If this is progress I don't think much . . .' She paused and looked out from the platform on which she was standing.

She looked first at the sea of faces pressed against the side of the wire netting and then at the place where the floor ought to have been.

'How nice,' said Karen Sawdust, 'to have a day-time run where you really can eat off the floor.'

'Safe from other animals,' added Mrs Sawdust.

'It'll help keep the grass short as well,' said Mr Sawdust. 'If she works hard I shan't need to cut it any more!'

Olga looked up. She was a polite guinea-pig and she felt it would be nice to say 'thank you', but words failed her.

Besides, she was a firm believer in the old guinea-pig saying that 'a piece of clover in the mouth is worth two on the lawn', and having just found a particularly juicy clump her mouth was very, very full.

From that day on Olga spent most of her waking hours on the lawn. If she didn't exactly manage to keep the whole of it short it wasn't for want of trying, and Mr Sawdust made sure that when he did use the mower he always left a corner uncut especially for her. It seemed as if every day was made up of sunshine and grass, and life could hardly have been sweeter.

It was on just such a day that Olga met Fangio.

It was late one afternoon. Karen Sawdust was at a place called school. Mr Sawdust was at another place called work, and Mrs Sawdust was busy indoors with her house.

Apart from Noel, who was chasing a fly in a nearby patch of heather, there was no sign of life whatsoever, and the only new object on the horizon was a kind of prickly round ball at the other end of the lawn.

Olga first noticed the ball when she was doing the rounds of her run clearing up the odd blades of grass before she was moved on to the next patch, and she was about to go round for the second time when she paused.

The ball wasn't in the same place! Without anyone kicking it, or even touching it, it had moved. It *definitely* wasn't where it had been the first time she saw it.

Noel gave her a superior look when she told him of her discovery. 'That's not a *ball*,' he said. 'That's Fangio. He lives in a garage down the road and they do say he has Argentine blood. He's a hedgehog.'

'A *hedgehog*?' repeated Olga. 'With Argentine blood? Wheeeee! What will they think of next?'

Fangio went past Olga's run several times, looking at her out of the corner of his eye, before he finally spoke. 'Who are you?' he asked suspiciously. 'I haven't seen you around before.'

'I'm a hedgehog-eater from Upper Burma!' Olga had a large stock of such words, most of which she'd seen written on the sides of boxes. She kept them by for use on special occasions and this seemed to be one of them. 'Wheeeeee!' she cried, in as loud and fierce a voice as she could possibly manage.

Fangio scuttled away and disappeared into the undergrowth.

He was gone some while and when he returned he looked at Olga even more suspiciously. 'You're not a hedgehog-eater at all,' he said. 'I've been making inquiries. You're a guinea-pig. You tell tales.'

'Sometimes,' said Olga carelessly, taking another nibble. 'When I feel in the mood and the sun is in the right direction.'

Fangio considered the matter for a moment. 'I could tell a few tales if I liked,' he said. 'All about the

Elysian Fields. That's where I'm off to now. I go there every evening.'

'The Elysian Fields?' Olga stopped eating. In spite of herself she couldn't help feeling interested. 'What are they when they're at home?'

'They're not *at home*,' said Fangio. 'That's the whole point.' He nodded vaguely in the direction of the shrubbery. 'They're over there. I can't think why you bother to stay cooped up in a cage when there's so much else to see. The world's a big place you know, and it's full of interesting things.'

'I'm happy where I am, thank you very much,' said Olga smugly. 'I have my run and plenty to eat. And I have a house on legs with a dining-room and a bedroom with a window to look out of.'

'I carry *my* windows with me,' said Fangio, blinking his beady eyes. 'And if I were to tell you some of the things I've seen through them it would make your fur stand on end.'

'I like my fur the way it is, thank you,' said Olga. 'Er . . . what things?'

'Trees,' said Fangio. 'Bushes, banks, leaves, rubbish dumps, bonfires, roads, lanes, vegetables, flora and fauna, copses, green meadows, mushrooms, ponds, streams, the springiest turf you could possibly imagine, puddles, strange insects, pheasants' eggs, hay, straw, molluscs, worms, shady nooks, holes in the ground . . . I could go on all night but I've so much to do I really can't spare the time.

'If I were you I'd be up and away. I wouldn't spend *my* life at the beck and call of others. I'd *do* things. Stand on my own four paws for a change.

'Think of it . . . instead of having to wait every day until someone feeds you you could do it yourself. Eat when *you* feel like it. What you like, *when* you like. They don't call it the Elysian Fields for nothing.'

'They've never forgotten me yet,' said Olga dubiously.

'Ah,' said Fangio darkly, 'but supposing they did? Suppose one day they weren't there and you were left shut up in your house . . .'

'Is it very dangerous in these fields?' asked Olga.

Fangio snorted. 'Dangerous? *Dangerous?* If anything comes along I don't like the look of I just roll myself up into a ball and wait until they go away again. There's nothing to it. I'd like to see the animal that would frighten me.'

'Even dogs?' asked Olga, who'd once seen a very large one from up the road. It was called an Alsatian and she hadn't liked the look of it at all.

'Dogs?' Fangio jumped. 'What? Where?'

'A great big one,' said Olga, making the most of it. 'Foaming at the mouth, with fangs as big as cucumbers . . . I'll tell you a story about it if you like . . .'

But Fangio had gone. Moving with a surprising turn of speed for his size he'd vanished into the nearby bushes as if his very life depended on it.

Olga sat staring at the spot for quite a while. Somehow she felt strangely unsettled and the grass which she'd been enjoying up until a minute or so before now seemed dull and tasteless.

It was not a very nice feeling and try as she might she couldn't shake it off.

'I do hope Olga's all right,' said Karen Sawdust later that evening after she'd put her to bed. 'She seemed very odd. Not at all her usual self.'

'I shouldn't worry dear,' said her mother. 'I expect guinea-pigs have their "off days" just as we do.'

And really she couldn't have spoken a truer word. For although Olga might not be having an 'off day' at that very moment she definitely had the thought on her mind, and as she closed her eyes and made ready for sleep she decided to have one just as soon as she possibly could.

CHAPTER SIX
Olga's Day Off

In her heart of hearts Olga didn't really expect to go roaming for quite some time, if at all, so she was doubly surprised when the opportunity came the very next day. Like most opportunities it happened un-expectedly, so that she had to make her decision at once before it passed her by.

In moving her run, someone – she wasn't sure who it was, for she was much too busy to notice – someone had been very careless and placed one corner of it on top of a small mound of grass. And this left a gap several inches high along part of one side.

Such a thing had never happened before and prob-ably never would again. So Olga was left with no choice: it was now or never.

As soon as she felt she was alone she eased herself

gently under the wooden frame, lowering her back and stretching herself out as far as she could, and suddenly she found herself on the other side.

She stood for a moment or two getting her breath back. All sorts of curious feelings were racing around inside her; part excitement, part fear, part elation at having done something so daring.

Even the air seemed different on the other side of her wire fence. Fresher somehow, and cleaner; full of the unknown.

Now she was ready for the big moment. The one she had been waiting for. The one she had dreamed about. She could start on her travels.

Which way should she go? Really, with the world at her feet and on every side as well it was hard to make a choice.

First of all she decided against the long, winding path leading back towards the house. There was no sense in risking capture quite so soon.

Then there was a vegetable patch near by, full of tempting cabbage leaves and lettuce plants, but she ruled this out too, for Mr Sawdust sometimes worked there and she might easily be spotted.

She wondered what Fangio would have done. Where was it he said he went to? The Elysian Fields?

They couldn't be that far away. Not if he went there
every evening.

Olga's mouth, which had been unusually dry until
a moment ago, began to grow moist with anticipation at the thought of the good things to come.

'Wheeeeee!' she squeaked. 'This is the life!' And
without wasting any more time she bounded across
the lawn in a series of short, sharp bursts until she
found herself in the shrubbery.

The shrubbery!

Although she wouldn't have admitted it, even to
herself, Olga found the shrubbery a trifle disappointing. From a distance it had always looked most
inviting, with shady nooks and branches which
waved gently in the breeze as if beckoning any passer-
by to pause awhile and sample the delights within.

But far from it being full of delights Olga found it
rather mucky, and very overgrown; chock-a-block
with weeds and sharp brambles which parted easily
enough but then immediately swung back again,
cutting off her return with a dense barrier of thorns.

The further she went in the worse it became.
Pushing, shoving, scrambling over dead twigs and
branches, Olga forced her way deeper and deeper into
the undergrowth.

It was all very well for Fangio. He had prickles to
start off with. A few more were probably neither here
nor there. But for a guinea-pig with only her fur to
protect her – fur, moreover, which she'd always
prided herself on keeping neat and clean – it was
quite a different matter.

Halfway through the shrubbery Olga's fur already
looked as if it had been dragged through a hedge
backwards, and by the time the first few chinks of
light appeared on the other side she hardly dared look
down at herself for fear of what she might see.

At last, battered and bruised, scratched and ruffled, she burst through the remaining mass of tangled foliage and lay panting with exhaustion while she took stock of her new surroundings.

'Elysian Fields indeed!' she exclaimed bitterly.

As far as she could make out Fangio's heaven on earth was nothing more than a rubbish dump, full of old tin cans and soggy bits of cardboard, and smelling strongly of bonfires.

As for food! Olga didn't really count two mangy looking thistles and a bed of old nettles as being fit for a compost heap let alone a hungry guinea-pig.

As she contemplated it she grew gloomier and gloomier.

And at that moment, as if to add to her sorrows, it began to rain. First one spot, then another, then several more. Ping . . . ping . . . ping, ping, ping, they went on the old tin cans.

Then faster still, and harder. Rat-tat-tat-tat-tat.

The spots became a downpour, the downpour a deluge. The burning embers of the bonfire sizzled out leaving behind an acrid smell. The nettles drooped beneath the weight. Trees added their drips to the cascade of water.

Olga made a dive for a near-by sheet of cardboard

and sat shivering beneath it. Never, in all her life, had she felt so wet and miserable, so . . .

There was a rustle from somewhere near by and a moment later a familiar head poked out from beneath some leaves.

'Enjoying yourself?' asked Fangio. 'Having fun?'

'*Enjoying* myself?' Olga stared at Fangio. 'Having *fun*?' she repeated. 'I've never so unenjoyed myself in the whole of my life! If this is the Elysian Fields the sooner I'm back on my lawn the better! I've never seen anything so . . . so dismal!'

'Beauty', said Fangio, 'is in the eye of the beholder. I must say that through *my* windows it looks lovely. Think of all the flies and insects there'll be when it stops raining.'

Olga shuddered. Fangio was welcome to his insects. She hadn't the slightest wish to stay and see them. 'If you ask me,' she said, '*your* windows need cleaning. Good night!'

'Second on the right,' called Fangio, as Olga stalked off, taking the long way home round the outside of the shrubbery. 'Third on the left, then right again. Only mind you don't fall in the . . . oh!'

He broke off as an extra-loud splash sounded above the rain.

'You might have told me!' wailed Olga, as she clambered out of a mud-filled hole.

'You didn't give me a chance,' said Fangio.

'Hedgehogs!' snorted Olga bitterly.

She had never felt so glad to see her run. Nor, for that matter, had she had such a welcome before. Judging by the whoops of delight that greeted her re-appearance, it seemed as if everyone in the neighbour-hood had been out looking for her.

'How nice to be back home,' she thought. 'How I could ever have wanted to leave I don't know.'

'Where *have* you been?' cried Karen Sawdust, as she gathered Olga up in her arms. 'We've been searching everywhere.'

Mr Sawdust held up an umbrella for protection.

'Pooh!' said Mrs Sawdust. 'She smells of bonfires.'

Olga took a deep breath. 'I've been to the Elysian Fields,' she squeaked. 'And I'm never, *ever* going there again!'

At least, that's what she meant to say, and if the squeaks themselves didn't exactly make sense to everyone around, the feeling that went into them made the meaning very clear indeed.

CHAPTER SEVEN

Olga Wins a Prize

After her dreadful experience in the Elysian Fields Olga decided it was high time she settled down for a while. She even invented a slogan, MORE EATING – LESS THINKING, and spent long hours outside in her run making up for the weight she felt sure she must have lost.

She always inspected her run very carefully each morning, making certain that there was no possible way in for any other creature, and that she herself couldn't get out by mistake either, but so much care was now taken over the placing of her run that there was hardly room for a centipede to crawl under the edge let alone a guinea-pig with a hearty appetite.

And then one day something unusual happened.

Hearing voices approach she hurried into the enclosed portion of the run in order to brace herself between the wooden floor and the back while it was turned on end. However, instead of being taken back home in the usual fashion, she found herself being

63

carried into the big house where the Sawdust family lived.

She was taken through the kitchen, along a passage, and into a big room, where she was placed on top of a thing called a 'table', a large area of very slippery wood high off the ground, with NO SIDES WHATSO-EVER.

Olga knew all this because Karen Sawdust, who had been carrying her, explained matters as they went along.

She sat very still, hardly daring to move, while everyone gathered round and began prodding, poking, staring, and even – biggest indignity of all – TURNING HER UPSIDE DOWN!

Olga was most upset. 'How would *they* like it', she thought, 'if someone came along and turned *them* upside down? It's not nice. It's not nice at all.' And she gave a passing nip to the hand which happened to be holding her.

After that she felt a trifle better.

It wasn't a really hard nip, but hard enough to leave a mark and to show exactly how she felt about the matter.

Then something even worse happened. A large object like a . . . like a . . . Olga tried hard to think just what it did remind her of, descended on her. A hedgehog! That was it. The object looked just like a hedgehog.

For a moment Olga thought Fangio had joined in the attack on her and she wriggled and struggled to avoid this latest outrage on her person.

'Come along, Olga,' said Karen Sawdust firmly, as she tried to hold her still. 'If you're going to be entered for a show you must have your fur brushed. You want to look your best don't you?'

Olga felt her heart miss a beat. 'Entered for a show! Me? In a show?'

She'd heard about SHOWS from some of the other guinea-pigs who visited her on occasions. Some of her friends even knew other guinea-pigs who had been in such things. One of them, Charles, boasted of a cousin several times removed who'd actually won a prize, but as no one had ever met the animal in question this was taken with a pinch of oats.

But it made a difference knowing the reason, and Olga lay back and let the brush ruffle through her fur. Really, it was quite a nice feeling. Tingling, but most pleasant, and very good for itches.

'Just wait until I see them next,' she breathed, thinking of all her friends. 'Just wait until I tell them!'

She went back to her house later that evening looking unusually spruce and well-groomed and with a definite air about her, for it never crossed Olga's mind for a second that she *wouldn't* win a prize.

It wasn't that she was particularly vain, or boastful, or even that she thought a lot of herself. It simply didn't cross her mind.

From the moment she heard she was going in for a show Olga thought of nothing else.

'I'm being Entered,' she told everyone who came near. She made it sound so important that even Noel began to treat her with unusual respect.

And there was so much to do. If she wasn't worrying about where she was going to put her prize – for it might turn out to be a large one – she was worrying over her diet.

'I *must* build myself up,' she kept saying. 'I *must* eat as much as possible. It's no good looking skinny.'

And eat she did. Grass, dandelions, groundsel, clover, paper, cornflakes – Olga was very keen on cornflakes, though she usually only got them on Sundays – oats, anything and everything that came within range of her mouth disappeared in a trice.

And every day her fur was brushed until it shone like the table top itself.

At last the great day came. Olga was up bright and early and after a final going-over with the brush and comb and a wash of her paws she was on her way.

Mr Sawdust had made a special carrying cage out of an old letter basket he'd taken off the front door of their house. Emblazoned across the front, in white letters on a blue background, were the words OLGA DA POLGA.

'Of course, the trouble with shows,' said Olga once she was settled next to a bored-looking rabbit in a neighbouring hutch, 'is all the waiting around. I mean they might just as well hand out the prize straight away and let everyone else go home. It would save all this mucking about.'

Really it was quite true. For every one person who came and stared at her and then went away again there were a hundred. Some made notes on pieces of paper. Others just talked. Then she was taken out of her box and made to stand on some things called 'scales'. Goodness only knew why. After which there was a lot of hemming and hawing and more chatter and note-taking.

'Talk! Talk! Talk!' muttered Olga. 'Why on earth don't they get on with it?'

'You should know by now,' said the rabbit, who was also getting a bit restive, 'that human beings *always* talk. They can't even dig a hole in the ground without discussing it first. Not like us rabbits.'

But at last the big moment came. The moment Olga had been waiting for. In fact, she was so quietly confident about the outcome of the contest she hardly batted an eyelid when one of the judges stepped forward and pinned something on her travelling hutch.

'Such a nice, intelligent man,' she thought, as everyone applauded. 'Not that he had much choice, of course, but he did it very nicely.'

'Mind you,' she mused on the way home, 'I'm not saying I wasn't helped by all the brushing I had. Credit where credit's due. But breeding always tells. It's bound to show through in the end.'

When she was being put back in her own house and caught sight of a blue rosette on the side of her travelling hutch she grew even more lyrical.

'A rosette!' she cried. 'A rosette! Wheeeeee! It's the story of the prince all over again.' And she looked round at herself to see if she had grown any more rosettes of her own.

She felt quite disappointed when she found she hadn't. Perhaps they took time to take root.

It wasn't until she caught something in the tone of Karen Sawdust's voice as she placed her carefully back in the straw that a slight feeling of doubt crossed Olga's mind.

'Fancy!' chuckled Karen. 'I've heard of guinea-pigs winning first prize for having the longest fur. I've heard of them winning first prize for having the smoothest and I've even seen awards for the longest whiskers . . . but *yours* . . .' The voice dissolved into gales of laughter as the door closed. 'It just serves you right for being so greedy!'

Olga sat for a while lost in thought. What *could* she have meant? *Me* . . . greedy? What sort of prize *had* she won?

She squinted through the window at the rosette still pinned to the travelling hutch and at the piece of card just below it.

Reading upside down wasn't Olga's strong point and although she had once, ages ago it now seemed, managed to spell out her name when there had been all the fuss about what to call her, new words were much more difficult and the writing on the card took a lot longer.

But then, FIRST PRIZE TO OLGA DA POLGA FOR BEING THE FATTEST GUINEA-PIG IN THE SHOW is a lot to get on to a very small card, especially when the reader is so indignant she can hardly believe her own eyes.

On the other hand, if it did nothing else it certainly cured Olga of being greedy. At least for the time being!

CHAPTER EIGHT

Olga Starts a Rumour

For a while the next morning Olga felt she hardly dared show her face.

However, a prize is a prize no matter what it's for, and it's certainly better than no prize at all. In fact, it needed only an hour or two outside in her run before she was as right as rain again.

'There's nothing like a spot of sunshine for taking your mind off things,' thought Olga. 'That and a good doze.'

She had several good dozes, partly to avoid being asked too many embarrassing questions about the show, and partly because the excitement of the previous day had left her feeling quite worn out.

In any case she soon had other things to occupy her mind. They were mostly to do with a round, stone-like object called Graham.

Graham was a tortoise and although he was 'known-about' he wasn't often seen on account of his being so slow.

Olga first caught sight of him making his way through the lettuce bed, but what with pausing for an occasional snack and stopping every now and then for a rest, it wasn't until mid-day that he finally drew level with her run.

'Where are you going?' asked Olga with interest, after they had exchanged a few pleasantries, for her new visitor had such a determined look on his face it was clear he had something important in mind.

'I'm getting ready to hibernate,' explained Graham. 'We tortoises do it every year. Sleep the winter away – that's the answer. It saves all the bother of trying to keep warm. Nothing like snuggling down under some leaves. It can snow, rain, freeze, do what it likes – it won't bother me.'

Olga looked at Graham and then at the sky. Although one or two clouds had certainly come up during the course of the morning and were now casting their shadow over the lawn, the weather didn't seem *that* bad.

'Hailstorms,' said Graham. 'No trouble at all. Thunder . . . lightning . . .'

'Aren't you a bit early?' broke in Olga. 'I mean . . . it's ages yet before winter.'

'When you are a tortoise,' said Graham, slowly and deliberately, 'you need to make an early start. It takes such a long time to get *anywhere*. I have to get up early to cross the road even, and if I want to come back again I have to get up the day before. Still, I shan't worry. Once I've found a good spot it can do what it likes. Gales . . . drizzles . . . showers . . .'

'But if you sleep all the winter,' persisted Olga, who was beginning to get a bit fed up with the weather as a topic of conversation, 'how do you know what's going on?'

'Nothing "goes on",' said Graham gloomily. 'That's something else you discover when you're a tortoise. You go to sleep in the autumn and when you wake up in the spring it's still the same old world. Nothing ever changes.'

'Nothing ever changes?' Olga stared at Graham as if she could hardly believe her ears. '*Nothing ever changes?*' she exclaimed. 'Why, things are changing all the time.'

'Name one thing,' said Graham. 'Name just one thing that's changed this morning.'

Olga gazed round the garden, for once at a loss for words.

'Well?' said Graham. 'I'm waiting. Only don't keep me waiting too long. I want to reach the other side of the lawn before it gets dark.'

'Er . . . yes . . . mmm . . . well . . .' Olga glanced up at the sky, trying hard to think of something to say, and as she did so a flash of inspiration hit her. It suddenly seemed a very good day to START A RUMOUR.

'I don't want to worry you,' she said casually, 'but did you notice anything funny about the sun this morning?'

'The sun?' Graham turned his head slowly to one side and squinted up at the sky. 'I can't see any sun.'

'No,' said Olga, taking a quick upwards glance to make sure it was still cloudy, 'and nor will you.'

She moved closer to Graham. 'It's changed places with the moon!' she whispered. 'It rose the wrong way this morning. Instead of appearing in the east like it always does, it rose in the west!'

Graham chewed this piece of information over in his mind for some time, and then gave a gulp as he at last swallowed it.

'If that's the sort of thing that goes on while I'm not looking,' he announced, 'I'm glad I'm hibernating,' and without so much as a good-bye wave Graham hurried on his way as fast as his legs would carry him, until by the middle of the afternoon he'd disappeared into the shrubbery.

By that time Olga had almost forgotten the incident, but shortly afterwards Fangio came rushing across the lawn, his eyes gleaming with excitement and his prickles standing on end like a porcupine.

'Have you heard?' he gasped. 'Have you heard? Something's happened to the sun. It's the wrong way round!'

Olga scarcely bothered to look up. 'Tell me something new,' she said.

'I did hear,' said Fangio impressively, 'that someone's pulled the plug out of the North Sea. All the water ran away and it's tipped the earth over.'

'Really?' said Olga, stifling a yawn. 'How interesting.'

Fangio looked at her admiringly. 'You're taking it very calmly,' he said at last. 'I must say I wouldn't like to be trapped in a cage at a time like this. I'm going,' and without further ado Fangio turned on his heels and ran.

Noel was the next to arrive.

'I know you're not going to believe this,' he gasped, 'but the sun rose the wrong way this morning. Someone pulled the plug out of the North Sea and all the water ran away. There was a terrible "glugging" noise. I didn't actually hear it, but they say it was dreadful. And it's all because of the humans. They've been taking all these things out of the earth for so many years . . . coal and oil . . . and gas . . . they've left this great big hole in the middle. That's where it's all gone!'

Noel paused for breath, but if he was expecting Olga to start rushing round her run shrieking for help he was disappointed. She simply went on eating.

'Aren't you going to *do* something?' he exclaimed at last.

'I may,' said Olga carelessly. 'On the other hand, I may not. I haven't thought yet. I don't believe in thinking too much on an empty stomach.'

'Your stomach hasn't been empty since the day you were born,' said Noel.

'Well! Well, of all the . . .' began Olga.

But Noel had disappeared.

A moment later the sun came out through a gap in the clouds. Olga looked up just to make sure it really was where it ought to be and then she went into the room at the back of the run, closed her eyes, and stretched out luxuriously on the floor.

Starting rumours was rather an amusing way of

spending one's day. Not unlike planting a seed and watching it grow before your very eyes. Really, there was no knowing what turn it would take next.

But the turn that it eventually took surprised even Olga.

In fact, it not only surprised her – it petrified her!

It seemed as though she'd hardly closed her eyes before the floor of her run suddenly began swaying in a most terrifying manner. It felt as if her stomach was being left behind while the rest of her rose into the air, twisting and turning, only to land on the ground with a simply dreadful thud.

Olga opened one eye to see what was going on.

Everything seemed all right.

She went outside.

The grass was still there.

She looked up.

The sun . . .

She gave a squeak of alarm.

The sun! *The sun had changed its position!*

When she'd gone inside her compartment it had been on her right. It had definitely been on her right. Whereas now . . . now it was on her left!

'Help!' she cried.

'Wheeeeee!

'Save me!

'I don't want to be the wrong way round!

'Wheeeeeeeeeeeeee!

'Man the pumps! Women and guinea-pigs first. I
mean ... guinea-pigs and women! Help! Save me!
Wheeeeeeeeeeeeee!'

Giving vent to a long and pitiful moan Olga collapsed into a heap on the grass.

'What's the matter?'

'Come along, Olga.'

'Good girl!'

The Sawdust family, drawn by the commotion,
rushed to comfort her. But it was no use. Olga lay
where she was, trembling in every limb, her eyes

tightly closed, her feet like jelly. And for the rest of that day nothing that anyone could say or do managed to stir her.

'I can't understand what's come over all the animals today,' said Mrs Sawdust later that same evening.

'There's Noel up a tree, absolutely refusing to come down. Fangio's acting like a scalded cat, and I've never seen Graham move so quickly. Everyone in the road says the same. They're all behaving like March Hares.

'As for Olga . . .'

'It's funny about Olga,' broke in Karen Sawdust. 'She seemed to be the only normal one until we turned her run round the other way, then she went like it too. What *can* it be?'

But no one ever did discover the answer, and the next day things were back to normal. Noel came down out of the tree, Fangio went back to his insect hunting, Graham carried on looking for somewhere to spend the winter, and all the other animals in the neighbourhood went about their business, so in time the matter was forgotten.

But it was noticeable, to those who notice such things, that many of them kept peering up at the sky in a most odd way, and for some time afterwards a certain guinea-pig remained very much quieter than usual.

And if there was a rumour going around the district as to why *that* was, it certainly wasn't started by Olga herself. Olga had definitely been cured of starting rumours.

CHAPTER NINE

Olga and the 'Surrey Puma'

One day towards the end of autumn a crisis arose in the Sawdust household.

Olga pricked up her ears as snatches of it came through the open kitchen window and floated past her house.

It seemed that the whole family had to go away unexpectedly, not just for a day but for a whole week-end. Friday night until Monday morning.

Noel was being looked after by a neighbour, but apparently there were problems over Olga herself – something to do with the time of year and the shortage of grass; a mysterious thing called 'not imposing on people', which meant nothing at all to Olga; and THE SURREY PUMA.

There had been talk of leaving Olga with a plentiful supply of oats and having someone call in just to make sure she was all right, but everyone seemed to think she would gobble all the oats up at once, and when the Surrey Puma was mentioned it was generally agreed they couldn't possibly leave her and she would have to stay with relations.

Olga was rather thankful when she heard this last piece of news as she didn't like the sound of the Surrey Puma at all.

For some months past there had been talk of a strange animal which had been seen roaming the area at night, killing sheep, chickens, and anything else it came across.

No one seemed to know quite what it was and the longer it remained at large the bigger it seemed to grow. It was rumoured that a young puma had escaped from a private zoo and had grown up running wild in a part of England called Surrey, so in the end it came to be called the 'Surrey Puma'.

Whether or not it really existed was a matter of great argument, but to be on the safe side many people in the neighbourhood began keeping their pets indoors at night.

Noel was one of the few exceptions. He had his own pussy-flap in the back door and was used to coming and going whenever he felt like it.

He kicked up such a fuss when Mr Sawdust barricaded his private door that he got his own way, though it was noticeable he didn't stay out quite as much as he had in the past.

The evening before she left, Olga went to bed in a state of great excitement. She'd never been away for a week-end before, and when she heard that the 'relations' she would be staying with were Karen Sawdust's grandparents her joy knew no bounds.

In fact, she was so excited by it all she scarcely bothered saying good-bye when she was collected, but ran round squeaking with delight when her house was lifted into the back of the car.

Her hopes didn't go unrewarded. For it was clear from the moment she arrived that Grandpa Sawdust intended taking his job very seriously indeed.

Scarcely an hour passed by during the course of that first day when he didn't arrive at her front door bearing some new delicacy or other: a handful of grass when none seemed to be around, a carrot or

two, slices of runner beans, groundsel and dandelions.
Goodness only knew where he was getting it all from,
for everyone else's supplies had dried up weeks before.

Olga made short work of everything that was put
before her. It seemed a shame to leave anything after
he had taken so much trouble. Though by the end of
the day even she had to admit that it was perhaps
possible to eat not wisely but too well.

'I'd sooner keep you for a week than a fortnight,'
said Grandpa Sawdust as he arrived with a fresh supply
just before dark.

Olga took a deep breath. 'And I would sooner stay
for two wheeeeeeek-ends than one!' she squeaked
happily as she began tucking in.

Though to be truthful by then she was so full that
she had great difficulty in crawling from her dining-
room to her bedroom, and once there it was as much
as she could do to open her eyes let alone say good
night.

Not that she was able to have her usual good
sleep. Instead, a rather uncomfortable feeling in her
stomach not only made proper sleep impossible but
gave rise to all sorts of queer half-dreams as well.
Dreams of finding herself trapped in the middle of a
huge forest of thistles and having to eat her way out;

of being chased by an enormous wolf-like animal with gleaming eyes and razor-sharp teeth, and then being caught in a bog, unable to move her feet . . .

Olga had no idea how long it all lasted – it seemed like hours and hours – but suddenly she woke with a start and the realization that *something really was outside her house!*

She caught her breath as a loud scratching sound came from overhead, and then froze in horror as a large, black shape appeared in front of her window, silhouetted against the moonlight, and looked in at her.

Olga closed her eyes and let out a shriek of terror.

'Wheeeeeee!' she shrieked. 'It's the Surrey Puma!
Wheeeeeeee! Wheeeeeeeeee! Wheeeeeeeeeeeeee!'

She shrieked so loudly and at such length that after
a while a light came on in one of the upstairs rooms of
the big house, then another, and a moment later the
back door flew open.

Opening her eyes again Olga saw to her relief that
the intruder had disappeared, and she collapsed
thankfully into the hands of Grandpa Sawdust as he
opened her door and reached in to rescue her.

'What a good job I squeaked loudly enough to
frighten it away,' she thought, feeling much braver
now that she was being carried inside the big house.
'Otherwise I might have ended up as a guinea-pig
with a tale. And not a very nice one at that!'

*

Olga's stock rose no end when she arrived back after
her week-end and told the others about her adventure
with the 'Surrey Puma'.

Animals from miles around came to hear the story
from her own lips, and Olga was only too happy to
oblige.

As the size of her audience grew and the story was

told again and again, so the 'puma' itself grew in size.

From being as large as a St Bernard, it became as tall as a horse, as fierce as a lion, as fleet as a gazelle, and as powerful as a grizzly bear.

She even managed to develop a kind of roar to go with the tale. It was far removed from her usual rather high-pitched squeak, for it started somewhere deep inside and went round her stomach several times, so that by the time it came out of her mouth it really was rather frightening.

Olga's audience listened with bated breath as she demonstrated how she'd used the roar to send her assailant packing.

'I'm not saying it *was* as big as an elephant,' she

remarked with a certain amount of truth, for even Olga felt she had to draw the line somewhere. 'On the other hand I'm not saying it wasn't.'

Fangio shivered. 'I'm glad I've got prickles,' he said thankfully.

Olga glanced at him patronizingly. 'I suppose they might be of *some* use,' she said. 'But if you can't roar at the same time they won't help a lot,' and to show

just what she meant she pressed her face against her front door and gave such a horrifying snarl all the other animals shot off into the night as if they were being pursued by a thousand fiery demons.

All, that is, except Noel.

Having jumped on to the roof of Olga's house for safety, he peered down over the edge and looked at her with interest.

'I suppose', he said, 'the puma must have come *after* I did.'

Olga, who'd been having some much-needed oats
after her long bout of story-telling, paused in order
to look up, and as she did so a rather odd look came
over her face, for there was something very familiar
about the shape silhouetted above her.

'I came all the way to see you,' explained Noel.
'There's nothing much to do these nights, what with
all the others being kept indoors, and I thought you
might like a bit of company.

'I tried to wake you by scratching on your roof,
but I think you were having a nightmare. You kept

giving these funny squeaks. Then all the lights came on again so I went back home.'

Noel looked wistfully at Olga. 'After what you've told us I'm rather glad I didn't stay,' he said. 'Though I wouldn't mind *seeing* a puma – just once. Tell me about it again.'

Olga gulped. 'I . . . er . . . there's nothing much to tell really,' she said at last. 'I may have exaggerated a little I suppose. They're rather like cats. I mean, once you've seen one you've seen the lot.

'Besides,' she added firmly, 'I've got a bit of a sore throat coming on. It's probably all the roaring I had to do!'

CHAPTER TEN

Disaster

Gradually a change came over the weather and Olga began to spend more and more time in her bedroom, only venturing out for meals. She was glad of the board which was put up over her front door every night, for it kept out the rain and the cold winds which had begun to blow. And she was even more thankful to have a window in her bedroom so that she could see what was going on outside without having to go into the chilly air too often.

Now, instead of stamping her hay flat as she'd done during the summer months she took to fluffing it up and burying herself deep inside where it was nice and warm, and on some mornings, when there was a frost, she even ate her breakfast that way, lying half in and half out of her bedroom.

Then one day a terrible thing happened.

Suddenly, with absolutely no warning at all, some great white balls, large as marbles and hard as iron, came raining down out of the sky, bouncing off the ground and beating down on the roof of her house like a burst of machine-gun fire.

Olga was so frightened by it all she nearly had hysterics. She rushed round and round shrieking her head off.

'Help! Help!' she shrieked. 'Wheeeee! Wheeeeee!'

She felt sure it was a war and that these were bullets. When she'd first started life in the pet shop some of the older guinea-pigs had told terrible stories about the war, and how noisy it had been. None of them had actually been fired at of course, but the stories had been handed down, and like most stories, added to.

At the time Olga had thought it all sounded rather exciting but now that she was actually experiencing war it was an entirely different matter.

'Wheeeeeee!' She shrieked. 'Wheeeeee! Help! Save me!'

Somewhere in the background a door opened and she vaguely heard voices calling her name. Then someone – it sounded like Mrs Sawdust – shouted for something called an umbrella, and a moment later her door was flung open.

Olga was so terrified by now she simply hurled herself at the opening. Anything to escape from being cooped up in her house, unable to defend herself.

Hands reached out to catch her, but in her terror Olga missed them completely.

She felt herself falling through space. It seemed to last an age, but could only have been a split second,

and then she landed with a thud on the wet concrete far below.

For a moment she lay where she'd fallen, fighting to get her breath back. Then, as she went to move, a terrible cold fear came over her, for an awful agonizing pain shot right through her body.

She tried to pull herself along with her front paws but struggle as she might nothing seemed to happen. The whole of the back part of her body seemed to be completely locked. She *wanted* to move, she strained

every muscle trying to move, but nothing happened.

Dimly she felt herself being picked up and carried, wet and bedraggled, into a warm room inside the big house, where she was placed in a towel and gently rubbed. But although it was all very comforting it did nothing to ease the awful ache which now seemed to cover her completely like a cloud.

From somewhere – it seemed miles away and yet she knew it must be close by – she heard Karen Sawdust's voice, sounding very tearful.

'Oh, Olga,' she said, 'what *have* you done? If only you could tell us what's wrong.'

Olga struggled against the pain as she tried to lift herself up but after a few faltering attempts she sank back exhausted.

'Oh, dear,' she moaned, closing her eyes as everything around grew misty. 'If only I *could* tell you. Oh, if only I could! But I don't even know myself. What *can* it be?'

Olga wasn't sure how long she slept but when she finally woke she found herself lying on a bench in a room she'd never seen before in her life.

There was an odd smell about it; not unpleasant, but somehow rather clean and safe. That was it! It definitely felt 'safe'.

Mrs Sawdust was there, and Karen Sawdust, and a man in a long white coat.

The man in white was holding something in his hand, a tiny white object about the size of a groundsel bud, and Olga pricked up her ears as he spoke.

'Give her a quarter of this every day,' he said, addressing Mrs Sawdust. 'Just in case she's suffering from shock. That's always a danger with guinea-pigs if they've had any sort of accident and sometimes it takes a day or two to come out. Keep her warm and dry. We don't want her getting any sores – especially as she can't stand up . . .'

Olga listened drowsily as the voice droned on.

Now that she'd been cleaned and dried and had a good sleep she was beginning to feel a little less dazed and the sharp pain in her back had almost disappeared. But it had been replaced by a kind of sleepy numbness, and she couldn't even feel her legs, let alone tell whether they were moving.

Instinctively she knew she was being taken good care of, and that she must do exactly as she was told if she was to get better, but she wished too that everyone would leave her alone so that she could get on with it.

Then she pricked up her ears again as she caught something new the man in white was saying.

'Her back's not broken, and her legs don't seem to be either . . .' Very gently he picked her up and ran his fingers over her body. 'There's no sign of any dislocation . . .'

'Oh, dear,' thought Olga. 'What a lot of things I *haven't* got. I do hope he finds *something* left.'

'Bruises,' said the man in white. 'She'll have plenty of those before she gets better.'

Olga suddenly wished she hadn't thought the question. She didn't know what bruises were and she didn't much like the sound of them either, but luckily for her peace of mind she fell asleep again before the vet's next remark.

'We'll give it a week,' he said. 'Unless there's any sudden change for the worse bring her back to see me in a week's time. Then we'll decide what to do with her . . . *one way or the other*!'

CHAPTER ELEVEN

The Dance of
the Sugar Plum Guinea-pig

A week went by, then another, and still Olga showed few signs of getting any better.

They were two of the longest weeks she had ever known. Every day she was taken into the big house belonging to the Sawdust family and placed in a basket on the kitchen table so that her legs could be massaged, and every day she was given her tablet and had her fur brushed smooth. As she couldn't bend she wasn't able to do it herself and it soon became terribly matted and unkempt.

The tablet was something of a problem at first. Olga found it impossible to swallow, although it was only a quarter of what was a very tiny one to start with, and the Sawdust family soon gave up the idea of forcing it down her throat for fear of hurting her.

In the end Mrs Sawdust decided to grind it into

powder and sprinkle it on her food, so each morning Mr Sawdust went out with a torch in search of a dandelion leaf.

Olga was pleased about the dandelion leaves. She was quite 'off' grass, and as for oats – if she never saw another oat again for the rest of her life it wouldn't worry her, for the effort required to bend over her feeding bowl was too much to bear.

But dandelion leaves were different. Something deep inside Olga told her that of all the food she could possibly have – and in the winter there wasn't a great deal of choice – dandelions were probably best of all.

News of Olga's misfortune quickly spread and Noel began paying regular morning visits so that he could issue bulletins to the others.

Fangio came to see her several times, and once he even brought her a piece of thistle he'd found in the Elysian Fields. But her house was much too high off the ground for him to give it to her, so he ate it himself and after a while went away again.

Even Graham came out of hibernation to see what was going on, and such a thing had never been known before.

After the first week Olga was taken to see the vet again, but he was still unable to make up his mind.

'Tell her to keep on taking the tablets,' he said, and then he explained that animals were like human beings in many ways and that sometimes if they'd had a bad fall or something which he called a 'slipped disc' the pain was so great that they were too scared to move, long after they were really better.

'Perhaps she needs a change,' he said, during their third visit. 'Something to take her out of herself.'

Olga felt this was much the most sensible remark she'd yet heard. Her present self felt so old and useless and painful she would have given almost anything to be taken out of it. It would be a pity to lose her fur, of course, especially after all the time she'd spent keeping it clean, but . . .

And then she heard Mrs Sawdust explain to her

daughter on the way home that what the vet really meant was that Olga ought to have a change of scene, not a change of body, and she became gloomy again.

'What's the use of new surroundings,' she thought, 'if I'm not well enough to enjoy them?'

However, shortly afterwards Olga did get a change of scene. Not a very big one to be sure, but certainly a break from her present humdrum existence.

Each evening when her own house was being cleaned out she was taken into the big house and placed on a rug in front of the living-room fire. Not so near that she would miss it when she went back home, but close enough for her to feel the warmth licking her face.

At first Olga was in two minds about the whole business, especially as Noel was usually around too.

It wasn't that she didn't trust Noel, it was simply a fact of nature that cats can't help chasing anything that moves. But she lay so still on the soft wool rug that really there was no excuse for such a thing happening and in time she began to look forward to her evenings out.

One of the things she enjoyed most was a large box which stood by itself in one corner of the room, for often the front of it lit up and became filled with tiny moving figures, some of whom even *talked*, while often there was the sound of music.

Whenever this happened Olga would stop whatever it was she was thinking so that she could pay proper attention.

Noel explained that it was called a 'television'. He wasn't very keen on it himself because the only smell it had was a kind of warm, burny one which wasn't very interesting, and once when he'd sniffed it too close his fur had given off a funny crackling sound.

But Olga grew to like the television more and more.

'It's just the thing for invalids,' said Mrs Sawdust, when she saw her look of fascination. 'It helps pass the time.'

One night Olga was allowed to stay up much later than usual and for some reason the music seemed to her ears more beautiful than any she had ever heard

before. Mrs Sawdust said that it was something called
'The Dance of the Sugar Plum Fairy', and sure
enough, as Olga watched a fairy did indeed appear, a
tiny, silvery figure, floating to and fro in time to the

music like a piece of thistledown caught on a breeze.
Sometimes the figure came close so that Olga could
see it quite clearly. Sometimes it took fright and ran

away again. And once it stood on its toes and spun round and round like a top until it seemed as if nothing could ever make it stop.

For a long while Olga sat entranced, unable to tear her gaze away from the screen. Then she closed her eyes and in her dreams she, too, began to dance. Slowly at first, and then, as the music grew louder, faster and faster until she felt herself spinning round and round just like the fairy in the box.

'Good gracious!' Dimly, from somewhere miles away, she heard a voice.

'Did you see that?' There was a chorus of excited voices, much closer this time. 'Olga ... you're standing up!'

As the music stopped and the applause rang out Olga opened her eyes and then nearly fell over backwards in astonishment.

It was true! She really had been standing! Not on one back paw as she had been in her dreams; not even on two back paws; but certainly on all four. And what was even more surprising was the fact that it didn't seem to hurt at all.

'I've been taken out of myself!' she squeaked. 'I've been taken out of myself at last!

'How nice to be living in such a magical age,' she

added, addressing the world in general. 'How lucky I am to be sure!'

And if Karen Sawdust noticed a row of whiskery faces pressed against the outside of the glass door leading to the garden she wisely kept it to herself. They all appeared to be nodding their agreement, but when she looked again they had disappeared, and there are some things to do with guinea-pigs that are best left unsaid. Especially when they've just been doing the Dance of the Sugar Plum Fairy.

It was enough for one evening that Olga was on her feet again.

CHAPTER TWELVE

The Night of the Moon Rockets

Having got back on her feet at long last Olga made a rapid recovery. Her eyes sparkled, her fur took on a new gloss, and she started making the occasional leap in the air, in the way that guinea-pigs do when they want to show that all is right in the best of possible worlds.

Not that she was able to leap very far, for the weather remained cold and her outside run had long since been put away for the winter, so apart from occasional excursions into the big house she spent most of the time in her own quarters.

In any case the lawn was almost permanently

covered in a blanket of dead leaves and as fast as Mr Sawdust raked it clean a fresh lot appeared.

Then Olga noticed a sudden change in the routine. Instead of placing the leaves straight on the bonfire, Mr Sawdust began piling them in a quite different part of the garden, along with sticks, boxes of waste-paper, old tree branches, and goodness knows what else, until he had an enormous pile almost as tall as himself.

Olga was rather pleased about this as she wasn't very keen on bonfires, especially when the wind blew the smoke the wrong way and made her eyes smart.

Then, late one afternoon, there was another un-usual happening.

It began when Karen Sawdust went into a near-by shed and came out again a moment later carrying a large pile of hay in her arms.

At first Olga thought that her house was going to have an extra-special clean out and she was just getting ready for it when to her surprise Karen Sawdust dis-appeared from view again.

And that wasn't the end of the affair by a long way.

Some time later she returned carrying what looked like a little old man on her shoulders. She went straight past Olga's house and placed the figure ON TOP OF THE PILE OF LEAVES.

Although Olga hadn't much liked the look of Karen Sawdust's new friend, for he had a red face which seemed to be tied on with string, and was very badly dressed, it did seem a little out of the ordinary to say the least.

But before she had time to dwell on the matter, let

alone put any of the two and two's together, Mr Sawdust appeared on the scene and with the help of his daughter picked up Olga's house, legs and all, and started to carry it away.

'Oh, dear,' thought Olga as she swayed to and fro, 'I hope they're not going to put *me* on the rubbish dump as well.'

But to her relief she found herself being taken round the side of the house and into the large room with big double doors where Mr Sawdust normally kept his car.

'It's only for this evening,' explained Karen Sawdust. 'You'll be much safer in here. We'll leave the door open in case Noel wants to come in out of harm's way.'

Olga poked her head out from beneath the hay.

'Safer?' she echoed, as the footsteps died away. 'Out of harm's way?' She peered up at the garage window. 'Dear, oh dear! What's going on now?'

The thought was hardly out of her mind when there was a flash and a whoosh and something shot past outside.

Olga nearly jumped out of her skin, but before she had time to recover from this first shock, there was a loud bang from somewhere overhead and what seemed like a million tiny stars suddenly appeared in the corner of sky she was able to see through the glass.

A moment later there was a scurry at the door and Noel shot through the gap, panting slightly and with his tail between his legs.

'Wheeeeeee!' shrieked Olga. 'Wheeeeeee! What's going on?'

'Goodness only knows,' said Fangio as he joined them. 'If you want my opinion everyone's gone mad. Bangs . . . crashes . . . hums . . . pops . . . rub-a-dubs. My spikes are all of a quiver!'

'Wheeeeee! Wheeeeeeee!' Olga's shrieks grew louder and more desperate with every passing minute as Fangio, his voice punctuated by more explosions from outside, went on to tell of some of the many narrow escapes he'd had before he'd reached the safety of the garage. 'Wheeeeeeee! Wheeeeeeeeeee!'

Noel glared at her. '*Must* you make that awful noise?' he asked. 'I came in here for some peace and quiet. It's worse than it is outside. You guinea-pigs are all the same. Squeak. Squeak. Squeak.'

Olga opened her mouth and then thought better of it. 'It's better than roaring,' she said stiffly. 'Or grunting. Or moaning. Or meowing like *some* I could mention!'

'You make it sound as if the world's coming to an end.' Noel, recovering from his fright, began to look rather superior as he had a quick wash. He peered out of the window as some more stars burst in the sky. 'It's probably only the humans going to the moon again. They're always at it. They go on things called rockets.'

Noel was often rather knowledgeable about things in general on account of his getting around a lot and coming across bits of information hidden away in dustbins.

With a great effort Olga pulled herself together. 'Guinea-pigs', she said, 'squeak because they've always squeaked. And as for going to the moon...' she paused, not wishing to be outdone by a mere cat, 'as for going to the moon, I don't see why the Sawdust people bother. We guinea-pigs did it years ago. In fact, that's how we got our squeaks.'

Noel and Fangio exchanged glances.

'All right,' said Fangio, settling down on an old pile of sacking. 'Tell us. At least it'll help take our minds off things.'

Olga took a deep breath and closed her eyes. 'It was the year One B.D.,' she began.

'Don't you mean B.C.?' interrupted Noel.

'I know what I mean,' said Olga, getting into her stride. 'B.D. stands for *Before Dandelions*, which was a very, *very* long time ago.

'As I think I've mentioned before, there were a lot of guinea-pigs in Peru at the time, and food had been getting more and more scarce. Had they known that dandelions would be discovered the next year they probably wouldn't have bothered, but as it was they decided one day to go to the moon to see if they could find any grass.

'Now in those days there weren't such things as . . .
er . . . dockets.'

'Rockets,' broke in Noel. 'It's spelt with an R.'

Olga opened one eye and fastened it on her audience.
'There weren't any R's either,' she said sternly. 'They
hadn't been invented.

'Anyway, to cut a long story short. Since there
weren't any dockets, or R's, or even any ladders small
enough for a guinea-pig, yet long enough to reach
the moon, they did the only thing possible. They
stood on each other's shoulders!'

Fangio stared at Olga open-mouthed. 'But the
moon's ages away,' he exclaimed. 'It's even farther
than the shrubbery!'

'If you really *want* something in this world,' said Olga simply, 'you'll never get it by sitting down and waiting. But if you go out and *do* things there's no knowing where you'll end up.

'They waited for a suitable night when there was a gap in the clouds and no wind and then they set off.

'First they all stood in a line – shortest on the right, tallest on the left. Then they chose the fattest and the strongest one of all to stand at the bottom.

'Then the next biggest climbed on to his back.

'Then the next biggest climbed on to the second one's back. Then the fourth, and so on and so on until at long last, just before dawn, the smallest guinea-pig of all started the long climb up to the top.

'They say it was an awesome sight. Animals from miles around came to watch and to wonder.

'And when word came down that the last guinea-pig of all had actually set foot on the moon such a roaring and barking and neighing and braying broke out there were some who thought the world had come to an end.

'It was then,' said Olga sombrely, 'that disaster struck.

'Strong though he was, the weight of all the other guinea-pigs had pushed the first one lower and lower

into the ground until his head was level with the surrounding turf.

'Suddenly a dew drop which had formed on a nearby blade of grass rolled off the edge, carrying with it a speck of dust, and landed on the end of his nose.

'He tried to lick it off but his tongue wasn't long enough.

'He tried shaking his head, but he couldn't.

'He tried holding his breath and thinking of other things.

'But it was no use.

'His nose began to twitch, and before he had time to warn the others of the danger he gave the biggest and loudest sneeze you could possibly imagine.

'The huge tower of guinea-pigs rocked and swayed most awesomely. For a second or two it seemed as though it might steady itself again, but then gradually a wavy motion set in and began to snake its way upwards. The line started to crumble and a moment later it collapsed and all the guinea-pigs fell to the ground.

'Fortunately the surrounding earth was very soft so none of them were badly hurt, but they were considerably shaken and it stopped all their moon

plans, for none of them felt strong or brave enough to
go through the experience again.

'It was a nasty moment – very nasty indeed.'

'It's very interesting,' said Noel doubtfully, breaking the silence which followed, 'but I still don't see
why guinea-pigs go "wheeeeeee".'

Olga stared pityingly at the others. 'You'd go
"wheeeeee",' she said, 'if you fell all that way.'

Noel and Fangio looked at each other. 'Ask silly
questions,' said Fangio, 'and you get silly answers.'

'We've been doing it ever since,' continued Olga
dreamily. 'Our *wheeeeeee*s have been handed down.
Why, do you know . . .' She opened her eyes, but
like the sparks from the fireworks her audience
seemed to have faded away.

Olga gave a sigh as she went back to her oats.
Taking others' minds off things was really most un-
rewarding at times. She sometimes wondered why
she bothered.

CHAPTER THIRTEEN

An Unexpected Visit

Olga was in trouble. Not serious trouble, but the kind where everyone else grumbles and you can't do a thing about it and even if you could there wouldn't be much point because no one would take any notice anyway.

It was all to do with her water bowl.

Each morning it was surrounded by a miniature lake, and unfortunately she kept getting the blame for knocking it over.

Olga got very fed up with all the fuss that went on, for only she was low enough to the floor to see the almost invisible hair-line crack in the side which was causing all the trouble.

'There are no two ways about it,' she decided. 'I simply must get rid of it. There'll be no peace until I do.'

But when you live in two rooms without so much as a back yard let alone a dustbin, getting rid of things isn't so easy. You simply have to rely on other people, and 'other people', being quite unaware of the problem, kept filling the bowl up again.

'I suppose', said Olga sadly, 'I shall have to spend the rest of my life tramping around with wet paws. I'll have rheumatism before I'm two most likely.'

And then one morning her chance came. For a brief moment she was left alone in her dining-room with the front door WIDE OPEN.

It needed only a tiny nudge and the job was done.

The crash brought feet running in her direction. The door was slammed shut and a very relieved voice called out 'Never mind . . . it's only her water bowl. Thank goodness *she* didn't fall out again!'

And Karen Sawdust replied, 'At least it's one problem solved. I'll give her a plastic bowl to be going on with and next week I'll put a note up the chimney.'

'*Put a note up the chimney!*' Olga stared through her window in disgust. 'What *are* they on about? *Really!*'

But she soon forgot the matter, for over the next

few days quite a number of equally strange things happened and her mind was awhirl trying to piece them all together.

For instance the very next evening Mr Sawdust came past her house carrying, of all things, a tree! She definitely saw him carrying a tree.

Then, a few nights later, there was the odd affair of the singing. Right outside her front door!

As far as she could tell it was Karen Sawdust and a group of her friends. It was difficult to make out the words, but it sounded very like 'While shepherds wash their socks by night'. It went on for some time, then there was a rattling sound as if something hard was being shaken about in a tin, and this was followed by some whispering sort of giggles as someone called out, 'We shan't get much there! Let's try next door.'

It was all very puzzling and most of the other animals had similar stories to tell.

Fangio related a fur-raising yarn of how he'd been pursued by an enormous van laden with parcels, which kept stopping and starting in the lane outside, and Noel, whose nightly prowlings took him over a wide area, reported that most of the other houses in the neighbourhood had suddenly taken to growing trees in their front rooms, and that not only were these covered with bits of paper and silvery string, but some even had coloured lights which flashed on and off.

Egged on by the others he had set off to investigate the one belonging to the Sawdust family, but in trying to catch one of the silver strings in his paw he'd brought the whole lot crashing down and had been banished from the house for the time being.

Olga voiced the thoughts of them all.

'Something', she said, 'is undoubtedly GOING ON!'

That very evening, long after it grew dark, there was an even more unusual happening.

Olga was in bed, safely tucked up in her nest of

hay, when someone opened her front door and began *cleaning out her dining-room.*

At least, that's what it sounded like. Scratchings, brushing noises, the smell of fresh sawdust being sprinkled on the floor; then a less familiar sound, rather like crackling paper. It went on for some while.

'Oh, well,' thought Olga, stifling a yawn, 'if they want to clean me out twice a day *I'm* certainly not stopping them.'

In any case her bed was much too snug to leave and in no time at all she was fast asleep again.

Whether it was because of all the excitement that had gone on during the past week, or whether it was partly the result of her disturbed night, Olga didn't know, but she slept much later than usual, and when she did finally open her eyes she found to her surprise that the shutter over her front door had already been taken down and the Sawdust family, Mr and Mrs Sawdust, Karen Sawdust, and both sets of grand-parents were gathered outside.

Another thing she noticed was that someone had tied a lot of green stuff outside her house – holly, it looked like, for she could see a cluster of red berries.

'Really!' she thought. 'Whatever next? There's no sense to it. You can't *eat* holly.'

So she yawned and stretched and was about to make her way through into the dining-room to see exactly what all the fuss was about, when she suddenly caught her breath and stopped dead in her tracks.

There was something odd about her floor. Odd, yet strangely familiar. Lines criss-crossing the sawdust. Lines which looked as if they'd been made with the aid of a stick. Lines which seemed to make up letters; letters which seemed to spell out . . .

OLGA DA POLGA!

Someone had written HER NAME in the sawdust. Just as she had done all that time ago when she had first come to live with the Sawdust family.

There was something else written below her name but Olga couldn't be bothered to read it. She ran round and round the dining-room squeaking with excitement, scattering the sawdust as she went.

'You see!' exclaimed Karen Sawdust triumphantly. 'She *does* know what it means! I told you so.'

'Yes, dear,' said Mrs Sawdust patiently, 'but I do wish she'd stop running around like that and open her parcel. It's cold standing out here.'

Olga came to a halt. 'A parcel? For *me*?'

She gazed round her dining-room and there, sure enough, in one corner was a small object wrapped in gaily coloured paper.

Olga liked paper. It seemed a very good idea to wrap a present in something you could eat. But she never really got the chance, for long before she'd taken the scantiest of nibbles the door opened and lots of hands came to help her undo her parcel.

As the last of the paper fell away Olga blinked in astonishment.

'Wheeeeee!' she squeaked, her eyes growing larger and larger. 'A new water bowl!'

And then she had a closer look. On the side of it, as clear and round and bright as possible, was written her name.

'You'd better take good care of this one,' warned Karen Sawdust as she carefully filled it. 'It's a present from Father Christmas and he only comes once a year.'

'A present from Father Christmas!' Olga sat staring at her new bowl long after the others had gone.

It was a truly magnificent bowl. It even made the water taste sweeter. And as for washing her feet – by doubling herself up there was almost room to do all four at once!

She could still hardly believe her eyes.

And if the cries of delight which greeted her ears every few moments were anything to go by she wasn't the only one to be pleasantly surprised that day.

Indeed, it wasn't long before Noel sauntered past licking his lips and smelling strongly of fish.

'Merry Christmas,' he said.

'Merry Christmas,' replied Olga.

Even Fangio had a bowl of milk put out for him.

'What a nice man Father Christmas must be,' thought Olga as she settled down in her hay after lunch. 'And how clever to know exactly what's wanted.' She gazed at the words on the side of her new bowl – OLGA DA POLGA. 'Even down to spelling a guinea-pig's name. No wonder he only has time to come once a year!'

Olga Meets Her Match

CHAPTER ONE

Olga Goes Away

Olga da Polga wasn't feeling well. She was far from being her usual self, and she hadn't been her usual self for several weeks.

Her condition was causing the Sawdust family a great deal of concern, and one morning Mr Sawdust decided something would have to be done about it.

Pausing on his way to work, he peered through the door of Olga's hutch and took a long, hard look at the ball of brown and white fur huddled deep inside the hay.

'If you ask me,' he said, 'that guinea-pig needs

taking out of herself. Look at her – she hasn't moved for days. A change of air – that's what she needs.'

A second figure joined him outside the wire netting. 'It might be worth a try.' Mrs Sawdust sounded slightly doubtful about the idea. 'As long as it isn't a change for the worse.'

'Well, we must do *something*,' said Mr Sawdust briskly. 'The whole thing's been going on far too long. We'll take a trip to the sea-side this week-end. There's nothing like a good, stiff sea-breeze through your whiskers when you're feeling low. It'll make a new animal of her.'

Olga stirred as the muffled voices filtered through the hay. For a moment or two she wondered if her ears were working properly – so much of her wasn't these days. She'd never even heard of a sea-side before, and as for being made into a new animal . . .

Scrambling to her feet she hurried into the dining-room to protest. 'Wheeeee!' she shrieked at the top of her voice. 'Wheeeeeee! I don't want to be made into a new animal, thank you very much. I like being a guinea-pig.'

But she had left it too late. Mr and Mrs Sawdust were nowhere in sight and Olga found herself addressing the empty air.

For a moment or two she stared indignantly at the

spot where they'd been. Then, partly because the excitement had suddenly made her feel hungry, but also because she wanted to make matters harder for

anyone who tried to tamper with her present arrangements, she turned to her food bowl.

Olga could be very difficult when she chose, and she ate an unusually hearty breakfast by any standards. When she had finished her oats she polished off a large pile of grass, and then rounded things off by eating several dandelions followed by two halves of a freshly split carrot for good measure.

'Just let them try making a new animal out of me now,' she gasped. 'Just let them try.'

Olga's stomach felt as tight as a drum. It was as much as she could do to drag herself back into her bedroom, and once there she sank down into the hay with a sigh of relief.

It was the first proper meal she'd had in ages, and if her eyes had been bigger than her stomach to begin with they certainly weren't now.

Olga's poor health was mostly the fault of the weather. The winter had been long and damp, and towards the end of it she had caught a nasty cold which had left her feeling weak and listless. Her fur had lost its usual gloss and she hardly bothered to keep herself tidy, which was most unusual.

The Sawdust family had taken her to the vet several times, and on his advice they'd tried mixing a few drops of cod liver oil in with her oats, but as she'd hardly been near her food bowl this had been of no help at all.

Gradually the unexpected meal began to have its effect. Olga's eyelids grew heavier and heavier and she sank deeper and deeper into her hay, until in no time at all she was fast asleep again.

How long she stayed that way Olga didn't know, but when she woke it was to the sound of yet another voice. This time it belonged to Karen Sawdust.

'Perhaps it isn't the cold at all,' she was saying. 'Perhaps she just needs company. She looks very lonely all by herself.'

'If that's the case,' said Mrs Sawdust meaningly, 'the sooner we make a move the better.'

'Oh, dear,' said Karen Sawdust. 'I do hope she doesn't fade away before we get there. Animals do that sometimes. They stop eating and lose the will to live and they simply fade away.'

Olga put on her most woebegone expression ever as the door of her hutch swung open. 'That's it,' she groaned to herself. 'I'm fading away. I expect if I looked in my drinking bowl now I wouldn't be able to see myself in the water I'm so faded.'

'*Fading away?*' exclaimed Mr Sawdust as he reached inside and picked her up. 'You must be joking!' He

squeezed Olga's stomach, gently but firmly. 'Feel that! Solid as a rock. And look at her bowl of oats – she's been through the lot. I reckon she's been having us on.'

Olga stared up at the others in disgust. 'You should have squeezed me this morning,' she thought. 'Or *tried* to more like it. You wouldn't have been able to then there was so little of me.'

Olga was so upset by the remarks being passed about her she scarcely noticed what was happening, and it wasn't until she took a deep breath and gathered her senses again that she realized she was sitting in a cardboard box.

Not only that, but in the background she could hear the sound of an engine.

She was sitting in a cardboard box in a motor car. And that could only mean one thing. She was being taken somewhere.

Suddenly it all came back to her. She was going to the sea-side!

Usually the thought of doing anything new filled her with excitement, but in her present state all it did was make her wish more than ever that she hadn't eaten quite so much. She was glad the Sawdust family had thought to line the box with hay, for it stopped her banging against the side when the car went round corners, and after her heavy meal Olga was in no fit state to bang against anything.

She lay where she was for a while, listening to the drone of the engine and to the sound of voices.

Karen Sawdust's voice floated through the hole in the lid of the box first. 'I've packed her case,' she said. 'There's a bagful of grass – in case she doesn't like it where she's going. And some oats, and some cod liver oil, and her own water bowl . . .' The voice paused for a moment and an eye appeared at the hole above Olga's

head. 'I wonder what it's like, being taken everywhere in a cardboard box?'

'Hmmmm,' said Olga to herself. 'You may well ask. I might not even have *wanted* to go.'

'She may not even have wanted to go,' persisted Karen Sawdust. 'I wish we could read her thoughts.'

Olga began to feel very superior. 'You may not be able to read *my* thoughts,' she squeaked. 'But I can read yours!'

'I suppose,' broke in Mr Sawdust, 'it's much the same as if a great big giant came along and picked one of *us* up. Rather frightening.'

'Not if it was a nice giant,' said Karen Sawdust. 'One you could trust and you *knew* wouldn't harm you. One who always took you to nice places – like the sea-side. Oh, I *do* wish I knew what she's thinking.'

But by then Olga wasn't really thinking anything at all. She'd been with the Sawdust family for so long now it didn't need any talk about giants – nice or nasty – for her to know they wouldn't let any harm come to her. The heavy meal and the warmth of the car were making her feel sleepy again. And the experience of riding through the countryside was no longer new. She'd done it so many times before it was really rather boring. Everything went past at such a speed it was impossible to take it all in, and once you've seen one field you've seen the lot – especially if you can't stop and nibble it.

It was dark when Olga woke. At least, dark wasn't quite the right word; for it was a dark with lights on. Brightly coloured lights. Red lights, blue lights, green lights; lights of many different colours, hanging just above her head almost as if the sky had suddenly closed in on them.

She scrambled to her feet, hoping for a better look. 'Wherever have I got to now?' she breathed.

Licking her lips in anticipation, she gave a start and then licked them again. They had a strange, yet somehow very familiar taste. She'd come across it before somewhere. Then she remembered. It was called *salt*. That was it – salt. She'd once stepped in some by accident when she'd been left in the Sawdust family's kitchen while her own house was being cleaned out. And now the air was full of it.

139

'Well, Olga?' Karen lifted up the lid of the box so that she could have a better view. 'You're at the sea-side now. What do you think of it?'

'Wheeeeee!' Olga gave an excited squeak as she peered over the edge. 'I'm at the sea-side. And it's got lots of coloured lights and it tastes salty and . . .'

She pricked up her ears as a roaring sound filled the air. It was like nothing she had ever heard before; almost as if someone was pouring an enormous pile of stones out of a sack.

'There's the sea!' exclaimed Karen Sawdust. She tilted the box a little more. 'Look at all the waves breaking on the shore.'

Olga gave another squeak, partly with delight, partly with fear, as she saw a huge white-topped wall of water rushing towards her.

'Wheeeee!' she shrieked. 'Wheeeeeeeee! I'm going to get wheeeeeeett . . . I know I am . . . I . . .'

But Olga didn't get wet, for the wall of water suddenly appeared to change its mind, and with a deep sighing roar it collapsed in a heap on the beach. Olga never did know what happened to it after that, for just then Mr Sawdust did something to the car and they turned down a side street away from the sea.

She wasn't sure whether to feel pleased or sorry, but

as it happened she didn't really have time to feel either. A moment later they drew to a halt outside a large house and she felt her box bobbing up and down once more as the family climbed out of the car.

A light went on and for the next few minutes the air was alive with a babble of strange voices. Olga couldn't make out much of what was going on, but from the little she could understand it seemed they were staying with friends and that she, Olga, had a house of her own all ready for her.

'Fancy having a house of my own at the sea-side!' she breathed. 'Whatever next?'

But the 'whatever next' turned out to be something even Olga hadn't bargained on. She caught sight of it as she was being put into her room. It was written in large letters above the door. Just one word, but it set her mind awhirl.

After the others had gone Olga lay quite still for a long while thinking about it. She was so used to seeing her own name – OLGA DA POLGA – painted above her own front door she could still hardly believe she'd seen aright. But she knew she had. 'B – O – R – I – S' it had said. BORIS!

And then in a sudden blinding flash it came to her. 'They've made a new animal of me after all!' she squeaked. 'They've made a new animal of me – and

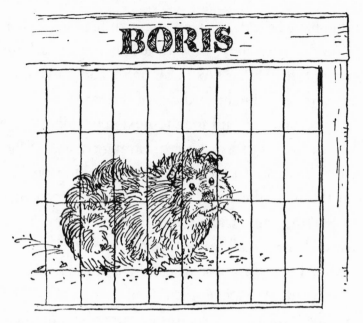

it didn't hurt a bit. In fact,' she ran round and round
her hutch several times just to make doubly sure,
'I think I feel better already!'

CHAPTER TWO

A Strange Meeting

Olga slept well that night, better than she had for a long time, and when she woke the following morning she felt unusually refreshed.

'How nice to be brand new again!' she squeaked, as she hurried into her dining-room.

Peering into the water bowl she half expected to see some strange new face staring back at her, but it looked much the same as usual.

'They've probably kept the best of the old,' she thought. 'And very wise of them too. I don't think I would really like to change that much and not be recognized.'

She ate a hearty breakfast, for the sea air was already having its effect, and then she sat back in order to study her new surroundings.

Her holiday house was not unlike the one she had with the Sawdust family. A little more cramped perhaps, and not quite as well cared for, but really very pleasant. Things weren't in their proper place, of course. But then other people's never were. The food bowl was on the wrong side of the dining-room for a start, but a few good shoves soon put that right. And the sawdust wasn't scattered entirely to her liking, but again that was quickly attended to.

Her housework done for the day, Olga turned her attention to the view through the window. Rather disappointingly, she couldn't actually see the sea, but in the distance she could distinctly make out the sound of waves breaking on the shore. And the smell of the sea was all around her. In the air, in the hay, even in the food she ate.

At the back of the house there was a lawn and a flower bed, and beyond that a strange low building quite unlike anything she had ever seen before.

It seemed to be made of stone and it covered quite a large area. The surrounding walls were about the same height as her own garden run at home, and apart from the main building, which stood at the far end, there were a number of towers, each one a miniature castle in itself.

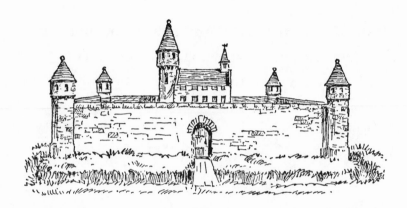

The whole area was covered by wire-netting – either to keep other animals out or to keep *something* in, and Olga spent some time wondering what on earth it could be.

In an odd kind of way it made her feel homesick, for she felt sure that given half a chance she could weave many a fanciful tale about the place, and the more she thought about it the more she wished that one or other of her friends – Noel the cat, or Fangio the hedgehog or even Graham the tortoise, had come with her on holiday so that she could try some of them out.

Tales of princesses locked in one of the towers – perhaps even a whole family of princesses – one in each tower, kept from ever seeing each other by some creature who lived in the big house.

Olga's imagination began to run riot. 'If only,' she thought, 'if only I could have a peep inside. Just one peep, that's all I ask.'

And then, hardly had the thought left her mind, than the strangest thing happened. A shadow crossed in front of the window, there was a click as the door catch was opened, and Karen Sawdust came into view.

'Olga,' she said, holding out both hands palms uppermost to make a cradle, 'I hope you're on your best behaviour today. You're going out visiting.'

'Visiting?' Olga's heart began to beat faster as she felt herself being carried across the lawn.

'The *castle*!' she squeaked excitedly. 'Wheeeee! I'm going to visit the castle. The Sawdust people must be able to read my thoughts after all!'

For a moment or two it all seemed too good to be true. But then, as they drew near, she began to have second thoughts.

The castle was surrounded by a kind of moat, and the only way in – or *out* – appeared to be by means of a plank of wood which led to a small door let into the side of one of the walls. Closer to, it looked somewhat dark and forbidding and she would have been perfectly happy to let matters rest there. A peep was one thing, but actually going inside such a place was quite another matter. In fact, if she'd had a tail to turn Olga would have turned it then and there and made a run for it. But she'd left things much too late. Before she could utter a single squeak of protest Karen Sawdust bent down, slid the door open, and Olga felt herself being bundled through the opening.

As the door slid shut behind her she crouched where she was, as still as the very stone the castle was made of, while she took careful stock of her new surroundings.

It was much brighter inside than she had expected. The walls were painted white, and rather unexpectedly the floor was made of grass.

After a moment or two, Olga plucked up courage and had a quick nibble. It was rather nice grass. Not quite the sort she'd been used to. For one thing it was too salty for her taste, but really . . . she took another nibble – folding the blade neatly in two so that she could test it twice as thoroughly, it was quite nice considering, and definitely eatable.

'If something *is* about to happen to me,' she decided, 'it may as well happen on a full stomach.'

Olga was extremely busy for the next few minutes. In no time at all she had cleared such a large patch in front of her she was almost up to the main building, and her mind was so at peace it was hard to believe it had ever been otherwise.

It was while breaking off for a well-earned rest that Olga suddenly had an odd feeling she was being watched. She looked round carefully, but apart from a few seagulls wheeling in the sky overhead there wasn't a soul in sight; and she'd just returned to her nibbling when she nearly jumped out of her skin with fright.

Just in front of her there was an opening in the wall of the main building which she hadn't noticed before, and standing barely a whisker's length away in the darkness beyond was another guinea-pig. It was so close, and it was staring back at her so unwinkingly, she might well have been looking at a reflection of herself in a mirror.

For a moment neither of them spoke, and then the other stirred.

'You must be Olga,' he said. 'I was told you were coming.'

Olga nodded, for her mouth was still too full to do anything else.

'You're not one of the Volga Olgas, are you, by any chance?'

Olga gobbled down the remains of the grass. 'One of the *Volga* Olgas?' she repeated, taken aback for the moment by this sudden and unexpected question. 'Most certainly *not!*'

'Pity.' The other guinea-pig made to leave and then paused. 'The Volga,' he said, looking back at Olga, 'happens to be a river in Russia. And if you'd been Russian I might have let you have a feed of my oats. As it is, I'm afraid I must ask you to leave by the next troika.' With that he turned on his heels and disappeared into the darkness.

Olga stared at the spot where he'd been for quite a while, trying to make up her mind about the matter. 'Volga?' she kept repeating to herself. ' *Troika*? What *can* he have been on about?

'Perhaps,' she thought, 'I was right after all. Perhaps there *are* some princesses being kept a prisoner. Guinea-pig princesses. Perhaps they have a mad father. Perhaps . . .'

And then she gathered herself together. 'Wheeee!'

she shrieked into the opening. 'This is a fine way to treat a sea-side guest. I wouldn't have any of your oats for all the groundsel in the world. I wouldn't . . .' She broke off as a figure appeared in the opening again.

'I'm sorry,' said the other guinea-pig. 'It was very rude of me. It was just that for one moment I thought perhaps . . .' A sad note crept into his voice, and then with an effort he pulled himself together. 'By the way, my name's Boris,' he continued, abruptly changing the subject. 'Boris Borski. Most people just call me Boris. I expect you saw it written above my hutch. This is my summer residence.'

Olga felt a pang of disappointment. She wasn't a new animal after all. 'Boris,' she repeated, putting on one of her superior expressions. 'That's very short.'

'I do have others,' said Boris grandly. 'But I won't bother you with them today. They're Russian and they all have *skis* on the end.' He gave a yawn. 'It's tiring having to go through the lot.'

'I have a *very* long name,' said Olga, not wishing to be outdone. 'And the Sawdust people said it's sort of Russian. It's *Olga da Polga*.'

'That's not *real* Russian,' said Boris scornfully. 'If it was *real* Russian it would have a *ski* on the end. It would be Olga da Polski. All Russians have a *ski* on the end of their names. At least, all the ones I saw last ni...' He broke off, as if he'd said something he hadn't meant to, and tried to cover his confusion by staring even more accusingly at Olga.

But Olga was hardly listening. While Boris was talking her mind had been racing on ahead.

'I *would* have had one,' she said, 'but it fell off when my ancestors were crossing the Alps. There were hundreds of them and it was bitterly cold at the time. It was so cold all the *skis* fell off the ends of their names and got left behind in the snow. That's why,' she continued wildly, remembering a conversation she'd once heard the Sawdust family having, 'even to this day they have places in the Alps called *ski resorts*. People go there from all over the world just to see where it happened. They've even tried using *ski lifts* to get them out, but it's no good ...'

Olga's voice trailed away as she suddenly realized she was talking to herself.

Looking most offended, she stared at the opening. Really, she wasn't used to such treatment when she was telling one of her tales, particularly when she was just about to get into her stride.

'If you like,' Boris reappeared again as mysteriously as he'd left, 'I'll tell *you* a story.'

'*You* tell *me* a story!' Olga could hardly believe her ears, and for a brief moment her indignation was so great she was hard put to think of a suitable reply. Then gradually her curiosity got the better of her. After all, it *was* a nice day, and she *was* on holiday, and ... 'If it gives you pleasure,' she said, not ungraciously.

'Mind you,' she added, as she settled herself down, 'it's quite possible I shall have heard it before. I know so many.'

'I doubt,' said Boris, 'if you've ever heard a story quite like this one. This story has been handed down!'

CHAPTER THREE

Boris's Story

'For this story,' said Boris, 'you will have to try and picture yourself living in Russia. This may not mean much to you, but my father used to be the Tzar. He ruled over the whole of the land. As far as the eye could see, from North to South, from East to West – it all belonged to him.'

Boris opened one eye cautiously in order to see how his tale was going so far. Olga returned his gaze with a mixture of surprise and admiration. She had to admit

153

it was the kind of beginning she would have loved to have thought up herself.

'To look at me now,' said Boris, 'you probably wouldn't believe I was once a six-foot-three prince with blue blood in my veins.'

'I certainly wouldn't,' agreed Olga.

Boris looked slightly put out. 'Would you believe a *five*-foot-three prince with pink blood?' he asked.

'I might,' said Olga, not wishing to put him off completely in case she missed something exciting.

Boris settled back into himself. 'When I think about it,' he continued, before Olga had time to change her mind, 'it seems only yesterday that I used to sit on the steps outside my father's palace listening to the bala- leikas. Afterwards we would all go for long rides through the snow on a horse-drawn sledge. I can still hear the sound of the bells tinkling in the moonlight. We had a real moon in those days. A great big one – not like that thing they've got up there now.'

He gave a sigh. 'All that was a long time ago, of course. Before I came down to this.'

Olga looked about her. 'It seems all right to me,' she said. 'I don't know any other guinea-pigs who have a castle all to themselves.'

'But it's not what I've been *used* to,' said Boris.

'That's the thing. Not even a hook for a chandelier – nothing. Once you're *used* to these things it's hard to make the change.'

'I was brought up in a pet shop,' said Olga. '*I* made the change all right.'

'A pet shop?' echoed Boris. He gave a hollow laugh. 'A *pet shop*? Do you realize that when I was small we had more servants than there are blades of grass in this run? I never had to lift a finger. I just *thought* what I wanted and it happened. My every wish was granted.'

'We were cleaned out every day,' said Olga. 'And we always had food. I don't see what else there is to think about.'

'I'll tell you what there was to think about,' said Boris grandly. 'Nothing! All day long there was nothing to think about – except having fun. And every evening, after dinner, there was a ball. People dressed up in their finest clothes and wore their most precious jewels, and we danced, and we sang, and we ate until we could eat no more.

'And next morning the troikas would draw up outside the palace gates carrying fresh supplies of grass from the near-by plains. Then it would begin all over again.'

'*Grass?*' repeated Olga suspiciously.

'In those days,' said Boris hurriedly, 'even humans

liked grass. Besides, it wasn't ordinary stuff. We had our own special fields, where the blades were as tall as a man and twice as thick as the arms of those who were sent out to gather it.'

Olga tried hard to picture the kind of grass Boris had just described compared with the sort Mr Sawdust brought in from the lawn each morning. 'If it was all so nice,' she said, giving it up as a bad job, 'what made you come and live here?'

'I'm very glad you asked me that,' said Boris, looking as if he felt quite the opposite.

'Well?' demanded Olga impatiently.

'You probably won't believe this next bit,' said Boris, 'but the people – the very same people my father had looked after all his life – they held a revolution and they all rose up and attacked the palace!'

'I don't find it a bit hard to believe,' said Olga bluntly. 'Not if you kept on telling them what a fine time you were having. I expect they wanted one too.' In point of fact Olga herself was beginning to tire of Boris's story with all its harping on the good things of life.

'That's all very well,' said Boris, 'but the thing is I was about to be married.' A dreamy look came into his eyes. 'My bride-to-be had light-blue eyes and hair the colour of ripening oats. She was said to be the most beautiful princess in all the land . . .'

'Story princesses always are,' said Olga knowledgeably. 'I've never ever heard of an ugly one.'

Boris chose to ignore the interruption. Instead he began running round and round in circles as he warmed to his tale.

'It was early morning when the first attack began, and it was all over within the hour. The guards held out as long as they could, but they were heavily outnumbered. Boom! Boom! Bang! Bang! Bang! One by one they fell at their posts, and gradually the mob got nearer and nearer, until at last they were inside the palace grounds and hammering on the door.'

He paused in mid-run and turned to Olga. 'What do you think my father did then?'

'I've no idea.' Olga tried hard to make it sound as if she didn't care either, but without much success. Although one half of her wasn't sure whether to believe Boris or not, the other half was only too eager to try. 'What *did* he do?'

'He sent for the Court Magician,' said Boris, 'and he ordered him to change us both into guinea-pigs. We were put into separate hutches in the Royal guinea-piggery for safety, and there we stayed.

'I expect you can guess the rest,' he said sadly. 'The Magician was supposed to change us back again when it was all over, but he was killed in the fighting, so there we were – stuck.

'After a day or two we were each set free at different times and went our separate ways. It's said that only if we both meet up again will we ever change back into our real selves. That's why, when I heard you were coming to stay, I thought perhaps . . .' Boris's voice trailed away and then with an effort he pulled himself together again. 'To think,' he said dramatically, 'all those diamonds and things in Russia really belong to me. Why, just one of them would probably keep me in oats for the rest of my life. But when you add up all the guinea-pigs there must be in the world . . .'

Olga looked at him thoughtfully. 'How will you know your princess when you meet her?' she asked.

Boris gazed back at her. 'I suppose,' he said carefully, 'you *could* ask the same thing of her.'

Olga took a deep breath and put on one of her far-away expressions. 'You know,' she said, 'I think *I* have a story coming on now. Shall we go over in the corner? You never know who might be listening, and it's really rather special.'

Olga had enjoyed Boris's tale, but more than that it

had set her own mind awhirl. Now she felt it was most
definitely her turn.

When they had settled down again she began to talk.
She talked and she talked and she talked; all through
the morning and on into the afternoon as well. She
talked so much neither of them even glanced at the
grass all round them, let alone ate any; and when she
had finished they lay for a long while basking silently
together in the afternoon sun.

'Fancy,' said Boris at last, 'I've waited all this time.'
He snuggled closer to Olga. 'And now you're here,
my princess.'

'Now *we're* here,' said Olga pointedly. 'How nice
it's going to be to share everything.'

Olga felt very pleased with herself, and she could tell that Boris was very impressed too. All the best story tellers believe in their own tales and by now Olga was convinced hers was true.

She wondered what it would be like living in Russia, and whether the Sawdust family would come and visit her. No doubt she would soon get used to all the servants.

They stayed for a while longer without saying anything, then she looked up at the sky. Goodness alone knew how long they had been together, for the sun was already sinking behind the far wall.

'I wonder how long it takes to change back into a princess?' she remarked dreamily. 'I hope the Sawdust people take me out of here first. There won't be room to stand and I don't want to get my golden locks caught in all that wire netting.'

But for some reason Boris had suddenly become restless. He didn't seem at all concerned about possible damage to Olga's hair.

He grew more and more impatient, and as the sun finally disappeared from view he jumped to his feet and hurried across to the front door.

'Is anything the matter?' asked Olga.

'They're late,' said Boris crossly. 'It's getting dark and they're late.'

Olga badly wanted to know who and how and why, but by then Boris was looking so worried she didn't dare ask for fear of upsetting him even more. In any case she didn't get the chance, for at that moment Karen Sawdust came down the garden path, and before she could utter so much as a goodbye 'Wheeeee!' Olga found herself back in her hutch.

Shortly afterwards the people they were staying with went past carrying Boris.

Olga called out, but Boris obviously had his mind on other things, for he either didn't hear, or if he did he couldn't be bothered to answer, and a moment later he'd disappeared into the big house along with the others.

When all was quiet again Olga peered at her reflection in the water. It had been a strange day. She felt quite different after it. Somehow, she had the feeling things would never be the same again. As for Boris . . . she gave a deep sigh . . . he was really rather handsome. A trifle gloomy perhaps – which, if all he'd said was true, wasn't surprising – but very handsome. The rosettes in his fur were quite the nicest she had ever seen – apart from her own, of course. Looking at him it was easy to believe he might once have been a prince. He would make a very suitable husband.

Stirring at last, Olga scrabbled about in her hay for a moment or two, fluffing it up to make it more comfortable. As she did so she wondered if it would be her last night in a hutch, and how she would take to the feel of silken sheets.

She'd seen sheets hanging on the line at the Sawdust family's house and she'd often wondered how anyone could possibly sleep in them. Perhaps she would soon find out.

When she'd finished making her bed Olga spent some time trying to make up her mind which way to lie. In the end she decided to sleep half in the dining-room, half in the bedroom, in order to leave plenty of room for expansion.

It would hardly do for a princess to begin her life

stuck inside a guinea-pig hutch and suffer the indignity of having to be sawn out.

Soon she was fast asleep.

CHAPTER FOUR

A Rude Awakening

In contrast to her first evening away from home, Olga
didn't sleep at all well that night. She seemed to spend
most of the time dreaming. If she wasn't listening to
balalaikas she was riding through snow on horse-
drawn sledges, or dancing or climbing in and out of
troikas. When she woke she felt quite worn out by it
all.

Worse still, for a second or two she had a job to
move, and for a dreadful moment she thought she
really had changed into a princess and was stuck inside
the hutch. But it turned out she had somehow or other

got her head stuck beneath an old ash branch Boris kept in a corner for his teeth.

Once free and properly awake she could hardly wait for the moment when they would be together again, especially when she heard Mr Sawdust say it was their last morning at the sea-side, and when at long last she was put in the outside run she hurried eagerly towards the tower in the far corner.

'Wheeeeeee!' she squeaked. 'Wheeeeeeeee! I'm here! Boris, I'm here!'

A familiar face appeared in the opening and regarded her without so much as a flicker of recognition.

'Morning all,' said Boris, in a polite but unusually gruff voice. 'What can I do for you?'

Olga stared back at him. This wasn't the kind of welcome she'd expected; if indeed it could be called a welcome at all.

Seeing that it was up to him to make the next move, Boris cleared his throat and made a sort of grunting noise. 'Er . . . to look at me,' he said, 'you probably wouldn't think I was once a six-foot-two policeman.'

'A six-foot-two policeman?' echoed Olga, as if in a dream.

'In my cotton socks,' said Boris. 'I was a lot taller in my boots.'

He stared accusingly at Olga. 'Where were you on the twenty-ninth?' he demanded.

'Where was I on the twenty-ninth?' Once again Olga found herself repeating Boris's words, for the simple reason that for the life of her she couldn't think of anything else to say.

'You'd better have an answer by the time I get back,' said Boris sternly. 'Otherwise I may have to take down your particulars.'

'Take down my particulars!' wailed Olga. 'But I haven't got any particulars. I'm Olga da Polga. Your princess . . . remember?'

But Boris not only showed no sign of being aware of Olga's new position in life, he didn't even appear to remember a single thing that had taken place the previous day.

'If you like,' he said, 'I'll tell you a story. It's all about a detective. It's very exciting.'

Olga stared back at him open-mouthed. For once she was completely at a loss for words. Then she gave him a look. It was the most withering look she could manage. It was so withering it ought by rights to have gone straight through Boris and out through the concrete wall behind him as well, and it left her feeling quite weak.

'That's the last time I ever talk to anyone at the sea-side,' she announced to herself, as she turned her back. 'And it's certainly the very last time I let anyone tell me a story. Why, there wasn't an ounce of truth in it from start to finish. How anyone can tell stories like that I just don't know . . . I shall never believe anything anyone tells me again.'

In her indignation Olga hardly knew whether she was coming or going. All she wanted was to get back home again. Thank goodness it was her last morning away. She couldn't wait to leave. Even the grass had a nasty taste and kept getting stuck in her throat.

Altogether Olga was so upset by the outcome of her

week-end with Boris she hardly squeaked a word on the journey home and even the Sawdust family began to look worried.

'I do hope she hasn't had a relapse,' said Karen Sawdust. 'She was looking so well first thing this morning. Perhaps I shouldn't have put her out with Boris.'

'That,' thought Olga, 'is the first sensible thing I've heard said today!'

'Maybe,' said Mrs Sawdust, 'she's missing him. They seemed to be getting on terribly well together.'

'And *that*,' thought Olga, 'is so far from being the

second most sensible thing I've heard, it just isn't true. *Me* – miss *Boris*? Really! Humans haven't got much sense at times. I don't give a "Wheeee!" if I never set eyes on him again!'

And she let out such a cry of disgust at the very idea Mr Sawdust nearly lost control of the car and drove them all into a ditch.

On the other hand, although she kept thinking these things to her 'outer self', Olga had very different thoughts deep inside her. In spite of everything, her 'inner self' still couldn't help thinking about him, and when she heard his name mentioned she pricked up her ears at once.

'Funny chap, Boris,' said Mr Sawdust. 'Very independent. Probably comes from living in a castle.'

'More likely all that television,' said Mrs Sawdust. 'It can't be good for him. I've never seen an animal stay quite so glued to a screen before. He looked most upset yesterday evening when they turned it off before the programme finished.'

'It's the same every night apparently,' broke in Karen Sawdust. 'They have a job to get him away from it. He runs up and down in front of the set when it's a cowboy film, and he sits very still when it's a story. He really seems to take it all in. It must have an effect.'

'I suppose it's a bit like Olga was with the ballet that

time,' agreed Mrs Sawdust. 'After she'd had that fall.
It wasn't until she saw *The Dance of the Sugar Plum
Fairy* on the television that she began to get better.'

'Two of a kind really, I suppose,' said Mr Sawdust.

Olga sank back into her hay as the voices droned on.

So that was it. Television! That box with moving
pictures the Sawdust people had in their home. Boris
led a different life each day according to the kind of
programme he'd seen the night before. One day a
Russian prince, the next day a detective. She understood perfectly now.

Any disappointment Olga might have felt about not
being a princess after all was more than made up for by
knowing the truth of the matter. Goodness only knew

what Boris would be tomorrow. She suddenly wished she was back with him so that she could find out.

If only she'd been more understanding. If only . . . but it was too late now. *Much* too late. Olga resolved there and then never to jump to conclusions again.

'Fancy us being two of a kind!' she squeaked. 'Wheeeeeeee! How exciting!'

Now that her mystery had been solved she was dying to get back home so that she could tell the others. Considering all the things that had happened to her she felt sure that she could make up a tale fanciful enough to impress even Noel the cat, let alone her other friends, Fangio and Graham.

CHAPTER FIVE

Olga Solves a Mystery

The rest of the journey seemed to take an age, but as soon as she was safely inside her house she rushed to the front door and called out in order to let the others know she was back.

A moment later Fangio and Graham, who'd obviously been hanging about inside the shrubbery, came out to greet her.

'You'll never guess where I've been,' squeaked Olga as they drew near. '*I've* been to the sea-side. *And* I stayed with a prince! He was a detective prince, and there aren't many of those left!'

Olga had decided there was no need to tell the others *everything* about her week-end. Some stories were all the better for what was left out rather than what was put in.

But as it happened, before the others had a chance to reply, the back door of the big house opened and various members of the Sawdust family came outside and began shouting and whistling and calling for Noel.

Olga felt rather pleased, not only because she liked a big audience, but also because she'd been rushing

about so much she really needed time to compose herself. 'I may as well wait for him,' she said carelessly. 'I know he'll want to hear all about my adventures.'

'You'll be lucky,' said Fangio gloomily. 'I haven't seen him since the night you went away.'

'You've not seen him?' Olga felt her heart suddenly miss a beat.

'I haven't either,' agreed Graham. 'Not that *that* means anything of course. When you're a tortoise you can sometimes go for days without seeing anyone if you happen to be facing the wrong way.'

Olga looked from one to the other, hardly able to believe her ears. 'But he was left in charge of someone,' she wailed. 'He was left in charge of a neighbour. They were coming in to feed him and make sure he

was all right. I heard the Sawdust family talking about it.'

'Well, he's not there now by the sound of it,' said Graham bluntly. 'They wouldn't be out looking for him otherwise.'

Fangio nodded. 'If you want my opinion,' he said ominously, 'it means one thing, and one thing only. Noel's missing.'

'Perhaps,' suggested Fangio, as the Sawdust family went indoors again, 'he got on a lorry by mistake and was driven off. He could be anywhere by now.' Living as he did in a garage, Fangio was very motoring minded.

'He might even have been run over,' said Graham gloomily.

Fangio considered the matter for a while. 'It's

possible,' he said dubiously. 'Although I should have thought we'd have heard something if he has. Still, I'll make inquiries.'

Being used to death all around them, on the roads and in the woods and hedgerows, Graham and Fangio tended to look on Noel's disappearance as being part of the general pattern of things. They were sorry of course, but being sorry didn't change things and tomorrow would be another day, full of other problems to worry about.

'These things happen,' said Fangio comfortingly, as he caught sight of the look on Olga's face. 'It happens to us hedgehogs all the time. Take a simple thing like crossing a road. You look right, you look left, you look right again. And what happens? Whizz, bang, wallop . . . in between looking left and looking right something comes rushing up from behind and squashes you flat as a pancake. I tell you, you're much better off living in a hutch. You're not safe anywhere these days.'

'It's worse if you're a tortoise,' said Graham. 'If you live in a round shell like me and haven't even got a right or a left to start with you don't know where you are.'

The others digested this piece of information. Graham had a habit of coming out with odd state-

ments from time to time, and they somehow felt
there was a flaw in this particular one. But neither of
them could put their paw on it and they were too un-
sure of their ground to argue, so soon afterwards the
meeting broke up.

Olga sat where she was, staring into space. It was
all right for Fangio and Graham; they were able to
roam the countryside at will, wherever and whenever
they wanted to. But she relied entirely on having visitors and the thought of never again seeing Noel made
her sadder than she would have dreamed possible.
The world suddenly seemed a colder place and for a
long while she stared unblinkingly at the spot where
she'd last seen him in the hope that he might reappear
as if by magic.

Catlike, Noel often disappeared for hours on end. Sometimes for a whole day. But he always turned up again. No one knew where he went to on his rambles, and the only time Olga had ever questioned him he'd put on such a superior expression she'd decided never to give him the pleasure of hearing her ask again. Now she wished she had.

Noel had survived many adventures, but as the day wore on and there was still no sign of the familiar black shape wending its way slowly up the garden Olga grew more and more unhappy. What with chasing birds and investigating various crackles in the undergrowth it sometimes took him ages to reach the house, but he'd never, ever, taken this long before.

The evening started to draw in, but still she didn't move. She refused to believe that anything had happened to him. She simply refused to believe it. She knew . . . she just knew, he must be somewhere around. The thing was . . . where? And how could she, shut inside her house, ever hope to find out?

For the umpteenth time Olga found herself wondering what Boris would have done. Boris, the detective, would have known what to do. Boris, the detective, would have looked for clues. Boris would have . . .

'Oh, Olga!' Karen Sawdust, her voice strangely subdued, appeared at the door. She opened it and held out her hands for Olga to climb into. 'I wish you could come in with us. But Daddy's lit the fire and he piled so much coal on before we left it's roaring away like nobody's business. Mummy thinks you'd get roasted alive and you wouldn't like that. Besides, I couldn't bear it if anything happened to you as well.'

She gave Olga her supper and then said goodnight before putting up the wooden front over the door to keep out the chilly night air.

When she was alone again Olga had a quick nibble of her oats and then wandered slowly and thoughtfully into her bedroom.

Something Karen had said was on the tip of her mind. What could it have been? She went over the conversation a dozen times. It had been mostly about fires and coal and being roasted, catching a cold . . . She tried turning the words about, sideways, back to front, every possible way . . . fire, coal, roasted, coal, roasted, fire, coal . . . And then, just as she was about to give up, she let out a squeak of excitement. 'Wheeeeeeeee!' It was there! It was there! Her first clue.

Her heart pounding away nineteen to the dozen, Olga turned her thoughts over in her mind several times. If Noel had been taken off on the back of a lorry then there was nothing she or anyone else could do about it, but if he *was* still somewhere around, then it was just possible . . . She came to a decision.

Hurrying across her room, she pressed her nose hard against the window and gave a loud squeak. 'Wheeeeeeee!' There was no reply. 'Wheeeeeeeeeeee!' She tried again, louder this time, but still without success. Filling her lungs so full of air they felt as if they would burst at any moment, she gave one last, long, loud squeak. 'Wheeeeeeeeeeeeeeeeeeee!' It was really dark now. Dark and still, and the sound echoed eerily round the buildings before it disappeared into the night.

Olga lay back in her hay and listened, hardly daring to breathe for fear she might have been wasting her time. But sure enough, a moment later there came a faint answering meeow. It was a strange kind of meeow – a mixture of all kinds of things; relief, hope, frustration, bad-temper, impatience; but it definitely belonged to Noel, and in the circumstances it was the kind of meeow Olga would have expected him to make.

She closed her eyes, a look of quiet satisfaction on her face. Two clues in one evening was a very good start to being a detective. She felt even Boris would have been pleased with her efforts.

As for the rest; that would have to wait until morning. She had done all she could for the time being, and she would have a fine tale in the morning.

All about the clue she'd had the night before when Karen Sawdust had put her to bed . . . and the meeow in the night; plus a lot more things she'd made up, to do with tracks and pawprints. And of the long hours she'd had to wait until she'd been taken out for her daily run on the lawn. And how when she'd got near the outhouse she'd kicked up such a fuss Mr Sawdust had been forced to unlock the door and look inside . . .

*

'He's back! He's back! Noel's back!' Fangio, anxious to be first with the news, hurried up to Olga's outside run and peered through the wire netting.

'Is he really?' Olga pretended to sound rather bored by the news.

'He came back this morning,' chimed in Graham. 'Apparently he's been at a "meeow-in" all the time!'

Olga gave a start. 'A *what*?' she repeated.

'A meeow-in,' said Fangio knowledgeably. 'He's just been telling us all about it. It's something humans do all the time – only they call them "sit-ins" and "think-ins" and "teach-ins".'

'Noel's been holding one for all the cats in the district,' said Graham. 'It's like a "think-in" only instead of thinking they all sit in a circle and meeow. It's a wonder we didn't hear it.'

Olga stared at the others, a half-eaten blade of grass hanging from her mouth . . . 'I can tell you why you didn't hear anything,' she squeaked indignantly when she got her voice back. 'A *meeow-in* indeed! A "*shut-in*" more like it! Next time he tries to tell you that ask him why he smells of coal dust. You realize where he was? Locked in the coal cellar! He's been in there ever since I went away, only he's too ashamed to admit it. Of all the . . . why, if it hadn't been for me he would still be there . . . and serve him right . . .' Olga broke off. The others had gone.

'Cats!' she squeaked bitterly. 'Wheeeeeeeee! Of all the ungrateful, scheming, self-satisfied . . .' Words failed her. 'I shall never, never, detect for one again!'

CHAPTER SIX

The Night of the Long Dance

'I suppose,' said Noel condescendingly, 'one advantage of having short legs is that when the weather's bad you can crawl under the nearest stone and keep dry.'

'I'd sooner do that,' replied Fangio, 'than get sopping wet every time it rains.'

'Who wants long legs anyway?' said Graham darkly. 'I don't. You sometimes see things you'd rather not. I stood on a mole-hill once and I didn't like what I saw at all. No wonder moles live underground.'

Olga chuckled to herself as she listened to the conversation going on to one side of her run.

The subject of legs had come up earlier that day when Fangio happened to pass a remark about the way Noel walked. Noel was a particularly beautiful cat. He was much given to taking up poses – draping himself on tree stumps or tops of walls in order to show off to the best advantage – but he was proudest of all about the way he walked, and Fangio's comment had set him going.

Although Noel secretly liked to be noticed he was a little upset by the fact that he had been, and he spent some time listing the countless advantages enjoyed by those who were lucky enough to have long legs, and the many, many drawbacks suffered by those who only had short ones.

Olga chuckled again as she basked in the afternoon sun. Although she still hadn't forgiven Noel over the episode with the coal shed, she had to admit that when he was on form he could be quite amusing in his superior kind of way.

Noel's voice suddenly broke into her daydreams. 'And what's *your* excuse?' he said.

Olga gave a start and looked around the garden. She hadn't realized they had been joined by someone else and she wondered who it could possibly be.

'Well?' Noel put his face against the wire.

Olga stared at him. 'Are you addressing me?' she asked coldly.

'Your legs are so short,' said Noel, 'I can't even see them.'

Slowly and carefully Olga drew herself up to her full height until she was practically standing on tiptoe. 'I keep them tucked under me for safety,' she said. 'Besides, I happen to have unusually long fur.'

'I suppose being so short has its uses,' said Noel, turning back to the others. 'I mean, it keeps the place tidy. You can sweep up as you go along.'

Fangio made a noise which sounded suspiciously

like a giggle, but it was quickly suppressed when he saw the look in Olga's eye.

'I admit,' Olga sank to the ground, because try as she might she couldn't hold her pose a moment longer, 'I admit that my legs could perhaps do with being a trifle longer – *if* I wanted to go around on stilts. But at least we guinea-pigs know what it's like to have long legs. We haven't always been like this. We guinea-pigs used to have the most beautiful legs imaginable. Long and slender and . . .'

'When was that?' demanded Noel. 'I've never seen a guinea-pig with long legs.'

'Oh, it was a long time ago,' said Olga vaguely. She picked on the thought that happened to be uppermost in her mind. 'It was in Russia.'

'Russia?' repeated Noel. 'Guinea-pigs don't come from Russia.'

'We may not *come* from there,' said Olga, 'but we've *been* there. You'll find guinea-pigs wherever they value breeding and good looks and . . .'

'Oh, *do* get on with it,' exclaimed Noel impatiently. In truth he was feeling a little put out that his afternoon's entertainment at the expense of Fangio and Graham had been interrupted.

Olga took a deep breath. 'For this story,' she said, taking a leaf out of Boris's book, 'you will have to try and picture yourself living in Russia at the time of the revolution.

'In those days the Tzar kept hundreds of guinea-pigs for his special pleasure, and they were said to have

the longest and most beautiful legs of any animal in the world.

'For a long time,' she added as an afterthought, 'they did try to breed some cats with legs half as long, but they never quite succeeded. Something always seemed to go wrong. They either bent the wrong way at the knees or else they fell off . . .'

Noel gave a loud snort.

'After the revolution,' continued Olga hurriedly, 'the people who had taken over the palace didn't know quite what to do to pass the time. They weren't used to the life, you see, and they soon got fed up with listening to ballylaikas all day . . .'

'Don't you mean *bala*laikas?' asked Noel suspiciously. Routing around in dustbins as he did Noel was apt to know about these things.

'If you'd had to listen to them all day long you'd have called them *bally*laikas too,' said Olga.

'Anyway, at last, when they could stand it no longer, their leader called on the Royal guinea-pigs to entertain them.

'At first the guinea-pigs didn't know what to do. Usually it was *they* who were entertained and not the other way round. But like guinea-pigs the world over, they were very gifted. The problem really was to decide which of their many talents would be most suitable.

'And then the sound of the music gave them an idea. Having such long and beautiful legs they were particularly good dancers, so that's what they did. They danced. Not the kind of dancing we know today, but special Russian dancing. They stood on their hind legs and they folded their front paws across their chests and away they went.

'The audience had never seen anything like it.

'"Moreski!" they cried. "Moreski! Moreski!"

'And the louder they called out the faster the musicians played; and the faster the musicians played the faster the guinea-pigs had to dance. On and on it went. On into the night – hour after hour.'

'Show us some,' broke in Fangio.

Olga gave him a long, hard look. Really, she wondered for a moment whose side he was on – hers or Noel's. 'I will,' she said at last, 'after that aeroplane has passed over. It really is most distracting.'

'What aeroplane?' asked Noel.

'The one behind you,' said Olga.

Olga's audience turned and looked up at the sky.

'I can't see any aeroplanes,' said Noel, as they turned back again.

'It was going very fast,' said Olga. 'It was going almost as fast as the dance I just did for you.'

The others stared back at her in disbelief.

'Well, now the aeroplane *has* gone,' said Noel, 'perhaps you can do it for us again.'

'It's a bit difficult on grass,' replied Olga, playing for time.

'There's a bare patch right behind you,' said Graham.

Olga suddenly gave a quick shuffle. 'Tarrraaaaaaa!' she exclaimed as a small cloud of dust rose into the air.

'Was that it?' demanded Noel scornfully.

'I didn't see a thing,' said Fangio.

'Nor me,' agreed Graham.

Olga gave a deep, deep sigh. 'Russian dancing is very quick,' she said. 'If you *will* look the other way or blink every time I'm afraid you'll never see it.

'Now,' she said wearily, 'I *must* get on with my story. Really, all this dancing has quite worn me out.

'Dawn,' she continued, 'was beginning to break when gradually the audience in the Tzar's palace noticed a very strange thing. In the beginning they'd been able to look out from their seats straight at the dancers; now they were looking down on them.

'The guinea-pigs,' said Olga dramatically, 'had danced so much they'd worn out their legs – right down to the ground.

'And that's why, to this very day, guinea-pigs – although they have very beautiful legs, also have rather short ones.'

The others fell silent for a moment or two, and Olga took the opportunity to go back to enjoying the sunshine, closing her eyes and snuggling down into the warm grass.

'Look,' Noel banged on the side of her run with his tail, 'if they stood on their back legs like you said, and danced them away, why haven't guinea-pigs got great big front ones still?'

'Here! Here!' echoed Fangio and Graham.

Olga opened one eye and put on her pained expression. There were some questions she just didn't choose to answer.

'If you don't mind,' she said, 'I happen to be fast asleep.'

CHAPTER SEVEN

Olga Takes the Plunge

One Saturday, soon after the week-end at the sea-side, Mr Sawdust set to work on the garden and began digging a hole. The animals watched with interest from a safe distance, for at first they weren't at all sure what he was up to. Clearly it was going to be a large hole, and equally clearly Mr Sawdust intended leaving it there, for he carted all the earth away in a wheel-barrow and dumped it at the bottom of the garden.

Graham, the tortoise, was particularly upset by it all. 'This garden's big enough as it is,' he grumbled. 'Fancy making a hole *that* size. If I go round it I shall have to walk twice as far, and if I go down inside I may never get out again.'

But the next day all was revealed. Olga had barely finished breakfast when Mr Sawdust staggered past her house bent almost double beneath the weight of what looked like an enormous grey bath. She was so taken aback she sat where she was with her mouth wide open trying to take it all in.

After Mr Sawdust had turned the bath on its back, he placed it carefully into the hole and then began mixing a lot of sand and water and grey powder stuff together, which he then poured between the bath and the sides of the hole.

Whatever it was he'd been doing he seemed very pleased with the result, for when he stood up again he called out for the others to come and see.

Olga thought perhaps he'd been building a water bowl for some enormous new pet the Sawdust family were getting, but Noel soon scotched that idea.

'It's not a water bowl,' he said scornfully. 'It's a pond. I know lots of houses where they've got one. You wait; in a few days' time they'll be putting fish and pots of plants in it. I know a pond when I see one.'

Noel was right, and as it began to take shape even Olga had to admit that Mr Sawdust's pond was really rather a splendid affair. It was built into the side of some sloping ground, and over the next few days he added three more smaller pools, each higher than the one before and overhanging it slightly, so that the whole formed one long waterfall.

After he had surrounded the pools with paving stones, Mr Sawdust spent some time connecting a thing called 'a pump', and there was great excitement one evening when he set it all in motion and water began cascading down from the topmost pool to the bottom.

Olga decided she liked Mr Sawdust's pond. It was near the spot on the lawn where she usually had her outside run and she found the sound of running water very soothing, especially on warm afternoons. But she enjoyed it just as much in the evenings, when all was still and the only sound was the soft plop-plopping of the fish as they surfaced in search of insects.

However, as with most things, everyone soon began to take Mr Sawdust's pool for granted and after a while it became so much a part of the normal scenery Olga almost forgot what the garden had been like without it.

It wasn't until a couple of weeks later that she was reminded of it in no uncertain manner.

She was enjoying a quiet nibble on the lawn when

all of a sudden she heard a tremendous scurrying in the near-by bushes. There followed a whirr of flapping wings and a moment later a bird – Olga was much too startled to take note of what sort – but it was definitely a bird, flew past her run with barely an inch to spare. It was hotly pursued by a black shape she had no trouble at all in recognizing.

It was Noel, and whether he was so intent on the task in hand he didn't see the pond, or whether in the excitement he'd forgotten all about it, or whether he thought he could clear the water in one bound, Olga didn't know. The fact remained that Noel didn't make it. He hurled himself into space, lost speed somewhere near the centre, hovered in mid-air for a fraction of a second, and then landed with a loud splash just short of the far side. Wild-eyed, he clawed des-

perately at the slippery edge for what seemed like an age, and then slowly sank back into the water, where he floundered around looking for a suitable paw-hold.

'Very good,' said Olga, when he finally managed to scramble out. 'What a bit of luck it wasn't any deeper. You might have drowned.'

Noel paused and gave her a look as he shook himself dry. 'If it had been you,' he said witheringly, '*that* would have been that!'

Olga bristled. 'Are you suggesting,' she exclaimed, 'that guinea-pigs can't swim?'

'No more than hedgehogs can fly,' snorted Noel, as he hurried up the garden towards the house.

'I'll have you know,' called Olga indignantly, 'that guinea-pigs happen to be very good swimmers. They're noted for it!' She peered through her wire at the pool. 'Why, two or three powerful strokes and I'd be at the other side and back while you were still thinking about it.'

But Noel didn't stop to argue. He disappeared through his pussy flap and there was a bang as it fell shut behind him.

A few seconds later there was another loud commotion and he came flying out again. It had something to do with wet paws and the fact that the kitchen floor had just been scrubbed, but whatever the reason Noel was obviously in an even worse mood than before as he came stalking down the garden.

'Two or three powerful strokes indeed!' he snorted as he reached Olga's run. 'Why, with legs like yours it'd be more like two or three hundred. Or two or three thousand. Or two or three ...' Noel broke off, unable to think of any more figures.

Olga gave a sigh. 'What a pity I'm stuck here inside this run,' she said. 'If only I *could* show you. If only I was outside I'd jump in. If only ...'

A wicked gleam came into Noel's eyes. He looked over his shoulder and then around the garden to make sure no one was watching, and then he sidled up to Olga's run and leant against it.

'What are you doing?' squeaked Olga nervously. As the bottom rose into the air she ran towards the boarded-up section at the back and scrabbled around anxiously. 'Wheeeeee! Watch out! You'll have me over if you're not careful.'

'Hurry up,' gasped Noel. 'I can't stay like this all day.'

'But I couldn't,' cried Olga. 'I really couldn't. I mean, *they* wouldn't like it.'

'*They* aren't watching,' said Noel. 'Come on, before I tip you right over.'

Olga hurriedly squeezed herself out beneath the side and watched forlornly while Noel lowered her run again.

'I really ought not to be doing this,' she said, clutching at straws. 'I've been very ill. That's why I was taken to the sea-side. I'm not at all well, really I'm not ...'

'I'm waiting,' said Noel menacingly.

Olga looked at his expression and then at the water. Of the two she infinitely preferred the latter. The pond had a placid look about it which was entirely absent from Noel's face.

'I won't do my best strokes to start with,' she said, peering over the edge. 'I may just play around for a while until I get used to the feel of the water.'

'In !'

Olga gave a gulp as Noel advanced towards her. There was something about the way his tail was brush-

ing to and fro on the ground she didn't care for at all.

Taking a deep breath she closed her eyes and slid gently forward on her stomach. The next moment she felt herself falling, and an icy shock as the water closed over her.

'Wheeeeeee!' she shrieked as she rose to the surface. The pool was twice as deep as she had expected, and the sides suddenly seemed an impossible distance away.

'Wheeeeeee! Help! I can't touch the bottom!' How anyone could possibly swim in a pool where they couldn't touch the bottom Olga didn't know. Nor, for that matter, did she greatly care. All she wanted was to get out of it and on to dry land again. But the more she struggled the worse her plight became. She felt herself going round and round in circles. First Noel came into view, then the house in the far distance, then her run, then Noel again.

'Wheeeeeee!' She gave another despairing shriek as she felt herself sinking for the second time. In vain she clutched at a near-by lily, but it came away in her paw and everything went black.

How long it all lasted Olga never knew. It felt like a lifetime, and she'd long since given up all hope of ever being rescued when she felt a familiar pair of hands close around her.

She had never been so thankful in the whole of her life.

'Olga!' Karen Sawdust lifted her, dripping and bedraggled, from the pool. 'Olga, what *have* you been

doing? And how on earth did you ever get out of your run?'

Olga lay panting, struggling to get her breath back, utterly unable to give even the faintest of squeaks in reply.

Karen Sawdust looked at Olga's run and then at Noel. There was something about the way he was avoiding her gaze that struck her as highly suspicious.

'Noel!' she exclaimed. 'You naughty cat! Have you got anything to do with this?'

But Noel didn't reply either, and for an equally good reason. He was no longer there.

Gathering Olga in her arms, Karen Sawdust hurried indoors and ran up the stairs to the bathroom.

'You poor thing,' she said, as she wrapped Olga in a large and fluffy towel. 'Why, you might have drowned.' She held her up to a round mirror which stuck out from the wall on a long arm. 'Just look at you. Have you ever seen anything like it?'

Olga stared at herself. Karen Sawdust was right.

She did look a mess. Her fur was matted and stuck up in spikey tufts all over her head. Even her whiskers seemed to be sticking out at a funny angle.

Although it wasn't the first time she'd been shown her reflection, Olga had never been quite so close to herself before. She began to wish she looked better for the occasion. It really was the biggest 'her' she had ever seen.

'Never mind,' said Karen Sawdust. 'We'll soon have you back to normal.' And with that she pushed the mirror to one side and began rubbing the towel briskly up and down.

Olga felt a pleasant warm glow enter her body. It started somewhere near the middle and gradually made its way through the rest of her until even her toes began to feel as warm as toast.

She was just thinking to herself that perhaps swimming wasn't quite such a bad thing after all, when she suddenly let out a gasp of alarm.

'Wheeeeee! Wheeeeeeeeee!' she shrieked. 'Whee-eeeeeee!'

Karen Sawdust stopped rubbing and looked down at her with concern. 'What's the matter, Olga?' she asked. 'What's wrong?'

But Olga was much too busy looking at her reflection in the mirror to hear.

'I've shrunk!' she wailed. 'Wheeeeee! Wheeee! Wheeeeeeee! I've shrunk!'

And it really did seem as though she had, for whereas when she'd first seen her reflection it had filled the whole of the glass, now it barely covered a quarter of it.

Olga sank back into Karen Sawdust's hands. 'It's the water,' she moaned. 'It's the water. I knew I shouldn't have gone swimming. Now I've dried out and I've shrunk!'

CHAPTER EIGHT

Olga Gets Her Own Back

Karen Sawdust held Olga up to the mirror with one hand and with the other she twisted the glass round until it faced the other way.

'Is that any better?' she asked.

Olga sat up and stared at her reflection in amazement. Not only was it better, but she had actually changed back into her old size again. Or rather, into the extra-big size she'd seen earlier on, for now that she looked at herself more closely she realized it was very much larger than life.

'It's Daddy's special shaving mirror,' explained

Karen Sawdust. 'One side is just like an ordinary mirror – see,' she turned the glass round and Olga suddenly became smaller again, 'the other side makes you look much larger. That's so that you can see your whiskers properly when you shave them off.'

It took Olga some while to absorb this strange piece of information; partly because she couldn't picture anyone in their right senses actually wanting to shave their whiskers off, and partly because she found the whole effect so exciting she couldn't draw herself away.

'You had me worried for a moment,' said Karen Sawdust. 'The way you were behaving I really thought I'd done something awful to you. Though if you ask me, I think I've come off worst.'

Sucking one of her thumbs, she examined Olga's paws and then looked her straight in the eye. 'Your toe-nails need cutting!' she announced.

'Now, you can either go to the Vet, or you can sit here quietly and let me do it. I promise I won't hurt, and it's quite safe as long as I only cut off the dead bits at the end – you can tell by the colour. But if they aren't done soon your nails will just carry on growing and bend right round until they dig back into the skin. You won't like that at all.'

It didn't take Olga very long to decide that although having her toe-nails grow back into her didn't sound very nice, having them cut was ten times worse, especially as the first choice had to do with something that was very much in the future, whereas the second choice was happening to her there and then.

'Why, oh why, can't toe-nails grow shorter instead of longer?' she moaned. 'It would save so much trouble. Wheeeeeeee!'

'Really!' exclaimed Karen Sawdust. 'No wonder they call you "Restless Cavies" in my book about guinea-pigs . . .'

Olga stopped struggling for a moment and pricked up her ears. 'A book?' she thought. 'About guinea-pigs?'

Olga knew all about books. The Sawdust people had lots. Rows and rows of them. And once, when she'd been left all by herself in their front room while her own house was being cleaned out, she'd actually had a nibble at one or two. And very good they'd been – just the thing for keeping teeth nice and trim. But she hadn't realized there was one all about her.

'Mind you,' she thought, 'I'm not surprised. It's probably very popular.'

Olga was so taken up by the thought of books that she almost forgot to squeak while the rest of her nails were being cut, and she looked very thoughtful indeed as she was being carried back downstairs to her run.

When she was settled in Karen Sawdust put a large rockery stone on top of it for safety. 'There,' she said, 'that won't get pushed over in a hurry.'

But Olga was much too busy with her thoughts to answer. In fact, she was so quiet for the rest of that morning that Noel began to look concerned.

'Are you all right?' he asked, peering through the wire at her. 'I haven't heard a weeeeeek out of you since you fell in the pond.'

Olga gazed up at him with a faraway look in her eyes. 'I'm busy,' she said carelessly, running her paw round a patch of dry earth to form a vague letter. 'I'm . . . er . . . I'm writing a book.'

'A book?' Noel looked at her in disbelief. '*You . . .*
write a *book*? Guinea-pigs can't write books.'

'Guinea-pigs,' said Olga stiffly, 'can do most things.
We can do things you cats haven't even dreamed of.'
And she turned her back on him to show the conversa-
tion was at an end.

But the trouble was, although she knew she *could*
write a book if she tried, she hadn't got an idea yet.
It really needed peace and quiet, and these were two
items she obviously wasn't going to get that day, for
having disappeared into the undergrowth, Noel
returned shortly afterwards followed by Fangio and
Graham – both eager for news of the latest happening.

'Have you finished it yet?' called Fangio. 'Is it true
it's all about swimming?'

'Wait for me,' cried Graham, as he hurried along
behind. 'Don't start without me.'

Noel jumped on top of Olga's run and peered down

at her. 'Don't worry,' he called. 'There's no hurry. I think she's run out of weeeeeeks. She used them all up in the pond this morning. You should have heard the noise . . .'

Olga grew more and more restive as Noel's voice droned on. Really, just lately he'd been getting very much above himself. It was about time he was taken down a peg or two. The way he kept on about her swimming anyone would think he was the world's best. Just because his whiskers had dried out he'd forgotten what a sight he'd looked. It was a good job he hadn't seen himself in the bathroom mirror. It would have turned them white. It would have . . . Olga paused for a moment as an idea entered her mind.

'If you like,' she said, taking the plunge, 'I'll start my book now. I haven't actually *written* it yet, but I can tell you what it's about.'

Olga waited for a moment or two, partly to allow her audience time to settle down, and partly to get her own thoughts straightened out.

'This story,' she began, when all was quiet, 'took place one fine summer's day in autumn.'

'I don't believe that for a start,' broke in Noel. 'You can't have a fine summer's day in autumn. It doesn't make sense.'

Olga gave him a look. 'Spring,' she said, 'had been a

little late that year. It was late because everything was the wrong way round. The world woke up one morning and found that left had become right, up had become down, black was white, and mornings were evenings.'

She lowered her voice. 'But something much, much worse had happened. Can you guess what?'

The others sat in silence for a moment or two trying to think of the worst possible thing that could happen.

'The fish man took the fish away instead of leaving it?' hazarded Noel.

Olga clicked her tongue impatiently. 'Food!' she exclaimed, taking a quick nibble at the grass. 'That's all some animals ever think about.

'No, I'll tell you. Things started to grow the wrong way. Grass gradually got shorter and shorter, trees turned into bushes, toe-nails got smaller.

'At first everyone thought it was great fun, but then they discovered they were getting smaller too. Instead of growing older they were getting younger every day. And that, too, seemed fun for a while, because nobody really likes growing old. But when they found they were beginning to forget all the things they'd ever learnt – even how to talk, they began to get really worried.

'The world was suddenly full of babies – and there was no one left to look after them.'

The others gave a shiver as they tried to picture the scene. 'I don't want to grow young,' moaned Graham. 'I want to stay as I am. I'm too old to die.'

'It won't happen, will it?' asked Fangio anxiously. 'I mean, it *is* only a story.'

'Perhaps,' said Olga cautiously, 'and perhaps not.'

She glanced across at Noel, who was sitting in a patch of noon-day sun. 'I haven't liked to say anything until now, but it has struck me you've not been looking quite so fat lately.'

Noel sat up. 'What do you mean?' he blustered.

'Have you noticed your shadow?' asked Olga. 'It's really very short. They do say that's the first thing to go when things start getting smaller. Shadows first – whiskers and fur last of all. I daresay yours will start dragging on the ground any day now. If I were you I'd make the most of things while you can.'

'But it's going to take me longer than ever to get anywhere,' wailed Graham.

'Cheer up,' said Olga. 'Think of all the things you'll be able to do when you get there. Things you've never done before.'

'Such as?' demanded Noel, who was beginning to believe the story in spite of himself.

'Go through gaps for a start,' said Olga. 'You won't have to rely on the width of your whiskers to see if you can get through or not.' She fixed him with a beady eye. 'Why, I bet there are gaps in that fence over there you could sail through already. Gaps you haven't been able to get through in years.'

'Go on,' exclaimed Fangio eagerly. 'Have a go!'

'Quick, before it's too late!' cried Graham.

'I don't want to,' said Noel.

'Coward!' said Olga accusingly.

Noel gave her a long, hard look, and then he turned on his heels and stalked off without so much as a backward glance.

'Do you think he will?' asked Fangio.

'Will what?' asked Olga innocently, as she turned to examine a particularly succulent-looking dandelion.

'Have a go,' said Fangio.

'Get through the gap,' chorused Graham.

Olga considered the matter, but before she had time to reply there was a long-drawn-out yowl from somewhere near by.

'I think,' she said, when the noise had died down, 'the answer is "yes", and then again "no".'

Noel's yowl had had a particular quality about it which she found very rewarding. It was a yowl of surprise and indignation rather than of pain, and it more than made up for the indignities she'd suffered earlier in the day.

Olga took a long nibble from her dandelion. All in all, she felt it was a most satisfying note on which to end a story.

CHAPTER NINE

Olga to the Rescue

One evening, a week or so later, Olga had a strange experience.

She was sitting quietly in her hutch enjoying the last of the day, when she heard an unusual noise. It had a kind of rasping note and every now and then it was punctuated by a loud smack.

Oddly enough, although she could tell that it came from somewhere near the Sawdust family's kitchen she couldn't for the life of her see what was causing it.

There was a glass panel in the door and when the light was on, as it happened to be that evening, Olga could often see shadows flittering back and forth.

The shadows and the clinking sounds that usually accompanied them were very comforting and she was always sorry when they stopped.

But the present noises had nothing to do with the Sawdust family, for they were most definitely coming from somewhere *outside* the kitchen, not within.

As Olga turned the matter over in her mind she gradually became aware of another very odd thing. Usually when the light was on it attracted insects – flies, gnats, moths; all kinds of annoying creatures she could have well done without. But for once they seemed few in number, and they were getting fewer all the time.

It was while she was idly following the progress of one of these denizens of the night that Olga solved her mystery.

As the insect swooped low past the bottom of the door a large greeny-yellow creature with bulbous eyes and an enormous mouth to match suddenly rose up out of the darkness. There was a snap and in one swift movement victor and victim disappeared from view as the former sank down on to its haunches and merged once again with the shadows.

Olga's eyes nearly popped out. It was all over before she'd had time to say 'sliced carrots' once over forwards, let alone twice over backwards.

She was about to let out a warning squeak for the benefit of anyone else who might be around when the kitchen door opened and Mr Sawdust came into view carrying a pile of rubbish.

'Thank goodness for that!' breathed Olga, as he crossed in front of her on his way to the dustbin. 'Now perhaps it'll go away – whatever it is.'

Brief though her glimpse had been, she had no wish to see the creature again. It was quite the ugliest she had ever come across. In fact she was just wondering whether or not she ought to warn Mr Sawdust himself when she suddenly realized he was talking to someone. Someone or some*thing*.

'Hullo, old chap,' he was saying.

Olga gave a start. Don't say he was actually speaking to the object? She could hardly believe her ears.

But it was true. In fact, not only was Mr Sawdust talking to it; he was even inviting others to do the same.

'I say,' he called. 'We've got a visitor. Do come and have a look.'

Mrs Sawdust appeared in the doorway. 'Ugh!' she exclaimed. 'I knew something like this would happen. It's that wretched pond of yours.'

Olga nodded approvingly. At least she had someone on her side.

Mr Sawdust stood up. '*My* wretched pond?' he repeated indignantly. 'I like that!

'Anyway,' he continued stoutly, 'I'm rather fond of toads. They've lots of character.' He bent down again. 'I must say he's quite a specimen and he looks very venerable. I bet he's twenty years old if he's a day. I wonder what he's doing here?'

'Probably after the insects,' said Karen Sawdust, joining the group. 'It's because we have a glass door. The light attracts them, and toads like insects. I expect he'll be coming here every night for his supper from now on.'

'In that case,' said Mr Sawdust, 'we'd better leave him to enjoy it. We don't want to give him indigestion.'

The voices died away as the Sawdust family went back indoors. It seemed that the toad had also decided it was time to leave – either because he'd been frightened or because he felt sufficiently full for one night, for there was a swish and a plop as he went past Olga's house, then another swish and a plop and he was gone.

In spite of everything Olga couldn't help admiring the way he moved. The sudden leap into space without any warning whatsoever, and the absolute stillness that followed.

Carefully making sure no one else was watching she tried a few practice leaps herself, but the most she could manage was a couple of inches and even then she ended up by banging her head against the side of her hutch.

Of course, having so much space must give toads a tremendous advantage, and ugly though they were, large eyes must be quite a help. You could see things before they actually hit you.

All the same, she felt most impressed.

Olga was very quiet the next day. Truth to tell she was looking forward to seeing her new friend again, and remembering Mr Sawdust's words she decided she would call him Venerables.

She tried out the word several times and decided she liked it. It had a nice 'old' sound to it that went very well with a toad.

Olga waited impatiently for night to fall. It had been a hot, cloudless day, and the sun took an age to disappear behind the trees at the bottom of the garden. Normally Olga was rather sad to see it go, but tonight she just couldn't wait.

As the gnats and the midges began to beat against the kitchen door she almost gave up hope, when suddenly there was a familiar swish and a plop and a snap and it was just as it had been the night before.

Olga peered through her wire netting. 'Good evening, Venables,' she called. Somehow, although she knew this time she hadn't got the word quite right, she felt it sounded even better.

'Venables!' she called, trying it out again. 'Wheeee-eeeeee! Venables!'

There was no reply. Venables was either too busy or too intent on his supper to answer.

'I've decided to call you Venables,' said Olga, 'because I think it suits you very well. Everyone should have a name. Being a toad, I don't suppose you've ever thought about it, but if you've a name it will make you different from all the other toads, and that could be very useful . . .'

Olga paused for a moment as a sudden thought struck her. 'You *are* the same toad who came last night?' she asked.

Faintly through the darkness there came an answering croak, though whether or not it was in reply to her question Olga never did find out, for just then the kitchen door opened.

'He's here again,' said Karen Sawdust excitedly. 'I told you he would be.'

'Leave him be,' called Mrs Sawdust. 'Dinner's almost ready and we don't want him leaping about the kitchen.'

From somewhere inside the house Olga heard Mr Sawdust give an answering laugh. 'Might be rather apt,' he said. 'All things considered.'

And then he made a remark that sent a cold shiver running down Olga's spine. It was so unlike anything she had ever heard him say before that really, she wondered if she had heard aright. But Karen Sawdust's next words confirmed her worst fears.

'Oh, Daddy!' she exclaimed. 'What an awful thought. How could you?'

As the door closed again Olga peered out of her hutch, her mind in a turmoil. Why on earth didn't Venables make a run for it – or hop for it – or whatever toads did when their lives were in danger?

'Wheeeeeee!' she shrieked. 'Wheeeeeeeeeeee! Wheeeeeeeeeee!'

But it was no good. No matter how hard she shrieked, Venables either couldn't or didn't want to hear, and gradually it was borne on her mind that perhaps he couldn't understand what she was saying anyway.

It wasn't long before her cries brought Fangio and Graham hurrying onto the scene. They were closely followed by Noel.

'It's Venables!' shrieked Olga. 'You *must* warn Venables! Do something. For goodness sake *do* something!'

'Do calm down,' said Noel, stifling a yawn. 'Anyone would think you were being murdered.'

'Venables may be if you don't hurry,' gasped Olga.

'Venables?' repeated Fangio. 'Who's *Venables*?'

'Venables,' said Olga, when at last she'd managed to get her breath back, 'is a very close toad friend of mine who happens to be in great danger. Very great danger indeed. In fact,' she lowered her voice, '*he's about to be eaten by the Sawdust people.*'

'A toad?' said Graham. 'Fancy anyone wanting to eat a toad. Mind you, humans do funny things.' He turned to Fangio. 'I have heard they're very keen on hedgehogs. They wrap them in clay and bake them. Then, after a couple of hours good roasting they break open the clay and all the prickles come away.'

Fangio took this piece of information with a

distinct lack of enthusiasm. 'Where is this friend of yours?' he asked, hurriedly changing the subject.

'Right behind you,' said Olga. 'At least, he was just now. Venables! Venables! Wheeeeee! Are you there, Venables?'

The answering croak made even Noel jump. He examined the cause of it dubiously. All his instincts called for him to reach out a paw and administer a pat if only to see what happened, but he stopped short at the sound of Olga's voice.

'We *must* stick together,' she said. 'We *must* make Venables a hideaway.'

'*We?*' Fangio looked up at her suspiciously.

'I shall be here to direct you,' said Olga grandly. 'And I shall keep watch in case the Sawdust people come.'

'Sometimes,' murmured Graham, 'I wish I lived in a hutch.'

'You're very welcome to climb up and open my front door,' said Olga, whose sharp ears missed nothing. 'I shall be only too pleased to help.'

Faced with this impossible task the others had no choice but to give in.

Noel took one last hopeful look at Venables and then made his way towards the shrubbery. 'Come on,' he called grumpily. 'Let's get to work. I'll do the digging. You can fetch the leaves and things.'

For some time the only sound to reach Olga's ears was the soft scratching of earth and the occasional snapping of a twig as the others busied themselves in the undergrowth.

It all took much longer than expected and the moon was high in the sky by the time the job was done. As the others limped wearily into view Olga had to admit to herself that she wasn't altogether sorry she'd been unable to join in, for they were so covered in dirt and leaves they were barely recognizable. Noel's fur in particular looked as if another dip in the pool wouldn't come amiss.

'I hope you're satisfied,' he gasped, as they drew near her hutch.

'They won't find him in that hole in a hurry,' said Fangio.

'A hole?' echoed Olga. 'A hole? Don't say you've put Venables down a *hole*?'

The others looked at her. 'What's wrong with that?' demanded Noel.

'But that's what the Sawdust family were going to do!' wailed Olga. 'I heard Mr Sawdust say so. He said "What a bit of luck Venables was outside the kitchen door because that was what they were having for supper – Toad in the Hole." Karen Sawdust was very upset.'

Olga broke off and peered out at Noel. For some reason or other he appeared to be having a kind of fit. He really was behaving most strangely. Unless her eyes were deceiving her he was almost foaming at the mouth, and some of his meeows were quite blood-curdling.

'Toad in the Hole!' he said bitterly. 'Toad in the Hole! I'll give you Toad in the Hole!'

'Thank you,' said Olga primly, 'but I happen to be a strict vegetarian.'

'"Toad in the Hole,"' spluttered Noel, 'is what human beings call *sausage in batter*.'

Olga looked from one to the other of her friends.

'Well,' she said at last, 'if the Sawdust people will give things silly names like that they must expect misunderstandings. Why, they might just as well call a dish "Guinea-pig in the Hole" . . .'

'That,' said Noel, as he turned away in disgust, 'is something that can always be arranged, and one of these days most likely will. Goodnight!'

CHAPTER TEN

Olga and the Chinese Dragon

Although Olga had lived with the Sawdust family for quite a long time – almost a year in fact, and although there was much that she'd come to take for granted, there was one thing she never grew tired of – and that was the view from her hutch.

The memory of her early days in the pet shop had grown hazy, but if she tried hard she could still picture what it had been like cooped up with all the other animals, and often when she looked out of her bedroom window she felt very lucky, for there was always something interesting going on.

232

The Sawdust family's house was perched on the side of a hill and from her own house she could see right across the valley. There were houses dotting the hill on the far side too, and in the evening, when the lights were on, they looked like fireflies twinkling amongst the trees. On really dark nights there were so many lights it was impossible to count them all. Olga had once got up to five, but then she became confused, and by the time she'd gone back over them again it was late and some were already being turned off.

The view was equally pretty in the daytime, and from her window she was able to watch in comfort the gradual coming and going of the seasons; the long winter months when the ground was covered with snow and people slid down the hillside on sleighs and toboggans, their whoops of joy echoing across the valley; and the coming of spring, when the whole countryside changed from brown to green.

In many ways Olga liked the spring, for it meant fresh grass and other delicacies; but the most beautiful mornings of all were undoubtedly those when the whole valley was filled with mist, and it felt as if she was looking down on some vast and mysterious sea of cotton wool. This took place mostly in autumn and early spring, but sometimes, when the weather was in a particular mood, it happened in summer too.

It was on just such a day that she chanced to overhear a remark passed by one of the neighbours as Karen Sawdust went in search of some early-morning dandelions.

'It's real dragon weather this morning,' she called over the fence.

'Dragon weather?' Karen Sawdust's voice floated back.

'In China,' explained the lady, 'they say dragons come out of the mist on mornings like this.'

The voices faded away leaving Olga busy with her thoughts. She peered out through her door in the hope of seeing something unusual. But not a ripple disturbed the scene below, and the only sound came from a building site down in the valley as the men started work for the day.

The building site, from all Olga could gather, was a bit of a thorn in the flesh of the Sawdust family. It seemed that some land had recently been sold and some new houses were being built. They were unlikely to spoil the view, for they were below the skyline, but it did mean a shattering of the normal peace and quiet for the time being as trees and hedges were uprooted, and strange things called concrete mixers and bulldozers began to arrive.

'Perhaps,' said Olga to herself, 'a dragon will come

and gobble them all up before they've finished.'

She made the remark almost without thinking, and it had hardly left her lips when her eyes grew wide with astonishment. For a second or two she sat transfixed, unable to move let alone utter a squeak. For there, rising out of the mist, was an enormous giraffe-necked creature the like of which she'd never seen before. A long thin tongue emerged from its tiny head and swung gently to and fro as if in search of something, and then, ever so slowly, it disappeared from view again.

'I see they have a crane on the building site now.' Karen Sawdust's voice brought Olga back to earth with a jolt.

'Let's hope it gets the job finished twice as quickly,' said her mother. 'It's been going on long enough.'

'A crane!' Olga sank back into her hay. For a moment, for one dreadful moment, she'd thought it was a dragon. She felt very pleased she'd found out the truth of the matter, and she felt doubly thankful some while later when she was put out in her run on the lawn. Goodness knows how she would have felt if she hadn't known what it was. She looked around to see who else was about, but the only sign of life came from the direction of the rockery, where Graham was basking in the early morning sunshine, and *he* wouldn't have been much good in an emergency – especially when it came to fighting dragons.

The top of the crane came and went several times and Olga began playing a game with herself as she set about clearing the patch of grass. She made up a spell which she timed to·say just before the crane rose into view. Then she made up another one to send it away again.

She was so busy doing this she didn't notice Fangio creeping up on her and she had quite a turn when he spoke.

'Are you all right?' he asked.

'Of course I'm all right,' replied Olga crossly.

'I thought I heard you talking to someone,' said Fangio.

'Where are you going?' asked Olga, quickly changing the subject.

'Oh, into the bushes,' said Fangio vaguely. 'I might go up the hill. On the other hand, I might go down it. I shall have to see how the fancy takes me.'

Olga looked at him thoughtfully as he turned to go. 'I wouldn't go down into the valley if I were you,' she called. 'Not while the dragon is about.'

Fangio stopped in his tracks. 'Dragon?' he repeated. 'What dragon?'

'Haven't you heard?' asked Olga carelessly. 'Everyone's out looking for it. It's been loose in the valley all the morning, and it's *very* hungry.

'It's a Chinese dragon,' she added in a louder voice for Graham's benefit. 'As tall as a house and with a roar that shakes the ground. It lives on a diet of hedgehogs and tortoises, with,' she added as she spotted Noel coming across the lawn, 'an occasional mog thrown in when it feels like a treat.'

'What's this? What's this?' Noel broke off his wanderings to join them.

Graham stuck his head out of his shell. 'There's a dragon loose in the valley,' he called. 'It's eating all before it. Better pass the word around quickly.'

Noel stared at Olga. 'It sounds to me like another of your tales,' he said suspiciously. 'If there really was a dragon, I can't picture you sitting there as calm as a cucumber for a start.'

Olga drew herself up. 'It just so happens,' she said haughtily, 'that the one thing all dragons are frightened of is guinea-pigs.

'We guinea-pigs,' she continued, lowering her voice, 'have magic powers over dragons. We can make them come and go as we please.'

'I shall believe that,' said Noel, 'when I see it.'

'All right!' Olga put on one of her expressions. 'I take a nibble of clover, and a morsel or two of grass, and I add a pinch of dandelion, then I say a few things that have been handed down . . .' She waited for the rattle of the crane and then, as it started to rise, she made a series of strange grunting noises, running round and round in circles as she did so.

The others sat petrified as the top of the crane rose into view. This time it had a big platform laden with bricks hanging from its 'tongue'.

'It *must* be hungry,' said Olga carelessly. 'Would you like me to make it go away again – just in case?'

'Yes, please!' called Graham, from somewhere inside his shell. 'I don't like it.'

Olga took a deep breath, 'Go away, dragon!' she cried. 'We do not like you. Go away before it is too late. Wheeeee!'

Olga timed it exactly right, for just as she gave her 'wheeeeee' the crane lowered the platform into a

new position and disappeared from view again.

The others stared at her in amazement, and for once even Noel could hardly find the right words.

'You never told us you could do that before!' he gasped.

'You didn't ask me,' said Olga. She turned her back on the others and carried on with her eating. 'There are so many things I can do I daresay there are quite a few I've forgotten to mention. If you like I'll do it for you again.' And closing her eyes she went through her grunting noises once more.

A movement somewhere behind him caused Noel to look round. Almost immediately he arched his back. 'That was quick,' he said.

Olga had a momentary feeling of surprise, for she'd missed the usual rattle that meant the crane was going up. 'My dragon spells,' she said, 'are very powerful. It'll probably keep coming back for quite a while. But don't worry, I can always make it go away again.'

'I wish you'd make it go away now then,' cried Fangio, his beady eyes agog. 'I don't like the look of it close to. It's bigger ... and more fierce ... and ...'

Something in the tone of Fangio's voice made Olga look round too. As she did so she nearly jumped out of her skin with fright, for she suddenly caught sight of an enormous green head with a yellow mouth and

large staring eyes heading towards them across the lawn.

'Quick. Do one of your spells,' hissed Noel, as the head rose into the air and bore down on them. 'Do something!'

'Wheeeeeeeeeee!' shrieked Olga. 'Wheeeeeeeee! Wheeeeeeeeeeee! Wheeeeeeeeeeeeeeee! Help! Help! Wheeeeeeeeeeeeeeeeeeeeeeeeeeeeee!'

Olga knew exactly what she was going to do and she did it with all possible speed. Regardless of the terrified cries from the others, she made a dive for the back of her run and buried her face in the corner as far as it could possibly go. She was conscious of the fact that she could hear a voice calling her name and that it was getting nearer and nearer, but she was much too scared to see who it was. There were times when closing your eyes and burying your head was the only possible thing to do and this was definitely one of them.

Karen Sawdust looked down at Olga's run. Really, animals were the strangest creatures. There was no telling how they were going to behave. Noel had scudded past her like a streak of greased lightning. Fangio hadn't been far behind. Even Graham had shown a surprising turn of speed as he'd disappeared into the shrubbery. And now Olga was acting in an equally odd manner. Anyone would think they'd come face to face with a real dragon.

'It's all right,' she said, holding up a large object on the end of a string. 'It won't do you any harm. It's only made of wood and paper. It's a Chinese kite. The lady next door lent it to me. Anyway, there isn't enough wind to fly it . . .'

But she might just as well have saved her breath, for if Olga did hear what she was saying it had no effect. She was past caring what the object was made of. Wood, paper, string . . . it was all the same to her. She would never, ever, say her dragon spell again.

CHAPTER ELEVEN

A Day to Remember

The meeting with the dragon left Olga feeling de-
cidedly queasy for several days afterwards. At first it
didn't bother her a great deal. After all, it wasn't every
day one met a dragon, and it would probably never
happen again. But as the days multiplied and she still
didn't feel any better she began to wonder if it really
was that. The early mornings were the worst. She
didn't actually feel bad, just off-colour, and somehow
slightly 'different'. Then there was the matter of food.
It wasn't that she was off food, it was simply that she
was forever wanting things that weren't there. If her

243

run was put on a patch where there were plenty of dandelions she had a craving for clover. If it was put on top of the clover she suddenly had a great desire for dandelions.

And there was the strange affair of THE NOTICE. It appeared one day on the front of her house; a piece of cardboard tied on with string across the front door. In some ways Olga rather liked it, for it made her more private and she suddenly felt the need to be by herself. But she was dying to know what it said, and she knew that it said *something*, for she caught sight of some words later that morning on her way back from the lawn.

But even her visits to the outside run suddenly stopped for some reason or other, so she had to rely on her friends – and they weren't much help.

With Fangio inclined to be short-sighted, and Graham having no idea how to read, it was left to Noel, and that evening he climbed up onto her roof in order to take a closer look.

Peering over the edge, he announced that the piece of cardboard said 'BRUTSID TON OD'.

It took him some while to work even that much out, for he was seeing the letters upside down and had to read them out one by one.

Olga played around with them for ages afterwards,

but she couldn't make any sense out of it at all, so in the end she gave it up as a bad job and contented herself with the thought that if you wait long enough most things have a habit of becoming clear in the end.

Then, a few days later, several things happened one after another. Things that were to make it a day to remember.

It all began when the postman arrived. Olga had often seen him before, but only in the distance, for he usually went to the Sawdust family's front door. The moment he arrived he was grabbed by Karen Sawdust and ushered round to the back of the house where he dipped into his bag and brought out six large envelopes for Olga to see.

'Morning,' he said gruffly. 'Happy birthday!'

'Happy birthday?' Olga stopped munching and gazed out of her front door in amazement. Fancy it being her *birthday* and she hadn't even realized.

'There's a card from Mummy and Daddy,' said Karen Sawdust, as Mr and Mrs Sawdust came out to join in the fun. She tore open the envelope and withdrew a piece of folded cardboard with a picture on the front.

'There's one from me,' she continued, tearing open the next envelope.

'One from Noel ...

'One from Fangio . . .

'One from Graham . . .

'And one from Boris. I don't suppose you remember *him*. He was the guinea-pig you stayed with earlier in the year.' She cast a meaning glance at the others. 'And in the circumstances I think sending you a card is the least he can do!'

'Boris!' Olga could hardly believe her ears. Fancy asking if she remembered him! To start with he was the only other guinea-pig she'd seen in months, so she could hardly *forget* him. But it wasn't *just* that. There'd been something special about her week-end with Boris that would have made him stay in her mind if she'd met a thousand others.

And then she pricked up her ears at something else Karen Sawdust was saying.

'He'll be here soon,' she said. 'They told us they would leave early. They're coming to stay for a whole week! Gosh. Wouldn't it be super if it all happened together!'

Boris! Coming to stay! With her! For a whole week! Sometime that very morning! Soon! Any moment now!

'Wheeeeeeeeee!' Olga ran round and round her house squeaking with excitement at the thought, until she suddenly had one of her dizzy spells.

'Oh dear,' she thought, 'I do hope I'm well enough to receive him.'

Olga's dizzy spell lasted longer than usual, but she roused herself quickly enough when the sound of a car engine heralded the moment she'd been waiting for.

Even then there were endless moments of chattering to be endured, but at long last the voices drew nearer and a familiar set of whiskers came into view.

'Hullo,' said Boris, as the door closed behind him. 'How are you? I see you've got your DO NOT DISTURB notice. What a thing to have hanging up on your birthday. Still, it can't be helped.' He looked at her critically. 'I hope you've got plenty of oats. It won't be long now before you've a few more mouths to feed.'

'A few more mouths to feed?' Olga looked at him incredulously as she suddenly realized the truth of the matter; the reason why she'd been feeling so strange for the past few days. What a ridiculous thing! And fancy not being able to work out that 'BRUTSID TON OD' was 'DO NOT DISTURB' backwards. Obviously the Sawdust family suspected something, otherwise they wouldn't have put the notice up in the first place. That was why they'd been fussing over her more than usual – not letting her go in her outside run. And all the time she'd hadn't suspected a thing! Really, she began to feel quite flustered.

Of course, the trouble was that what with one thing and another – going to the sea-side, detecting, thinking up new stories, rescuing Venables, swimming, not to mention making dragon spells, she'd been so busy she hadn't had time to think about anything.

'I really must pay more attention to myself in future,' she decided. 'I'm always doing things for others.'

'It's a good job I got here in time!' Boris broke into her thoughts. He looked round carefully and then moved a little closer. 'You might not think it to look at me,' he murmured, 'but I was once a very famous surgeon. If you like, I'll tell you a story about one of my operations.'

Olga gazed at him happily. As far as she was concerned Boris could go on telling stories for the rest of her life. She wouldn't believe a word, but she would never grow tired of hearing them.

It was a little later that same morning that she suddenly noticed a tiny movement inside her.

'I think you'd better finish your story later,' she said hastily. 'I may be busy for a while.'

Olga was true to her word. For the rest of that morning she was very busy indeed, and as she lay back at long last and looked down happily at the three small figures poking out from under the straw and felt them nuzzle up to her, she decided she was likely to remain busy for some time to come.

There was great excitement in the Sawdust family household when they heard the news. First Karen Sawdust, then Mr and Mrs Sawdust came to see her. There then followed a long procession of friends and neighbours. It went on for most of the day.

And to cap it all, there was still one more surprise in store for her.

Later that same evening Karen Sawdust headed yet another procession from the house. This time she was carrying a small, white object on a plate, and on top of it there was a lighted candle.

Olga gave a squeak of surprise. Whatever was going to happen to her now?

'It's to celebrate your birthday,' explained Karen Sawdust, as she drew near. 'You're one year old today. The cake's only made out of cardboard, I'm afraid; but if you nibble a hole in the side you'll find it's full of oats. And if you blow the candle out in one blow you can make a wish – which *may* come true.'

Olga had no idea how to blow, but she gave a loud 'wheeeeeee' instead, and with some help from the others the flame went out.

There was a round of applause and some cheering, and then all the Sawdust people sang 'Happy birthday, dear Olga, happy birthday to you.'

Olga didn't want to seem ungrateful, but by then she was feeling so tired she decided to wish that they would all go away, and lo and behold shortly afterwards they did. Only Noel, Fangio and Graham, drawn by all the noise, remained to say goodnight.

Olga snuggled up to Boris. One way and another it

had been quite a day – a day to remember. 'How nice to have furs and descendants,' she sighed, gazing proudly at her three offspring.

'Don't you mean *heirs* and descendants?' called Noel, who liked to get these things right.

Olga roused herself. 'No, I do not,' she said firmly, '*You've* never seen a guinea-pig with hair. They *always* have fur. Beautiful soft, silky, lovely fur . . .'

'Goodnight!' said Noel hastily.

'Goodnight!' echoed Fangio and Graham.

And from somewhere near the kitchen door there came a loud croak.

'Goodnight, Venables,' said Olga.

She settled down again next to Boris and closed her eyes. 'If you like,' she said graciously, 'you may tell us a story now. I've had such a busy day I don't think I could possibly manage one myself. Besides, it's a father's privilege!'

DO NOT DISTURB

Olga Carries On

CHAPTER ONE

Olga's Present

Olga da Polga was suffering from 'mixed feelings'.
That is to say, one half of her was feeling reasonably
pleased with life, the other half of her was feeling
quite the opposite.

The fact of the matter was her family had gone
away.

Of course, it had its good side; most things do if
you look hard enough. Since they had been born her
three children had grown and grown, so that just
lately her hutch had become very crowded indeed.

But when she thought of the weeks she'd spent
bringing them up; the number of times she'd . . . well,
not exactly 'gone without', but awaited her turn at
the feeding bowl, words failed her.

255

And what upset her most of all was the way it had happened; suddenly, without so much as a 'please', or a 'do you mind', or even a 'thank you very much' afterwards.

Karen Sawdust and her father had arrived outside her house soon after breakfast one morning carrying a cardboard box, and before she'd had time to gather her wits about her the children had been lifted out, the door slammed shut again and she'd found herself all alone in the world.

What with all the squeaking and shrieking which had gone on at the time, any explanations were completely lost.

And none of her friends were of much help either. As soon as the coast was clear and the sound of Mr Sawdust's car had died away, they came out of their various hiding places and gathered round in order to hear what was wrong.

'Is that all?' said Graham, the tortoise, when Olga had finished her tale of woe. 'I thought something terrible had happened.'

'I expect they've been given away,' said Noel, the cat. 'That's what usually happens to unwanted families.'

Olga's jaw dropped. 'Given away?' she repeated, hardly able to believe her ears. '*Unwanted?*'

'Think yourself lucky,' broke in Fangio, the hedge-hog. 'At least it means they've probably gone to a good home. Not like hedgehogs – left to fend for themselves, *and* as likely as not get run over the very first time they try to cross a road on their own.'

'Or drowned,' said Noel. 'That's what happens to kittens sometimes. I could tell you a few tales.'

Olga gave a shiver. 'I'd rather not hear them, thank you very much,' she squeaked.

Noel sniffed as he turned to go. 'I've never heard so much fuss being made over nothing,' he said.

But Olga had suddenly begun to remember snatches of conversation she'd heard that morning. Remarks that had passed unnoticed during the heat of the moment, and which were now flooding back.

For instance, she was sure Karen Sawdust had said she would bring something back with her. Yes, that was it, she'd said that when she returned she would bring a present!

Olga liked presents and she grew more and more excited at the thought.

'I wouldn't go yet if I were you!' she called.

The others stopped in their tracks.

'I may,' said Olga vaguely, 'have something for you soon.'

Noel looked at her. 'Something for *us*?' he repeated. 'What sort of something?'

'You'll have to wait and see,' said Olga mysteriously. 'But I'm sure it will be very nice. Karen Sawdust promised she would bring a present back with her.'

'Why are *we* getting one?' asked Noel suspiciously. 'They haven't taken anything away from us.'

'Not yet,' said Fangio ominously.

'I'm all right,' said Graham. 'They can't take anything away from me. I haven't got anything to take.
And if they try I shall go inside my shell and I shan't
come out again.'

'You'll all be getting a present,' said Olga patiently,
'because I shall be sharing mine.'

'At least,' she added, 'I shall be sharing it with
those who are still here.'

'Do you mean to say,' grumbled Noel, 'that we've

got to hang around here all the morning listening to you complaining?'

'Complaining?' repeated Olga indignantly. 'You'd complain if you'd just had your own flesh and fur taken from you . . . it's very lonely without them.'

Noel, who secretly knew when he was beaten, stretched out lazily on top of the coal bunker near Olga's hutch and closed his eyes. It was as good a way as any of passing a warm, sunny morning.

'The thing is,' began Olga, as she gave the matter some more thought, 'I'm sure my family won't have been passed on to just anyone. After all, they must be very valuable.'

'Valuable?' Noel opened his eyes and looked at her scornfully. 'How do you make that out?'

'Well, I don't want to boast,' said Olga, 'but I mean to say . . . look who their mother was.' She preened her whiskers in the reflection from her water bowl.

'I cost twenty-two and a half new pence when I was new, and that was ages ago. Mr and Mrs Sawdust are always saying how things are getting more and more expensive all the time. Even the price of my oats keeps going up, and I eat lots of those, so goodness knows what I must be worth now.

'I mean,' she added, warming to her subject, 'it's not like cats. You said yourself they often drown kittens . . .'

Noel looked at her in amazement. For someone who didn't want to boast Olga was doing remarkably well.

'If I'm worth ten times as much as I was,' she continued, 'there's no knowing what they'll get for my children.'

Noel made a noise which was halfway between a sniff and a snort and then closed his eyes again, but Graham and Fangio began to look more and more impressed.

'Well, if *I'm* to have a present, I'd like a THIS WAY UP sign,' announced Graham, getting in first. 'I've always wanted one of those. People keep on picking me up and turning me over. I once saw a sign on the side of a box,' he went on dreamily. 'It took me all the morning to work it out because it had been put on upside down – but that's what it said – THIS WAY UP.'

'I'd like a bowl of bread and milk,' said Fangio hungrily. 'A great big one. A *bottomless* one.'

Graham considered this for a while. 'If it didn't have a bottom,' he said at last, 'all the milk would run out.'

'I don't mean *that* sort of bottomless,' said Fangio.
'I mean one that went on and on with no end.' He
made a loud sucking noise. 'It needn't even be a bowl
– it could be a hole in the ground, and the more you
eat the more there is . . .'

Olga rustled her hay impatiently. 'I can't promise
what it will be,' she said. 'You'll have to wait and
see.'

As it happened the words had hardly left her mouth
when there was a click from the side gate and Karen
Sawdust came into view. She was carrying a small
handbag, and as she drew near Olga's heart missed a
beat. The big moment had arrived. What *could* be in
store for her?

If Karen Sawdust noticed three other pairs of eyes
watching her every movement she showed no sign.

'Poor Olga,' she said, as she opened the door. 'I'm
sorry we had to take your family away from you
without any warning, but there really wasn't room in
your hutch for *four*. It was high time we did something about it.

'Anyway, they've all gone to a good home with a
friend of mine. As I couldn't really ask her to pay
anything for them, I did a swop instead.' She opened
her handbag and took out a small piece of cardboard.

'My friend's father has a special camera that takes pictures while you wait, and he let me take one of your family in their new house.'

Olga watched in astonishment as Karen Sawdust took some sticky tape and fixed the piece of card-board to the wall of her dining-room.

She blinked, and then she blinked again – just to make sure. For there, gazing back at her, were three very familiar faces.

Karen Sawdust closed the door again and fastened the catch. 'Whatever else you do,' she warned, 'don't chew the edges. It's the only picture we took and there'll never be another.'

There was a moment's silence as she went away, and then as the kitchen door shut the hub-bub broke out.

'I'm hungry!' wailed Fangio. 'It's thinking about all that bread and milk.'

'I'm going,' called Graham, 'before anyone picks me up and turns me over.'

' A *swop*!' exclaimed Noel bitterly. 'Who wants a picture of a lot of guinea-pigs?'

Olga drew herself up to her full height. '*I* do,' she said, with as much dignity as she could muster. 'And they're not just any old guinea-pigs. They happen to be *my* family. It's quite the nicest present I've ever had.

'You're welcome to share it with me,' she called. 'You can come and see it whenever you like.'

But the others had disappeared.

Olga gave a sigh. Really, there was no accounting for some tastes.

She lay back and studied her present with care. She would miss her children – there was no denying the fact – but they had to go out into the world on their own at some time, and their new owners sounded very nice and kind. In a way, she had the best of both worlds; she could still see her family and yet she hadn't the bother of looking after them. It seemed a very good arrangement.

'I expect it was the only thing Karen Sawdust

could do,' she announced, in case Noel, Fangio and Graham were still within earshot. 'After all, some things in this world are so valuable you just can't buy them – and my family happens to be one of them!'

CHAPTER TWO

Olga's Tallest Tale

One day Olga made a discovery. She discovered she
was able to speak French. True, she could only say
one word, and it wasn't a very long one at that; but
as Karen Sawdust explained, it was more than a lot of
human beings managed to learn in a whole lifetime.

Olga made her discovery quite by chance.

Early that morning Karen Sawdust and some of her
friends came out into the garden in order to do something called 'rehearsing a play', and Olga was put in
her special run so that she could watch what was happening and enjoy a late breakfast at the same time.

At first Olga spent more time watching the
'goings-on' on the lawn than she did eating the grass
itself, but when she found the play had to do with
'The Wars of the Roses' she soon lost interest.

Olga knew all about the Wars of the Roses. They took place all through the summer, whenever Mr Sawdust came into the garden. In fact, as far as she could make out, Mr Sawdust spent more time battling with his roses than he did over anything else. If he wasn't cutting bits off the ends he was attacking them with something called a spray gun. Sometimes he fought battles against green flies; at other times he fought battles against black flies; and Olga had no doubt that if there had been any pink or blue flies on the roses Mr Sawdust would have found a spray for those as well.

Then there was some nasty white stuff called mildew, and something even worse called black spot. In fact, so many things seemed to go wrong with Mr Sawdust's roses Olga often wondered why he bothered to keep them at all. They were much more trouble than they were worth. It wasn't as if they did anything useful, for according to Fangio and Graham they weren't even nice to eat, and Noel was always grumbling about the sharp thorns they had all the way up their stems.

Another thing Olga didn't like about roses was the fact that often, if Mr Sawdust did his spraying on a day when the wind was blowing in the wrong direction, she wasn't allowed on the lawn for days at a time in case it made her ill.

Given her way, Olga would have had one really big War of the Roses and finished them all off for good. Giving a loud squeak of disgust, she turned her back on the proceedings and began tucking into the grass for all she was worth. There was no knowing if Karen Sawdust and her friends mightn't take it into their heads to do some spraying as well.

As it happened Olga's squeak was much louder than she had meant it to be, and it made the others stop what they were doing and look round at her in surprise.

'Did you hear that?' cried Karen Sawdust. 'Olga was speaking French! How about giving her a part in the play?'

'I don't see what the French have to do with the Wars of the Roses,' said one of her friends. 'It all happened in England.'

'But it was *after* the soldiers had got back from France that it happened,' insisted Karen Sawdust. 'They started fighting amongst themselves.' She picked up a stick and laid it on the grass. 'The bit between here and Olga's run can be the English Channel. Olga's run can be France. And Olga herself can look after it and make sure the fighting doesn't spread beyond the shores of England.'

They all crowded round the run, and feeling that something was expected of her, Olga lifted up her head and gave another loud squeak.

'There you are!' cried Karen Sawdust triumphantly. 'She said yes!'

'What a beautiful accent!' exclaimed someone else. And dissolving into gales of laughter, they all ran off again and went on with their play.

Olga felt very pleased with herself. 'Fancy me being able to talk in a foreign language!' she thought. 'And not only talk it, but make myself understood as well!'

Olga couldn't wait to tell her friends, but the play went on and on, so she had to keep the news to herself for the time being.

It was a very noisy play. There were several boys taking part – some with white roses pinned to their jackets and others with red ones, and they spent their time running up and down the lawn waving wooden sticks called 'lances', and shouting at each other. Whenever they fell over – which was quite often – Karen Sawdust and her friends took it in turns to help them to their feet and give them something called 'first aid'.

It was all very strange, but Olga did her best to join in. Each time anyone came near her run she dashed round and round in circles, squeaking as hard as she could.

'I think you defended France very well,' said Karen Sawdust, when the play came to an end at last and she moved Olga's run to a new spot on the lawn. 'You deserve some fresh grass as a reward for all your bravery.'

Olga felt very pleased with herself and she decided she would have to try and speak French more often.

'*French?*' exclaimed Fangio when she told the others about her discovery later that morning. 'What's French?'

Olga sighed. It really was most difficult trying to explain even quite simple things sometimes. 'It's another Sawdust language,' she said. 'It's spoken by people who live in France. People who live in other countries speak other languages.'

'I don't see why people have to speak another language just because they live in a different country,' said Graham. 'Why can't they all speak the same language?'

'Anyway,' broke in Noel, 'how do you *know* they

speak a different language if you've never even been there?'

Olga took a deep breath. 'I know,' she said wildly, 'because one of my relations invented French. It was my great-great-great-uncle, Sir Lancelot da Polga.

'That's how I come to speak such good French myself,' she added. 'Karen Sawdust said I do, and she should know.'

The others sat and digested this piece of information for a moment or two while they tried hard to think of a suitable reply.

It was Noel who broke the silence. 'If you're so good at French,' he said, 'how about telling us a story in it?'

'If I told you a story in French,' said Olga, 'you

wouldn't understand a word. But I'll tell you how it came about in ordinary language if you like.'

She looked round the garden for inspiration, thinking over the morning's happenings and putting them all together in her mind.

'It started,' she said, after she'd got her ideas sorted out, 'at the time of the Wars of the Roses. You see, the French people were frightened that the fighting might spread across the English Channel, so they planted lots and lots of rose bushes all along their shores to stop the English soldiers getting in. They put special stuff on the ground to make them grow quickly, and they sprayed the leaves every day to get rid of all the flies, just like Mr Sawdust does with his roses.

'In no time at all the roses became so thick and tall and prickly that no one, not even if they'd used the biggest pair of clippers in the world, could ever have entered France.

'The only trouble was, they made such a good job of it that when the war in England came to an end the French people found they couldn't get out of their own country.

'Of course they could hear voices on the other side of the hedges – lots of them: because people kept on

crossing the Channel to pick the roses. You see after
the war there weren't many left in England. But they
couldn't see anybody, and they couldn't make themselves heard either.

'They tried calling out "Help!" as loud as they
could, but it was no use, the hedge was much too
thick; and there were far too many thorns for them to
push their way through.

'They decided that the only way they would ever
attract attention would be by tying a flag to the top
of one of the rose bushes, but not even the tallest
Frenchman standing on the largest ladder in all
France could reach anywhere near it.

'Then just as they were giving up hope of ever being rescued, my great-great-great-uncle, Sir Lancelot
da Polga, came on the scene, bringing with him a tiny
basket which he and some of the other guinea-pigs
had made out of bullrushes.

'In those days,' continued Olga, 'guinea-pigs were
often called on in times of trouble because they were
so good at thinking up ideas. They were also very
brave and noble and . . .'

'Oh, do get on with it,' said Noel impatiently.

Olga fixed him with a beady eye. 'Uncle Lancelot's
idea was a very simple one,' she said, 'and when he'd

explained to the French people what he wanted they granted him his every wish.

'They called on their tallest soldier, mounted him on the largest horse they could find, and then tied the basket to the longest lance that anyone had ever seen.

'As Uncle Lancelot climbed into it and the soldier rode off to a point somewhere near the horizon you could have heard a blade of grass fall to the ground.

'When he reached his chosen point, the soldier turned his horse, lowered the lance and charged.

'They do say that even to this day the sound of horse's hooves brings people running from their houses.

'When he was within a stone's throw of the rose bushes he brought his horse to a halt in a cloud of dust, and Uncle Lancelot shot out of the basket like a bullet from a gun and flew through the air towards the top-most branch.

'As he clasped it, the crowd, which had been standing watching in silence, suddenly gave out a great cheer.

' "Can you see over the top?" they cried. "Tell us, can you see over the top?"

' "Yes!" Uncle Lancelot's voice echoed round the valley far below. "Yes! Yes! Yes!"

'And that,' said Olga, 'was how the French language came to be invented, and how my uncle came to be called Lancelot.'

She sank back on her haunches, nibbling absent-mindedly at a morsel of grass. Telling stories was very tiring work, and it had given her quite an appetite.

'Wait a minute,' said Noel thoughtfully. ' "Yes" isn't a foreign word. The Sawdust people say it all the time.'

'I've heard them,' broke in Fangio.

'Me too,' agreed Graham. 'I don't think very much of that as a story.'

Olga looked round carefully before replying. 'Well,' she whispered, 'the thing that no one knows – the thing that's never been told before . . . not until today, is that Uncle Lancelot didn't really say "yes".

'You see, when he landed on top of the rose bushes he caught his paws on some prickles. So what he really said was "Wheeeeeeeeeeeeee".'

And to show what she meant Olga opened her mouth as wide as it would go, and gave voice to the loudest cry in the best possible accent she could manage. 'Wheeeeeeeee! Wheeeeeeeeeeeee! Wheeeeeeeeeeeeeeeee!

'From that moment on,' she continued, 'the word "wheeeeee" has always meant "yes" in French.

'Of course, other people came along afterwards and thought up more words. Once the idea caught on it was easy, and they thought it might be nice to have their own language. But it was really my great-great-great-uncle Lancelot who started it all . . . and we guinea-pigs have been able to say "yes" in French ever since. "Wheeeeeee!" '

Olga glanced round, but to her surprise her audience seemed to have vanished.

'How useful it is to know a foreign language,' she thought. 'Especially when you want to enjoy your lunch in peace. I must remember to practise it in case I ever need it again!'

CHAPTER THREE

Olga's Best Effort

One day, Olga was sitting in her outside run on the lawn, enjoying a quiet nibble in the sunshine, when she smelt a smell.

There was nothing very unusual about this. The Sawdust family's garden was full of smells. The roses, the flower-beds, the shrubs, the heather-filled banks, the vegetables, all gave off some kind of odour for those with a nose to smell it.

Even each different blade of grass had its own particular scent; not to mention the occasional dandelion or piece of clover – *when* she could find them.

Olga counted the days when she found a clover or

a dandelion leaf on the Sawdust family's lawn as 'lucky' ones indeed, for Mr Sawdust worked hard to keep the grass free from what he called 'weeds'.

Olga had never quite got used to these odd ways of the Sawdust people. She couldn't understand what made them like one plant and not another, and why they should want to destroy perfectly good eatable things simply because they didn't like the look of them. There was no accounting for tastes, but if she'd had her way all lawns would have a liberal sprinkling of all sorts of nice plants besides grass.

But the smell she could smell that morning had nothing to do with anything immediately nearby. It wasn't a fresh, spring smell; nor was it a dusty summery one; it was almost an autumn smell – yes, that was the best likeness she could think of. It was the kind of smell that usually heralded the coming of autumn, when bonfires made up of dead leaves and branches were lit in the general clean-up before winter set in.

Olga wondered for a while if she could smell the smell because she was in a different part of the garden. The Sawdust family had arrived home late that morning from what was known as 'Saturday shopping'. There had been a great deal of rushing about and talk of a snack lunch of egg and chips. Olga had been put on the front lawn for a change – it had to do with Mr Sawdust having sprayed his roses in the back garden once again – and then they had all disappeared into the house.

She looked around, but apart from the familiar stone-like shape of Graham asleep under some bushes, there wasn't a soul in sight. Noel had gone out early that morning and probably wouldn't be back until much later, and Fangio was doubtless hiding away somewhere until it was time for his evening bowl of bread and milk.

Olga returned to her nibbling, but for once her mind wasn't on it. The smell was getting stronger all the time and it began to bother her more and more. Her nose twitched, and try as she might she couldn't rid herself of the feeling that something was very wrong.

There was little wind, but what there was seemed to be blowing the smell in her direction. She turned round in order to see if there was anything going on behind her and suddenly became rooted to the spot.

Her eyes bulged and she stared through the wire mesh of her run, hardly able to believe she was seeing aright. For there, not a dozen run length's away, was a great column of black smoke billowing out of the Sawdust family's kitchen window.

Olga had seen smoke coming out of their kitchen window in the past – usually on mornings when Mr Sawdust did something called 'burning the toast'. But when that happened, he always opened the door and waved a newspaper to and fro to get rid of it. On this occasion there was no one around, and it was all much, much worse than anything she'd seen before.

'Wheeeeeeeeeeeee!' she shrieked.

'Wheeeeeeeeeeeeeee! Wheeeeeeeeeeeeeeeee! Wheeeeeeeeeeeeeeeeeeee!

'Help! Fire!

'Wheeeeeeeeeeeeeeeeeeeeeeeee! Do something!'

And she ran up and down her run calling out as loudly as she possibly could.

'Wheeeeeeeee! Wheeeeeeeeeeeeeeee!' If only she could get outside. She felt so helpless shut in behind her wire.

But the only effect her shouting had was to waken Graham. He stirred in his sleep, looked around drowsily for a moment or two, and then ambled slowly in her direction.

'Is anything the matter?' he asked as he drew near.

'Is anything the matter?' repeated Olga. '*Is any-*

thing the matter? Can't you *smell* what's the matter? There's only a fire, that's all! The Sawdust family's house is on fire and no one's doing a thing about it!'

She ran around her run several more times and then stopped in front of Graham again. 'You'll have to raise the alarm!' she exclaimed.

'*I* will?' Something about the way Olga was behaving began to infect even Graham and he looked quite worried. He gave a sniff. Now that she mentioned it he could smell an unusual sort of smell.

'How? Why? What? Where?' he cried.

'I don't know!' squeaked Olga. 'Find someone else! Find Noel . . . or Fangio . . . or anyone. But do *something*!'

'Leave it to me!' said Graham. 'I'll be as quick as I can.'

Olga gave a groan as he lumbered past. 'No, not *that* way,' she cried. 'Wheeeeeeeeeee! Wheeeeeeeeeeeeeee! The fire's the other way!'

But Graham wasn't to be diverted.

With his head down he disappeared round the back of Olga's run, heading goodness knew where in the excitement of the moment.

Olga sank back on to her haunches and gave another despairing groan. Fancy! Of all the creatures

to be left alone with at such a time it had to be
Graham – the slowest one of all.

Suppose the whole house caught fire? And the
trees, and the grass . . . she might be burnt alive and
all her whiskers turned into umbrella handles. She'd

once got too near a candle on her birthday and had
had a terrible fright when one of her whiskers had
singed and rolled itself up into what Karen Sawdust
called an umbrella handle. It was something she had
never forgotten.

In her panic Olga began to dig at the grass.
'Wheeeeeeeeeeee!' she shrieked. 'Wheeeeeeeeeeeeeee! Wheeeeeeeeeeeeeeeeeeeeeeeeeeeee!'

Whether or not she would ever have tunnelled a
way out was hard to say, but long before Olga had a
chance to find out, things began to happen.

Karen Sawdust came running out of the house. Olga felt the run being lifted up, and then she was safely in warm hands and out of harm's way. After that so many things took place all at once it wasn't until much later that she could even begin to sort them out. All she could do was sit in her house and watch wide-eyed.

There were shouts and cries from the Sawdust family. More smoke – clouds and clouds of it. Flames, even, licking up the kitchen wall. Then there was the wailing of a siren; at first in the distance, but getting closer and closer all the time. Then more shouts, this time from lots of men in dark uniforms. And the pounding of feet, followed by mounds of white stuff like soap suds, which seemed to cover everything.

After that there was silence, followed by a very

poohy, pongy smell, much worse than anything that had gone before, but thankfully a much 'quieter' sort of smell – without the crackles and pops of the earlier one.

'We left a chip-pan on the stove and forgot to turn off the gas,' explained Karen Sawdust to one of her friends much later that day, as they cleaned Olga's house out. 'It caught fire while we were out of the room and then set light to Daddy's new wall panels!'

Olga took it all in. She knew about chip-pans. In fact she knew more about chip-pans than she cared to remember, for she'd seen Mr Sawdust rush past her house with one all covered in flames. And she knew about Mr Sawdust's wall panels as well, for she'd had many an afternoon's nap spoiled by his hammering while he was putting them up.

Karen Sawdust looked very black. In fact all the Sawdust family looked black, for they had spent the rest of the day cleaning up the mess.

'Thank goodness Olga raised the alarm,' said Karen Sawdust to her friend. 'I don't know where we would be if she hadn't.'

She closed the door of Olga's hutch, and then looked through the wire mesh. 'I told the man in charge of the fire brigade and he said he thought you ought to have a medal, so . . .' She felt in a pocket of her jeans and took out a small, silvery object. 'I've made you a special one all to yourself. It's an O.B.E!'

'An O.B.Wheeeeeeeeeeee!' squeaked Olga with excitement. She hadn't the slightest idea what it meant but it sounded very important.

'O.B.E.,' said Karen Sawdust, as she pinned the object on to the wire netting, 'is short for Order of the British Empire – or Olga's Best Effort – which-ever you prefer.'

Olga knew exactly which *she* preferred, and when Karen Sawdust went and fetched a large pile of dande-lion leaves and clover to make up for the lack of lunch earlier, she felt her day was complete.

Her mouth full of greenery, she gazed up at the medal long after Karen Sawdust and her friend had gone back indoors. One moment chewing rapidly, the next moment sitting stock still as if transfixed, she looked as if she could hardly believe her eyes.

The truth of the matter was she was longing to tell someone her good news, and there was just no one around.

Neither Noel nor Fangio had put in an appearance all day, and if the noise was anything to go by the Sawdust family were still busy with their cleaning operations. Anyway, they already knew about it. It was all most disappointing.

And then she heard a rustle in some nearby bushes.

It was Graham. But a very different Graham than the one she'd last seen that morning. His shell was covered with mud; his feet were black; and his eyes were red and rimmed with sweat. He looked in a truly dreadful state as he dragged himself slowly nearer and nearer.

'Am I too late?' he gasped. 'I went everywhere I could think of but I couldn't find anyone, and then I lost my way and . . .'

'Are you too late?' Olga gazed at him indignantly.

'Why, it's been ov . . .' She was about to launch into one of her best ever tales; all about her moment of glory and how she alone had saved the day; but she caught sight of Graham's eager face looking up at her and she paused.

Then she did a very noble thing.

'No,' she said firmly. 'You're not too late at all. In fact you're just in time. You're just in time to see our medal.'

'*Our* medal?' repeated Graham.

'Yes,' said Olga. 'It's an O.G.E. Some people get it wrong and call it an O.B.E., but it's not – it's an O.G.E. That means Olga and Graham's Effort.'

'Can you eat it?' asked Graham hopefully. 'I'm hungry.'

'No, you can't,' said Olga. 'And even if you could, it would be wrong. Medals are only given on very special occasions. But you *can* eat these . . .' And she carried the remains of her supper across her dining-room and began pushing it through the holes in the front door.

Graham blinked happily as it floated down and landed beside him. 'What a funny thing,' he said. 'I do believe it's raining dandelions.'

He started munching the greenery and then looked up. 'Wouldn't it be nice,' he added happily, 'if we could have an O.G.E. every day?'

CHAPTER FOUR

A Model Guinea-pig

Olga crouched in the middle of the Sawdust family's dining-room table and gazed around the room with a very superior look on her face indeed.

The curtains had been drawn; chairs taken away in order to make more space; and all kinds of strange objects – big, shiny things with wires hanging from them – had been brought in; all because of her.

It was most exciting, and when the door swung open and Noel strolled in to see what all the fuss was about she could hardly contain herself.

'Look at me!' she squeaked, as she ran round and round in circles. 'Wheeeeeeeeee! You'll never guess what's happening!'

But if she was expecting her words to have any effect on Noel she was disappointed. He took in the scene with one disdainful glance. 'It looks as if you're going to have your photograph taken,' he said, trying hard not to yawn.

'I should think you'd be a fiftieth of a second exposure at f8. Unless of course you keep running round and round in circles like that. If you do, they may have to change things – just to be on the safe side. Otherwise it will come out blurred.'

'f8,' repeated Olga. 'A fiftieth of a second exposure? What *are* you on about?'

'I was forgetting,' said Noel, in world-weary tones. 'You wouldn't know about these things. You've never had your photograph taken before. It's all to do with letting the right amount of light into the camera.

'Mind you, if Karen Sawdust's taking the picture she's got a camera with the places already marked. There's one for bright sunshine, and another for cloudy days, though I don't suppose there's anything marked "guinea-pigs" – there wouldn't be any call for it.'

'They're getting someone in specially to take *my* picture,' broke in Olga, trying to get a word in edgeways. 'And it's going to be in colour.'

'You mean there are other sorts?' asked Noel. 'What are they taking? Head and Shoulders?' He looked Olga up and down. 'Oh, I'm sorry, I forgot – you haven't really got any shoulders. Never mind, I expect they'll find some way of doing it. After all, it isn't as if you've got black fur like me.

'The trouble with black fur,' he continued, 'is that it soaks up all the light. Mr Sawdust says he has to *pour* the lights on sometimes and it all disappears – just like water.'

'If you've got so much light inside you,' said Olga crossly, 'why don't you show up when it's dark?'

Noel couldn't answer that one, and to Olga's relief he stalked out of the room. She was glad to see the back of him. Really, if he'd gone on much longer it would have upset her whole morning.

But she soon forgot the interruption in the general excitement as the rest of the family came back in and started making ready for the big moment.

As she'd told Noel, her picture was being taken by a friend of the family and it was needed for a SPECIAL PURPOSE. Karen Sawdust had told her so while she was giving her fur a brush that morning in order to make sure it was all neat and tidy. 'You're the only one who's just right for the purpose,' she'd said.

'Well,' thought Olga, 'it's quite understandable of course. I mean, they must be fed up with looking at pictures of cats. If you're going to take photographs at all it might as well be something worthwhile.'

And as the lights came on in all the shiny reflectors she turned to face the front. She'd never seen such bright lights before, not even in mid-summer, and for a moment or two they made her blink. In fact they were so bright she could hardly make out what was going on in the rest of the room. All she could see were vague, shadowy figures. But listening to what was being said she gathered they were busy doing something called focusing the camera.

'We shan't be long now,' said Karen Sawdust, as she came round in front of the lights and turned Olga so that she was sideways on. 'But we have to make sure you come out nice and clear.' And she put some dandelion leaves on the table to make certain Olga stayed where she'd been put.

Olga was a bit disappointed she was only having a sideways picture taken of her. She'd always considered her face was her best part. But she thought it over while she sat chewing the leaves, and decided it was probably the best way of getting all of her in.

However, as it turned out the Sawdust family's friend took not one, but lots and lots of photographs. Most of them were from the side, but there were quite a few from different angles as well. Some from the front, some from the back, and one from right overhead. Then she took some measurements with a long piece of tape, and afterwards she even drew a life-size picture on a big sheet of white cardboard, which she then coloured with a special box of paints.

At last it was all over. The lady thanked Olga very much and said how good she had been; the lights were switched off; the curtains drawn back; and Olga was returned to her own house.

After so much time spent under the hot lights it seemed cold and dark; even – though Olga hardly liked to admit it – a trifle dingy. If it hadn't been for the fact that Karen Sawdust brought her out a special feed of oats she would have felt very miserable indeed.

'That's a present for being such a good model,' said Karen Sawdust as she filled the bowl.

'A model!' squeaked Olga. 'Wheeeeeeeeeeeeee!' And she lost no time in telling the others all about it.

'A model what?' asked Noel suspiciously.

'Er . . . a model guinea-pig,' said Olga lamely. 'I expect they want to stand one in the garden like a gnome.' Olga had once seen some plastic gnomes in someone's garden when she'd visited Boris at the seaside.

'I don't like gnomes,' said Fangio darkly. 'I've seen some up the road. Nasty things. You can't tell what they're thinking.'

Olga had a sudden thought. 'Perhaps it's a statue,' she exclaimed. 'The Sawdust people are always putting statues up to remind them of famous deeds.'

'Famous deeds?' repeated Noel. 'What famous deeds have you ever done?'

'I was thinking,' said Olga, with as much dignity as she could manage, 'of what happened with the fire.

They might want to stand a statue of me in the front garden just to remind them.'

'Oh, *that!*' Noel suddenly lost interest and wandered away. He was still upset at having missed all the fun, and he was also tired of hearing the same old story retold so many times.

'Well, if it *is* a statue,' said Graham, 'I expect they'll want to do one of me as well. Perhaps I'd better go and wait by the back door just in case.'

Olga returned to her oats. 'I think,' she said, in her 'its-high-time-we-changed-the-subject' voice, 'we shall just have to wait and see.'

But as things turned out Olga had a very long time to wait before she heard any more news about her photograph. Several weeks went past, and she had almost forgotten about it when one morning Karen Sawdust arrived outside her house carrying a mysterious-looking brown paper parcel under her arm.

It was an unusually long parcel. Olga couldn't remember ever having seen such a long one before, and she watched eagerly while Karen Sawdust unwrapped the paper.

'What do you think of that?' asked Karen Sawdust, as she held up a long, furry object. 'Do you recognize yourself?'

'Do I recognize myself? Wheeeeeeeee . . . . . .!'
Olga started to squeak in surprise and then broke off
as the rest of the paper fell away and she stared at the
object in front of her.

She had never felt so disappointed by anything in
the whole of her life. Words failed her. There wasn't
a squeak in her entire vocabulary which could have
possibly expressed her feelings at that moment.

True enough the face wasn't bad: quite good
really. Not like the real thing, of course – the whiskers
were much too coarse – but then that wasn't really
surprising. And the rear end, as far as she could judge,
was reasonably true to life.

But as for the body . . . it was too long by miles.
Why, it was longer than her hutch. It was practically
as long as two hutches put together. How anyone
could possibly make such a mistake she couldn't begin
to think. There was only one thing to do in the circumstances. She would ignore it. That's what she

would do – ignore it. And she turned her back on it without so much as a further glance.

Karen Sawdust went back into the house. 'I don't think Olga liked it very much,' she heard her say to her mother.

'Never mind,' Mrs Sawdust's voice floated back. 'It's ideal for what we want. Just the right length.'

Olga pricked up her ears. 'Perhaps,' she thought, 'it's been made that long so that as many people as possible can see it. That's it . . . there probably aren't enough guinea-pigs to go round to please everybody, so that's what they've done.'

Olga felt better. She even began to wish she'd taken a longer look at the model of herself, whatever use the Sawdust people intended putting it to.

But it was Noel who finally solved the mystery. There was a bang from the pussy-flap later that evening as he came hurrying out.

'Here!' he called. 'You'll never guess what they're using your statue for.'

Olga looked at him suspiciously. There was something about the tone of Noel's voice, not to mention the look in his eye, which she didn't much care for. 'If I'll *never* guess,' she said, 'there's not very much point in my trying . . .'

'They've put it against the dining-room door to keep the draught out,' said Noel. 'I only found out because I tried to push the door open just now and there was this great long thing in the way. It's called a draught excluder and it gave me a fright, I can tell you.

'The Sawdust people are always worried about draughts. It's because they haven't got any fur. Their legs get cold and it makes them cross and . . .'

He looked up, but Olga had gone into her bedroom. She didn't want to hear another word.

'That's the very last time I let anyone take *my* photograph,' she thought. 'And if they do try I shall run round and round and round so fast there won't be a camera made that will ever, ever catch me!'

And with that she buried herself deep inside her hay to keep out the draught and went to sleep!

CHAPTER FIVE

A Mystery Solved

'Tell me again,' said Olga. 'Slowly, and from the very beginning.'

Noel stood up, curled his tail neatly round himself, and then settled down again.

'There's a guinea-pig trapped in a pipe down near the shops,' he said. 'We had to stop on the way to the vet this morning and I heard it calling out. It was still there on the way back, squeaking away like mad.'

'What was it saying?' asked Olga. 'It must have been saying *something*.'

Noel gave himself a quick lick. 'That's the funny thing,' he said. 'It wasn't really saying anything. I mean, it *sounded* like you – as if it needed oiling, but there was nothing that made any sense.'

'Then how do you know it wanted help?' asked Olga. 'It might be very happy where it is.'

'Because it only calls out when people get near,' said Noel. 'As soon as it sees a crowd of people it starts going "Wheeeee! Wheeeeeeeeee! Wheeeeeeeeeeee!"; and when they've gone again it stops, so it must be trying to attract their attention. If it was happy it would go on squeaking all the time.'

'Perhaps it's invented another foreign language?' suggested Graham. 'Like your great-great-great-uncle Lancelot.'

'But what makes you think it's trapped in a pipe?' persisted Olga, ignoring the interruption.

'Because I happen to have very good hearing,' said Noel. 'And I *know* that's where it's coming from.'

Olga sat back and considered the matter. She had to admit that although any list of Noel's good points would have been fairly short, the one thing he was good at was hearing things. Noel could hear a bird

clearing its throat at the other end of the garden, and if he said the sound was coming from inside a pipe then there could be no doubt that it was.

'Well,' she said at last. 'I don't know. I'd like to do something to help, I really would. But without knowing what it's saying I don't see what I can do.'

'We can't leave him there,' said Fangio. 'That's for sure.'

'If only I could get out of my house,' said Olga. 'I'd go down there straight away. Nothing would keep me away. *Nothing.*'

Noel looked at her thoughtfully. 'I know one way you could get there,' he said.

Olga's jaw dropped. 'You *do*?' she exclaimed.

'You could get there the same way that I did,' said Noel. 'If you get yourself taken to the vet you're bound to go past. Mr and Mrs Sawdust always go that way. I should know. I've been enough times.'

In saying he frequently went to the vet, Noel was making the understatement of the year. There were occasions when it seemed as though he practically lived there, and Mr Sawdust was always grumbling about the bills. If he wasn't having injections for one thing he was being given tablets for something else. His present visit had to do with a fight he'd been in the previous night. No one knew who his opponent had been, and Noel himself was very vague about the whole affair, but he'd lost quite a lot of fur off one of his back legs and was really looking rather sorry for himself.

'I'm not getting into any fights,' said Olga firmly.

'It doesn't have to be a fight,' said Fangio. 'You could have an accident. Perhaps you could scratch yourself on one of the wire netting ends in your hutch.'

'There aren't any wire netting ends in my hutch,' replied Olga. 'Mr Sawdust was very careful when he made it.'

'You could let Noel give you a nip,' suggested Graham.

'Certainly not!' said Olga, before Noel had a chance to reply. She didn't like the way he'd suddenly started licking his lips, and she went back to her bowl of oats with the air of someone who'd declared the conversation at an end.

'If you're frightened of getting hurt,' said Noel, breaking the silence, 'there *is* one other way.'

Olga looked up at him suspiciously.

'You could stop eating,' said Noel. 'Mrs Sawdust is bound to think there's something wrong with you if you stop eating – she always does.'

'What a good idea!' said Fangio.

'If Olga stopped eating,' said Graham wisely, 'there *would* be something wrong with her.'

Olga, her mouth full of oats, gave him a withering look. 'I think it's a perfectly silly idea,' she said. 'If I stop eating I shan't have any strength left to do anything at all. I shall be no use whatsoever.'

'You don't need any strength to listen,' said Noel, pressing home his point. 'And you won't have to *do* anything except go without food long enough to get yourself taken to the vet. You can make up for it later. I bet once you start eating again you'll be given lots.'

'Dandelion leaves,' said Graham.

'And fresh clover,' added Fangio, encouragingly. 'I remember once when I was ill I had cream off the milk for days afterwards. I was sorry when I got better again.'

'I'll just finish off my breakfast,' said Olga casually, 'then I'll think about it. I can't think on an empty stomach.'

'You won't get taken to the vet on a full one,' said Graham bluntly. 'That's for sure.'

Olga began to look more and more gloomy. It was all very well for Graham to talk. Having a shell meant that no one would ever know what state his stomach was in.

'The sooner you start,' said Noel, 'the sooner you finish. Besides, think how *you* would feel trapped inside a pipe.'

Olga struggled with her conscience for a moment or two longer before finally giving in. And really, as she sat back basking in the congratulations that followed she began to feel rather noble.

It was only when she returned and caught sight of her bowl of oats, still half-full from breakfast, that she began to wonder if she was doing the right thing after all.

'Don't worry,' said Noel, cheerfully. 'It won't take the Sawdust family more than a few days to see that something's wrong.'

'A few days!' Left on her own, Olga hardly knew what to do with herself. Never had her food bowl looked quite so tempting. And the closer she got to it the worse it became. In the end she could stand it no longer and she disappeared into her bedroom and lay down in the hay with her back to the world.

Even when Karen Sawdust came to see her later in the day she still didn't budge.

Instead, she sat listening to the familiar sound of the dustpan and brush as the floor of her dining-room was cleaned out. Then, to her relief, she heard Karen Sawdust call out to her mother. 'Olga hasn't eaten very much today,' she said. 'I hope there's nothing wrong with her.'

'Perhaps she's tired of oats,' called Mrs Sawdust through her kitchen window. 'It may be the warm weather. Try giving her more greenstuff.'

Olga groaned inwardly a few minutes later when Karen Sawdust returned carrying a pile of assorted tit-bits. Her nose twitched as she smelt the good smell of freshly picked grass, and dandelion leaves, and clover – all the things she liked best in the world. She was supposed to get them *after* she'd been to the vet, not before!

To make matters worse, Karen Sawdust seemed to be taking extra-special care over everything that evening. She emptied out the food bowl, washed it carefully, and then filled it to the brim with fresh oats. Even the water bowl had never looked quite so clean and sparkling before. Olga could see it all out of the corner of her eye. But even though the pile of greenstuff was placed temptingly outside her bedroom door, she steadfastly refused to take any notice.

'I hope you feel better in the morning,' said Karen Sawdust, as she shut her up for the night. 'If you don't we'll have to take you to the vet.'

Although in one way the words were like music to Olga's ears, in another sense they were no comfort at all, for 'tomorrow' was a long, long way away.

'If I feel like I do at the moment,' she thought, 'I may not even *be* here in the morning!'

But if that day had seemed long, the night was much worse. Sleep was a long time coming, and even when she did finally nod off it was only to dream of food and yet more food; all tantalizingly just out of her reach.

Really, she didn't know which was worse, dreaming about food or seeing the real thing and being unable to touch it.

To make matters worse Noel gave her no peace. His pussy-flap hardly stopped banging as he kept coming outside to make sure she was sticking to her bargain.

At long last dawn broke, and then – rather earlier than usual – Karen Sawdust came to see her.

'Poor Olga,' she said, when she saw the pile of

uneaten food. 'You *must* be feeling off-colour. I've never known you to leave your food for as long as this before.'

'And you won't ever again,' thought Olga. 'Not if I have my way. Not ever and ever again. If I go on like this I shall be so off-colour I shall be white all over.'

But to her dismay there was worse to come. Instead of taking her out of the house as she'd expected, Karen Sawdust went through the whole business of cleaning it out again and fetching still more fresh food and water. Really, it was unbearable. She couldn't stand it any more. Karen Sawdust had promised to take her to the vet the very next day and now, here she was, still sitting in her house surrounded by food.

'It's Sunday,' said Noel, when he came to see her again.

'Sunday?' repeated Olga. 'What do you mean, Sunday?'

'The vet doesn't open on Sundays,' said Noel. 'Except for very special cases. They'd forgotten about that.'

'I'm special!' squeaked Olga. 'I'm very special!'

'Well, they've decided to leave it until tomorrow,' said Noel. 'I heard them talking about it at breakfast this morning. Mr Sawdust thinks you've got plenty of fat to live on until then.'

'Plenty of *fat*?' Olga could hardly believe her ears. 'How does he know what I've got underneath my fur? Wheeeeeeee!' She tried to give a squeak of disgust, but words failed her.

How she got through the rest of that day and the following night Olga never did know. She had lots of visitors, and her food was changed several times, but by then she was feeling too weak and miserable to care. In fact, she'd almost forgotten the real reason for her fast, and it wasn't until she felt herself being picked up and placed into her travelling box that it all came back.

The thought put new life into her, and as they drove

off she had a quick nibble at the hay which had been put in the box to protect her from the jolting.

She felt the by-now-familiar swaying motion as Mr Sawdust drove the car up the short driveway and into the lane outside, then down the long, winding hill leading to the shops and the spot where Noel had said he'd heard the cries for help.

Olga braced herself as they turned into the main road, and sure enough, a moment later she felt herself plunge forward as they drew to a sudden halt.

This must be it. This must be the place where Noel said they always had to stop.

Straining her ears to the utmost, she pressed herself against a small airhole in the side of the box. She could hear the sound of other cars. A screeching of brakes as they, too, came to a halt. The sound of hurried foot-steps, and of people talking. But there was no sign of a guinea-pig, only a high-pitched 'bleep, bleep, bleep'. In fact the 'bleeping' was so loud and urgent-sounding, Olga wondered how even Noel, with his keen sense of hearing, could possibly have heard anything as small and delicate as a guinea-pig's voice.

'I expect it's been without food for so long now,' thought Olga, 'it's just like me. I don't suppose it has the strength to say anything.'

And then she pricked up her ears again as she heard the Sawdust family talking.

'This new pedestrian-crossing idea certainly seems to be working,' said Mr Sawdust.

'It's such a simple idea too,' agreed Mrs Sawdust. 'I mean all you do is press a button, the lights change, the traffic stops, and "bleep, bleep, bleep" . . .'

'Everybody starts hurrying,' broke in Karen Sawdust. 'It always makes me get a move on. I even saw Noel on it the other day. Goodness knows where he was off to.' She laughed. 'Perhaps he thought it was Olga calling out. It sounds rather like a guinea-pig. Wheeeeeee! Wheeeeeeee! Wheeeeee!'

'How strange,' said Mrs Sawdust, as there was a rustling at her side. 'Olga must think so too. Listen . . . she's joining in.'

'Perhaps she's feeling better,' said Mr Sawdust as the bleeping noise outside stopped and they moved on their way.

'Joining in?' repeated Olga.

'Feeling better?

'Wheeeeeeeeeeeeeeeeee!

'To think . . . I've been going without food all this time just for the sake of a . . . a . . . *pedestrian crossing*!

'Cats! Wheeeeeeeeceeeee!'

And she dived into her hay and gobbled it down so fast that by the time they reached the vet there was hardly any left. And if it didn't entirely make up for all the food she'd been without over the past two days, at least it gave her more than enough energy to decide exactly what she would have to say to Noel when she got back home.

CHAPTER SIX

Some New Arrivals

One morning Noel tore out of the house in a state of great excitement. Or rather, to be more exact, the kitchen door suddenly shot open and he came flying out with his tail between his legs, uttering a yowl which caused all the other occupants of the garden to stop dead in the middle of whatever it was they happened to be doing.

As the door slammed shut again he skidded to a halt, slunk along the path for a couple of yards, then paused for a brief and highly unnecessary wash.

But even to the most casual observer it was clear he had something on his mind, and shortly afterwards, having recovered his dignity, he turned and strolled purposefully across the lawn towards the others.

'We've got some new arrivals!' he announced.

'Some new arrivals!'

'Who?'

'What?'

'Where?' Olga joined in the general excitement as the news sank in.

'They're called Fircone and Raisin,' said Noel, 'and I can't tell you *what* they are, but I know *where* they are. They're in Karen Sawdust's bedroom. The door was open when I went past just now and I saw them.'

Olga suddenly felt rather downcast. To have additions was bad enough, but to find out that they were being kept in Karen Sawdust's bedroom was rubbing salt into the wound. True enough, in the past, she'd often been taken there as a treat when her house was being cleaned out, or when the weather turned particularly cold – she could safely say she knew every nook and cranny, especially the best ones to hide in when it was time to go home again, but she had never, ever been invited to *live* there. It was all most unsettling. The very idea made the grass taste so funny she nearly stopped eating it.

Noel licked his lips. 'I thought perhaps they were a present for me,' he said hungrily, 'but I don't think they could have been. I wasn't even allowed a proper look. You should have heard the fuss that went on as soon as I put my head round the door.'

Noel had had his fill of investigating for the time being, and on the pretence of having better things to do he disappeared for the rest of that morning.

However, Karen Sawdust's room was on the ground floor, and several times during the next few days he managed to climb on to the outside window ledge without being noticed. In this way he gathered a lot of extra information, all of which he passed on to the others.

Gradually they found out what the new arrivals looked like. It seemed that Fircone and Raisin had golden brown fur, large eyes, and long tails – which they could be picked up by. They were very clean in their habits, and apart from tearing up bits of paper which they used for their bedding, hardly ever needed cleaning out. They had cost £1.20 and their favourite food was something called sunflower seeds, which came in a big, yellow packet. When they weren't eating these they spent a lot of their time sleeping.

'They don't *do* very much, do they?' said Olga, looking up from her feeding bowl one day. 'I mean, all they seem to do is eat and sleep.' And she went into her bedroom and lay down for a quick nap just to show her disapproval.

She was getting a bit fed up, not so much with Fircone and Raisin as with hearing Noel go on about them. Just lately he had talked of little else, and Graham and Fangio were more than eager to listen. Her position as story-teller-in-chief was in danger. Every time she opened her mouth to say something Noel was off again. If it wasn't about what Fircone and Raisin were actually doing, it was about where they were doing it.

If Noel was to be believed, their home was a very splendid affair indeed; painted dark blue, and full of every gadget and comfort you could think of.

There was an upstairs bedroom, reached by a sloping ramp, and on the ground floor there was a special tray which could be taken out without disturbing the occupants on the rare occasions when they needed cleaning out. There was a wheel which went round whenever Fircone or Raisin climbed inside it – Noel said it went so fast you could hardly see their legs move; and to cap the lot Mr Sawdust had made them a long wooden tunnel from a hollowed-out tree branch, which they could hide inside when they wanted to be alone. It made her own house seem quite drab by comparison.

But the unkindest cut of all came one morning when she overheard a conversation between the Sawdust family.

'Are you going to the pet shop this morning?' called Mrs Sawdust.

An answering 'yes' floated back from Karen Sawdust. 'I'm getting some food for Fircone and Raisin.'

'Well, don't forget Olga needs some more oats,' called Mrs Sawdust.

'I'll try not to!' came the answering cry.

'I'll try not to!' repeated Olga. '*I'll try not to!* Wheeeeeeeeeeeeeeeeeee!'

Her squeak of disgust was so loud it was enough to

make any pet-shop owner within miles rush to line his
counter with packets of oats, just to be on the safe side.

And then Noel made another discovery about
Fircone and Raisin. It seemed that when they were
upset, or cross about something, they made loud
drumming noises with their back legs on the floor of
their house.

Unfortunately for Noel this was something he
didn't find out about until it was too late.

After days of hanging around outside Karen Sawdust's bedroom he slipped in there one morning
while the Sawdust family had their backs turned, and
hid under the bed. No one knew just what evil
thoughts he had in the back of his mind, but his hour
of triumph was short-lived.

The combined efforts of Fircone and Raisin drumming their feet on the side of the cage brought the
Sawdust family running, and for the second time in a
little over a week Noel came flying through the kitchen door. Only this time there was a difference.
This time he hadn't escaped completely unharmed.
Pausing in order to have his usual wash in times of
trouble, he licked his paw, and when he took it away
again the fur on the end had gone an ominous shade
of red.

Someone or some*thing* had taken a bite out of the end of his nose!

Olga looked at it with interest. 'I shouldn't worry too much about licking it,' she said, trying hard to keep the note of satisfaction from her voice. 'I think it's going to rain soon. Anyway, fancy letting little things like that get the better of you. I *am* surprised!'

Noel arched his back. 'Little things?' he repeated stiffly. 'Did you say *little* things?'

Olga stared at him in surprise. Somehow, for no reason other than the sound of their names, she had always pictured Fircone and Raisin as being small. Certainly no larger than herself.

'How big *are* they then?' she asked.

Safe in the knowledge that he was the only one present who had actually seen them, Noel began to embroider his tale in the hope of regaining some of his lost prestige.

'I'm not saying how big they are,' he began, rubbing his nose again, 'but I wouldn't like to be any of you lot if they ever get out. They'd have you for breakfast for a start. Why, they've got whiskers as thick as the bars on their cage. And as for their teeth – they're like celery sticks, and sharp as needles. It's all those sunflower seeds they've been eating. It's made them grow and grow and grow. If you knew the struggle I had . . . I'll tell you all about it if you like . . .'

'No, thank you,' said Fangio hastily. 'I'm going.'

'Wait for me,' called Graham.

'If you really want to know how big they are,' called Noel, 'I'll try and show you.' He stared round the bottom half of the garden until his gaze lighted on an enormous rhododendron. 'Can you see that bush over there?' he asked.

But if Noel was expecting any reply from his audience he was disappointed. They were looking in completely the opposite direction, and a moment later he discovered the reason why.

'Noel,' said Karen Sawdust, as she placed a very small blue cage on the ground alongside Olga's run, 'you're a naughty cat. Fancy trying to frighten my gerbils like that. No wonder they bit the end of your nose. It serves you right and I hope it taught you a lesson. You ought to be ashamed of yourself.'

Encouraged by the sound of Karen Sawdust's voice, Fircone and Raisin came out from inside the pile of shredded paper in their bedroom and peered at the others. Then they ran down the ramp and clambered up the rails at the front of the cage, staring out inquisitively. They were scarcely bigger than a medium-sized carrot.

'Say hello to Olga, Fangio and Graham,' said Karen Sawdust.

Olga suddenly decided she liked the newcomers after all. Anyone who was so small and yet could stick up for himself and bite someone hundreds of times his own size must have some good in him. She decided to get in first.

'Wheeeeeeeeeee!' she squeaked. 'Welcome to the family.'

The squeak which Fircone and Raisin gave in return was very small and very high.

It was friendly, but there was definitely a note of warning to it. Noel, who'd been about to let his instincts get the better of him again, understood it only too well, and he promptly sat down for another wash.

Olga relaxed. She was a great believer in starting as you mean to go on, and it was perfectly clear that Fircone and Raisin felt the same way.

She turned to Noel. 'What was it you were saying about a bush?' she asked. And there was a warning note in her voice too.

Noel busied himself with his washing. 'Nothing,' he said meekly. 'I only asked if you could see it, that's all.'

CHAPTER SEVEN

Olga Writes a Poem

As the summer wore on, finding fresh grass for Olga
became more and more of a problem for the Sawdust
family. The weather had been warmer than usual,
with very little rain, so the grass in their garden was
soon used up. The lawn itself hardly grew at all, and
gradually they began to go further and further
afield in their search for fresh supplies.

Olga could usually tell at once where her grass

came from. If it was from a field then it was often quite eatable, but if it came from the side of a road – particularly a main road – then it tasted of what the Sawdust family called 'diesel fumes', and with no rain to wash it clean it could be most unpleasant. True, Karen Sawdust always apologized in advance for its state, but that didn't make it taste any better.

And then one day Olga had a nice surprise. Karen Sawdust arrived outside her house carrying a large plastic bag, which was full to the brim with some of the lushest and greenest-looking grass she had ever seen.

Olga's sensitive nose twitched as the front door swung open, and she uttered a loud 'Wheeeeeeeeee!' of approval. This was more like it! She could hardly contain herself.

'It's from Tennyson's Lane,' Karen Sawdust called out to her mother. 'There's masses and masses of it. I don't know why we haven't thought of going there before.'

'Well, Olga should be all right for a while then,' said Mr Sawdust thankfully. 'After all, it's National Trust – and that does mean no one can build on it.'

'What a sensible idea,' thought Olga, 'keeping grass in a National Trust especially for guinea-pigs.'

331

Not that she cared where the grass had come from; she was much too busy eating it. It really was the most delicious she had ever tasted, and while the rest of her house was being cleaned out she chewed happily away, hardly listening to what was being said.

But gradually she became aware that Karen Sawdust was talking. And not only talking, but talking in a very strange way. Olga usually understood most of the things Karen Sawdust said, and even if she didn't know what every word meant she could always put two and two together and make at least three – enough to get the general idea. This was partly because Karen Sawdust spoke very clearly, but also because she mostly talked about sensible things – like food and drink.

However, for once Olga couldn't make head or tail of what it was all about.

'*See what a lovely shell,*' said Karen Sawdust.
'*Small and pure as a pearl,*
Lying close to my foot,
Frail, but a work divine,
Made so fairly well
With delicate spire and whorl,

How exquisitely minute,
A miracle of design!'

Olga knew what shells were. The inside of Boris's castle at the sea-side had been decorated with shells. But even though she craned her neck as far as it would go she couldn't see any lying at Karen Sawdust's feet. It was all very odd. Unless she was standing on them it didn't make any sense at all.

Olga decided to go back to more important things, and she was still chewing away later that evening when Noel appeared. He was closely followed by Graham and Fangio, and all were ready and eager for their own suppers.

Noel looked enviously at Olga's house when he caught sight of some bits of grass sticking out through the side of her front door. He liked an occasional blade for medicinal purposes, and as he strolled past he reached up automatically to take one.

'I know where this came from,' he said after a moment's thought.

'So do I,' said Olga. 'It's from Tennis Lane.'

'Not Tennis Lane,' said Noel. 'Tenny*son's* Lane. That's quite different. I go there sometimes when I'm out for a walk.'

Olga pricked up her ears. Although she was perfectly happy in her house, firmly believing that if she waited long enough all that mattered in the world would sooner or later come to her, she always liked to hear about the comings and goings of others. This was particularly so with Noel; because he was often away for such long periods, and came back looking so tired, she felt he must go to interesting places.

'Tennyson,' said Noel; 'was a poet.'

Olga paused. 'A poet?' she repeated. 'What's a poet?'

'A poet,' said Noel vaguely, 'is someone who says things in a funny way so that you don't know what they're on about in the middle, but the end bits always sound the same. Karen Sawdust reads poetry when she does her school homework – that's how I know. It goes on for ages and ages sometimes.'

'So that was it,' thought Olga. 'Poetry. Karen Sawdust must have been doing her homework poetry while she was cleaning me out.'

'This Tennyson,' continued Noel, 'was very famous and he used to live near here. He had a special spot where he walked when he was writing his poetry, so that's why they call it Tennyson's Lane.'

'I expect that's why Karen Sawdust went there

in the first place,' thought Olga. 'How very lucky!'

She stopped chewing. 'To think,' she said romantically, 'I may be eating the very same grass Tennyson once walked on.'

'Ugh!' Noel made a choking noise, for he was rather fussy about his food. 'I hadn't thought about that!'

But Olga was miles away. 'I would like to write a poem,' she said dreamily.

Fangio looked up from his bread and milk. 'Animals don't write poetry,' he said bluntly.

'I wrote my name in the sawdust once,' boasted Olga, 'and it was all jumbled up in the middle for a long time. But the ends were very good. I'm sure I could write some.'

The others waited in silence for a while, but if they were hoping for any sign of the rhymes they were unlucky. Olga simply carried on with her eating.

'I'll . . . er . . . I'll try and have something for you tomorrow morning,' she announced. 'I can't do it straight away. I'm really rather busy.

'Perhaps,' she added as an afterthought, 'we could all think of a poem and see which one is best.'

'Oh, I couldn't write a poem,' said Graham. 'I don't think I could do that.'

'Neither could I,' agreed Fangio. 'I wouldn't know how to start, and as for the middle and the end . . .'

'You don't know what you can do until you try,' said Olga grandly. And she disappeared into her bedroom for some peace and quiet while she set to work.

Olga stayed awake late that night, making marks in her sawdust, scratching them out again, adding some things and taking others away. But she had to admit she hadn't a single idea in her head, and the

more she tried the harder it seemed. It was all very well for Tennyson – he'd had a walk with lots of grass on it where he could write *his* poems, but all she had was her own two rooms, and by now her sawdust was in such a state it would need a lot of work with a brush and pan to put it right again.

'Oh, dust!' she exclaimed at last. 'Dust and mogeration!' And she went back into her bedroom, closing her eyes in the hope that if she went to sleep something or other would happen during the night without her having to do anything more about it.

Olga slept much longer than usual. It was already well into the following morning when she woke. Her hutch had been cleaned out and a breakfast of oats and a further supply of the new grass was waiting for her. All signs of her efforts at poetry writing had long since disappeared.

As she came out of her hay, blinking in the strong light, she discovered Noel, Fangio and Graham waiting outside her house.

Fircone and Raisin were there too. Their cage had been put on a table outside the Sawdust family's back door, so that they could enjoy the morning sunshine as well.

'There you are,' said Noel. 'We were wondering where you'd got to. How's your poem?'

'Poem?' repeated Olga. '*Poem?*' For a moment or two she wondered what on earth Noel was talking about, and then it all came back to her. 'Oh *that*,' she said carelessly. 'I didn't want to write too many in case I got so far ahead you never caught up. You can have more time if you like . . .'

'Don't worry,' broke in Fangio eagerly. 'I've done lots. I did them while I was having supper last night.'

'So have I,' said Graham. 'You were quite right. You don't know what you can do until you try.'

'How about this one?' said Fangio. 'It's all about a carrot.

> '*The goodness they hold,*
> *Makes you lively and bold.*'

'Mine is about a bumble bee,' said Graham.

'A bumble bee,
Is hard to see,
When you are not very well,
And you live in a shell!'

'*Cats,*' said Noel, trying to get a word in edgeways,
'*Don't wear hats.*'

'I've got another one,' exclaimed Fangio. 'I've just remembered it.

> '*Shrubbery*
> *Sometimes tastes rubbery!*'

'I've done one about crossing a road,' called Graham. 'It's a bit long, so I hope I get it right.

> '*If I was a toad,*
> *I would hop over the road,*

But as I'm not,
I don't go out a lot.'

'*Cats*,' said Noel,
'*Are good at catching rats.'*

'I've got another one,' said Fangio.

'*There are ants*
In the cucumber plants.'

'We've done one as well,' called Fircone and Raisin. 'We did it between us.'

'*Sunflower seeds,*' said Fircone,
'*Are a bit like weeds.'*
'*We know,*' added Raisin,
'*Because we've watched them grow.'*

'There are some in the bit of ground outside Karen Sawdust's window,' he explained. 'I expect she dropped them there one day when she was cleaning us out, but we couldn't get all that into a poem.'

'*I can't run very fast,*' broke in Graham,
'*So I'm always last.*'

His voice trailed away as he caught the look on Olga's face and mistook its meaning. 'I know they're not very good,' he said. 'But they're the best I could do in the time. I don't suppose they're half as good as yours.'

Olga stared from one to the other full of indignation. How *could* they come out with such things when she'd been sitting up most of the night and hadn't a thing to show for it?

'Wheeeeeeeee!' she squeaked in disgust, making up the first words that came into her head. 'Wheeeeeeee! *Ombomstiggywoggles!* Wheeeeeeee! Wheeeeeeeeeeeeeeee! Wheeeeeeeeeeeeeeeeeeeeeeeeeeeee!'

Noel, Fangio, Graham, and Fircone and Raisin looked up at her admiringly.

'That's good,' said Fangio. 'That's very good. I like that.'

'The ends are the same,' agreed Graham. 'And the

middle doesn't make any sense at all. That's what I call a *real* poem.'

'I don't know how you thought of it,' said Noel grudgingly.

'Oh, it just came to me,' said Olga modestly.

She tried it out again. 'Wheeeeeeeeeee!' she squeaked. '*Ombomstiggywoggles* and Wheeeeeee! Wheeeeeeeeeeeee! Wheeeeeeeeeeeeeeeeeeeee!'

The more she said it the more she liked it. There was a very nice sound to it indeed. She was quite sure even Tennyson himself couldn't have done any better.

'How nice,' she thought, as the others went their separate ways and she was left to get on with her breakfast. 'How nice to think that Tennyson and I both like the same grass. I might never have thought of it otherwise!'

CHAPTER EIGHT

Olga Sets a Trap

Noel was in disgrace. And not just any old disgrace,
but a really big one.

His troubles started when Mrs Sawdust came downstairs one morning and found the waste bucket lying
on its side with its contents spread all over the kitchen
floor. The very next day the remains of 'something' –
no one ever did discover what – were found lying
on the mat. Rugs had been disturbed, cupboard doors
squeezed open, the larder raided; in fact one way and
another whoever was responsible had been having a
high old time.

344

Because he was the only one with a free run of the house during the night – able, because of his flap in the back door, to come and go as he pleased – the blame had fallen on Noel. He'd been threatened with all sorts of dire punishments – including being locked out for the night and having his pussy-flap boarded up.

Noel was very bitter about it all. 'I wouldn't mind if I'd done it,' he meeowed. 'I wouldn't mind at all then, but I didn't.'

'If you didn't,' said Olga one morning, after he'd been going on about it for rather longer than usual, 'then who did?'

'I've got my suspicions,' said Noel darkly. 'If you ask me it's "Stinker" Martin. He's found my flap and he uses it when I'm not there. I can tell by the smell.'

A wave of sympathy ran round his audience, and even those who had treated the matter fairly lightly up to that moment began to take a different view.

All the animals had their own territory, and poaching on anyone else's ground was very much frowned upon. It was the kind of thing to be expected from foxes and other lesser creatures who knew no better, but not from one of their own kind. However, they all agreed it was typical of 'Stinker' Martin.

'Stinker' lived a little way up the road, and although most of the time he kept himself very much to himself, there were times – when the moon was high, or he was feeling just plain bored – when he went on the prowl; and if that happened it was time to watch out, for he hadn't earned his name for nothing.

'Why don't you lie in wait for him?' suggested Olga. 'You could hide behind your flap and pounce on him when he's halfway through.'

'You'd be lucky,' said Noel gloomily. 'I can see *him* getting caught like that!'

'Perhaps if you're locked out,' said Graham, 'and it still happens, they'll see it wasn't you and . . .'

'If *I'm* locked out,' said Noel, 'then "Stinker"

Martin will be too – so they'll still think it's me. I tell
you, I'm done for!' And with that he stalked off into
the bushes, leaving the others to carry on the discussion without him.

'We must do something,' said Olga after a while.

'The thing is,' said Fangio, 'what?'

'Leave it to me,' said Olga grandly. 'I shall think of
a plan. I shall call it MY PLAN. You'll see.'

Fangio looked up at her scornfully. 'What can *you*
do,' he asked, 'shut up in your house all night?'

But Olga wasn't to be put off by such trifling
details. Once she had her mind set on something
there was no stopping her. 'I only said I would think
of A PLAN,' she remarked. 'I didn't say anything about
doing it. I mean, I would if I could, but I can't, so I
won't, will I?'

It was the kind of remark to which there was really
no reply, so while Olga settled down to think up her
idea the others went their separate ways.

Matters became even more urgent over the next
few days, for there were two more night raids on the
Sawdust family's house. During the first some tufts
were torn out of the dining-room carpet, and on the
second occasion a packet of butter was left half-eaten
on the kitchen table.

347

Unfortunately, Noel himself discovered the remains of the butter, and in doing so accidentally got some on to his own whiskers. He was caught in the act of licking them clean and from that moment on his fate was sealed. Threats which had been made more in fun than in anger suddenly became very real.

The only ray of hope was that Olga had actually seen the intruder leaving. Because it was dark at the time, she couldn't swear she'd recognized the shadowy figure as 'Stinker' Martin, but she could definitely say that it hadn't been Noel, simply by the sound of its voice.

In trying to leave as quietly as possible it had stepped on something sharp. There had been a muffled meeow and then it had disappeared into the night, leaving Olga wide awake and with the first glimmerings of an idea forming in her mind.

The next morning she called an urgent meeting with Fangio and Graham.

As soon as they'd settled down she asked her first question.

'What,' she asked, 'would you think is the most sensitive part of a cat?

'I know it's not an easy question,' she said, as the others tried their best to think of an answer. 'I mean, it's hard to picture them having *any* sensitive parts at all . . .'

'Their whiskers?' hazarded Graham. Not having any whiskers himself he'd always imagined there must be something rather special about them, particularly as Noel seemed to spend so much time keeping his own in order.

Olga clucked impatiently. 'They only use those for going through holes,' she said. 'They haven't got much sense so they need something to tell them how wide they are. There's nothing sensitive about a cat's whiskers.'

'I'd rather you told us about your PLAN,' grumbled Fangio.

With an effort Olga brought herself back down to earth.

'All right,' she agreed reluctantly. 'Well, it isn't their whiskers that's the most sensitive part . . . it's their paws!' And she went on to explain all that had happened the previous night.

'The thing is,' she said at last, 'suppose we wait until after it gets dark and the Sawdust people have gone to bed, and then put something sharp on the *other* side of the pussy-flap? As soon as "Stinker" Martin climbs through he'll step on it and kick up such a din he'll wake everyone up and they'll come down and catch him!'

Olga sat back feeling very pleased with herself. It was a masterly PLAN. A plan to end all plans. One that couldn't possibly fail.

'Something sharp?' said Fangio at last. 'What sort of sharp?'

Olga gave a sigh.

'I don't know,' she said impatiently. 'Glass . . . Sawdust people put broken glass on top of walls to stop other people climbing over. I've seen it.'

'Oh, I've got masses of broken glass,' said Fangio sarcastically. 'I mean, I carry it around with me all the time. Besides, he might not tread on any of the sharp bits. If broken glass was any good we hedgehogs would have had it years ago. Why do you think we're born with spikes on our backs? It's to protect ourselves. When anything tries to attack us we just roll ourselves up into a ball. Why, just one prick of a hedgehog's spike is enough to . . .'

Fangio broke off. He was about to curl himself up in order to show the others exactly what he meant

when he suddenly realized they were hanging on his every word.

'No,' he said firmly, looking from one to the other, 'I'm *not* being trodden on by "Stinker" Martin.'

'It's only *one* tread,' said Olga. 'Besides, if you don't they may get rid of Noel. Just think what that would mean. If they get rid of him there won't be anyone to chase the birds away. And if there are lots of birds there won't be any insects left. You won't like that.'

Fangio stared up at Noel's pussy-flap. 'It's much too high,' he announced. 'I'd never reach it.'

'You would,' said Olga slowly, 'if you stood on Graham's back!'

If Olga had announced that the world was about to collapse beneath them her words could scarcely have had a greater effect on her audience. But she wouldn't listen to any arguments. The more reasons Fangio and Graham thought up as to why they should have nothing to do with HER PLAN, the more reasons she thought up as to why they should.

Even the Sawdust family noticed.

'I can't understand it,' said Mrs Sawdust as they went to bed that night. 'Fangio and Graham haven't left Olga's hutch all day. They were still there when I locked up. They kept peering up at Noel's pussy-flap. Anyone would think there was something "going on".'

'There'll be something going *out* tonight, if we have any more trouble,' said Mr Sawdust grimly. 'And it'll be spelt N . . . O . . . E . . . L!'

'Perhaps putting him out early will help?' said

Mrs Sawdust hopefully. 'He may come back so tired he'll go straight to sleep.'

'That,' said Mr Sawdust ominously, 'remains to be seen.'

Noel had been sent out soon after tea that evening, and his several attempts at returning home had been rebuffed by some very firm 'shoo's' from the rest of the family, so that in the end he'd gone off in a huff, leaving them all feeling slightly guilty.

'I do hope he hasn't taken it too badly,' said Mrs Sawdust. 'I mean, I'd hate him to think he really wasn't wanted.'

But the only reply she got from Mr Sawdust was a grunt as he turned out the light. Mr Sawdust had other things on his mind, but even so it was safe to say that none of them came anywhere near picturing what was happening one floor below. If they had he would have been out of bed like a shot.

The fact of the matter was, Olga, Fangio and Graham were having trouble. Or rather, to be more exact, Fangio was having trouble, and neither Olga nor Graham could do a thing about it.

Olga's plan had run up against an unexpected snag. The first part had gone well enough. After a certain amount of effort Fangio had managed to clamber on

353

top of Graham's back, and from there he'd worked his way up to the hole in the door. It was then that the trouble had started. Noel's pussy-flap was made in such a way that it hinged from the inside. This meant that although it was easy to enter the house, anyone trying to back out again – especially anyone with prickles – tended to force the flap shut again.

Somehow, in trying to squeeze through the hole, Fangio had got himself well and truly jammed, so that he could neither climb back out again, nor, with

his back legs off the ground, could he push himself through into the house.

'I'm stuck!' he wailed, for what seemed like the fiftieth time. 'Help! Help ∎*Do* something!'

Olga tried another approach.

'I shouldn't be too long if I were you,' she called. 'I don't know, but I think I can hear "Stinker" coming!' And she lifted up her head and uttered a loud 'WheeeeeeoooooooooooooooW'.

In normal circumstances even Olga would have had to admit that it wasn't very much like a cat, but it had the desired effect.

Fangio, his back legs working away like pistons, made one last desperate bid to free himself. There was a hurried scratching sound, followed by a loud metallic bang and a dull thud, and then silence.

'I hope he landed the right way up,' said Graham.

'If he's so good at rolling himself into a ball,' said Olga, 'I'm sure he can do a simple thing like turning himself over. He's not like a tortoise.

'Anyway,' she added, 'I've done my bit. I can't do any more. All we can do now is wait for "Stinker" to come.'

Graham cast an anxious glance over his shoulder. 'You can wait if you like,' he said. 'I'm going. I've

355

done my bit too!' And without more ado he vanished into the darkness of the shrubbery.

Olga lay back in the hay and closed her eyes. She felt quite worn out from the strain of wondering whether or not Fangio would get through Noel's pussy-flap, and in no time at all she was fast asleep.

She woke suddenly to the sound of a tremendous howl. It was a howl fit to waken the dead, let alone a sleeping guinea-pig.

It went on and on and on.

It certainly woke the Sawdust family. Lights started coming on; there was the sound of running feet; and then voices – half-cross, half-scared, half-disbelieving – began to reach her ears.

Olga felt a glow of satisfaction. At last all her hard work was beginning to bear fruit. Now the Sawdust family would surely see the truth of the matter.

The back door opened and Mr Sawdust, wearing a dressing-gown and looking strangely ruffled, stood framed in the opening for a moment while he went down and placed something on the ground.

' "Stinker" Martin!' exclaimed Fangio bitterly, as the door slammed shut behind him. ' " *Stinker" Martin*!'

For the first time that night a doubt entered Olga's mind. 'Is something the matter?' she asked.

'I'll say,' said Fangio. 'It wasn't "Stinker" Martin at all. It was Noel! You forgot to tell him about your plan. He came back home and landed right on top of me. Now his feet are full of my prickles and he's got to go off to the vet again in the morning. There's a terrible rumpus going on.'

'Well,' said Olga, recovering her composure, 'at least we know my PLAN works. Perhaps we shall be luckier next time.'

'Next time?' exclaimed Fangio. 'Next time! There won't be a next time. Not for me there won't. And if you think I'm fed up, you wait till you see Noel!'

Olga gave a sigh as Fangio stalked off. When she thought of the amount of effort she put into helping others . . . and for what? Really, there was no gratitude left in the world. She decided she would go back to sleep at once and let them get on with it.

It was some two days before Olga saw Noel again, and when he did return from the vet, nursing two heavily bandaged front paws, he was strangely subdued.

He hobbled up to Olga's house and peered up at her.

'Er . . . thanks,' he said gruffly.

If Olga was taken aback she tried her best not to show it. 'That's all right,' she said.

'I still don't see how you knew,' said Noel.

'Well, er, wheeeeeeeeeeeee,' said Olga, playing for time, 'guinea-pigs are like that. They do know about things.'

'I mean,' said Noel, half talking to himself, 'with me at the vet's it had to be someone else, didn't it? I mean, when "Stinker" Martin broke in next night and I wasn't there they knew it must have been him all the time.'

Olga stared at Noel open-mouthed. It was the first she'd heard of another break-in, though now he mentioned it something had woken her up during the night, but at the time it had seemed like rain.

'I shouldn't think *he'll* be coming back again,' said Noel in tones of satisfaction. 'I hear Mr Sawdust threw a bucket of water over him. Was he very wet?'

'Well,' said Olga, feeling unusually truthful for once. 'I must admit I didn't actually see it.

'But I heard it,' she added hastily, seeing the look of disappointment on Noel's face. 'It woke me up with a terrible splash.

'The thing is,' she said, 'drawing up PLANS is *very* tiring work. Especially PLANS that work out right in the end. I'm afraid I was so worn out I went straight back to sleep again.'

CHAPTER NINE

Olga Learns a Lesson

Olga crouched by her bowl of oats and fixed her friend Boris with a beady eye. 'It's all your fault!' she exclaimed.

Boris looked a bit taken aback. '*My* fault?' he repeated. 'But I wasn't even here!'

'That,' said Olga sternly, 'has nothing to do with it.' And she pushed her feeding bowl into a corner out of his reach just to show how strongly she felt.

Olga's day had begun badly, and the fact that it was mostly her own fault didn't help matters. She was only too happy to lay the blame on someone else, and it was Boris's bad luck that he happened to arrive at the wrong moment.

It was all to do with the picture of her family which she kept hanging on her dining-room wall. Or rather, the picture which *had* been hanging on her wall; for that very morning she had somehow or other caught her claws in the edge and it had come away in her paws, falling, as luck would have it, slap bang in the middle of her water bowl.

Olga wasn't too sure what happened after that, but in trying to get it out of the water she'd stepped in her bowl of oats by mistake, and in no time at all she'd got herself in a terrible mess.

It wasn't until Karen Sawdust was cleaning it up for her that Olga learned she was receiving a visit from Boris. Boris, who was the father of her children, and with whom she had once spent a whole weekend in his castle by the sea.

'It's your fault,' said Olga, 'because you started it all.'

Boris peered at the sodden remains of his family. 'They look all squashed!' he exclaimed. 'What's happened?'

Olga told him in no uncertain terms. 'If you hadn't been the father,' she said, 'there wouldn't have been any children. And if there hadn't been any children there would have been no need for a photograph. And if there hadn't been a photograph I wouldn't be in the mess I'm in now.'

Boris thought the matter over for a while, and then wisely decided to let the matter drop. Instead, he made as if to join Olga at her feeding bowl, and then something about the way her back was arched made him

change his mind about that too. Olga was obviously in no mood to share anything at that moment, least of all her oats.

A thoughtful gleam came into Boris's eye. 'You know your trouble,' he said. 'You're too good-natured.'

Olga, some oat shucks dangling unheeded from her whiskers, looked up in surprise. 'I'm *what*?' she exclaimed.

'Good-natured,' repeated Boris. 'You mustn't let yourself get trodden on so.'

'That,' said Olga, 'is something that would *never* happen. Karen Sawdust is most careful.'

Boris gave a snort. 'I don't mean that sort of trodden on. I mean you mustn't let yourself be taken advantage of. You should stand on your own four paws and stick up for yourself.'

He licked his lips. 'Now, take a thing like that bowl of oats, for instance. If someone like ... er, well, like me, hungry after a long journey, came up to you and asked to share it, what would you say?'

Olga opened her mouth. She knew exactly what she would say, but before she had a chance to give voice to it Boris was away again.

'Because you are kind and generous,' he said, 'I expect you'd push the bowl across to me and say "help yourself". But that would be quite wrong.'

Olga gave a gulp. 'It would?' she squeaked, looking more and more mystified. It wasn't at all what she'd expected Boris to say.

'Oh, yes,' said Boris. 'Quite wrong. What you should really say is: "If you're hungry and want some oats you can come and get them yourself." If you like, I'll show you what I mean.'

Olga watched open-mouthed while Boris ran round and round her dining-room several times. Coming to a halt at last, he crouched in a far corner and gazed at Olga. 'I'm hungry,' he panted. 'May I have some of your oats?'

'Certainly not,' said Olga. 'If you're hungry and want some oats you can come and get them yourself.'

Boris hurried across to the feeding bowl. 'Thank you very much,' he said, pushing Olga to one side. 'You're getting the hang of it.'

'Now,' he continued, some while later, smacking his lips noisily as he ran his tongue round the bottom of the bowl, 'that was very good, but supposing – just supposing – the same thing happened with these carrots?' He glanced towards some fresh halves of

364

bright red carrot lying near the entrance to Olga's bedroom. 'Supposing I said to you "Those oats were very nice, but it would be nicer still if I could round things off with a carrot or two", I bet you'd say "Yes, go on, help yourself", or "You're very welcome – take as many as you like", or something like that. I know you.'

'I most certainly would not,' said Olga with feeling. 'I wouldn't dream of saying any such thing.'

'Good for you!' exclaimed Boris. 'What *would* you say?'

'I'd say "If you want some carrots you'd better go and get them yourself!",' announced Olga.

Boris didn't reply for a moment or two. His mouth was far too full.

'Now,' he announced, when he'd polished off the last of the carrots, 'I'll give you one more test. All this eating has made me very thirsty . . .'

'Look,' interrupted Olga impatiently, 'if you're *that* thirsty you know very well where the water bowl is . . .

'Really!' she went on, addressing the world in general as Boris dipped his nose in her water bowl, 'anyone would think I've nothing better to do than wait on you all day!'

Boris allowed a dribble of water to fall from his mouth as he glanced round. He'd fared so well he was beginning to find difficulty in moving. In fact it was as much as he could do to lie down.

He gave a contented sigh as he lowered himself gently into the nearest patch of hay. 'That's better,' he said. 'I haven't felt so good for ages.'

Olga had to admit she hadn't felt so happy for a long time either. All her bad temper had disappeared. It was quite like old times again.

'I'm glad you came,' she said, snuggling into the hay.

Boris gave an answering grunt which was very close to being a snore.

Soon they were both fast asleep.

How long it lasted Olga didn't know, but she suddenly awoke to the sound of her door being opened.

It was all over so quickly she barely had time to call out good-bye before Boris, too full to give much more than a token kick and struggle, let alone an answering squeak, disappeared from view in the direction of his travelling box.

A few minutes later there was the sound of a car drawing away. The noise gradually disappeared into the distance and then all was quiet again.

Olga stretched, made as if to settle back down into the hay, and then thought better of it. All the excitement made her feel hungry. In fact, not just hungry – but *starving*. She hurried into her dining-room. Come to think of it, what with one thing and another she hadn't even had a proper breakfast, let alone lunch. It was high time she made up for it. Her mouth began to water in anticipation of the good things to come. And then she paused.

'Wheeeeeeeeeeeeeeeeeeeeeeeeeeeeeee!' she shrieked.

'Wheeeeeeeeeeeeeeeeeeeeeeeeeeeeeee! Wheeeeeeeeeeeeeeeeeeeeeeeee!'

She rushed to her front door.

'Wheeeeeeeeeeeeeee! Wheeeeeeeeeeeeeeeeee! Wheeeeeeeeeeeeeeeeeeeee!

'Come back! Come back!'

She turned and gazed disbelievingly at her empty
bowls again.

'Wheeeeeeeeeeeeeee!

'The cheek of it!

'How could he?

'Wheeeeeeeeeeeee! Wheeeeeeeeeeeeeeeeeee! Wheeeeeeeeeeeeeeeeeeeee!'

'What ever's going on?' A familiar voice close at
hand caused her to stop in her tracks.

'Don't tell me that Boris has eaten all your food!'
exclaimed Karen Sawdust. 'Crumbs! That wasn't the
idea at all. The greedy thing.

'No wonder he felt fat when I picked him up!'

'Wheeeeeeeeeceeeeeeeeeeeeeeeeeeeeeeeeeeeeeeeeeeeee-
eeeeeeeeeeeeeeee!'

Olga's answering squeak was the longest she had
ever managed in one go. It left her feeling quite worn
out; but then she'd had a lot to pack into it.

It was the sort of squeak which said: 'Pleasemay-IhavesomemorefoodandwaterbecauseIthinkI'vebeen-takenadvantageofagainandIfeelveryveryhungryand-thirsty!'

But she needn't really have bothered, for Karen Sawdust had already disappeared.

When she returned she was carrying a bag of oats, a jug of water, and the biggest armful of grass and dandelions Olga had seen for a long while.

As she opened the door of Olga's house Karen Sawdust gave a squeak herself. 'Wheeeeee! There you are!' she said.

It was a very good imitation of a guinea-pig. It didn't make sense, of course, but then one couldn't expect the Sawdust people to do everything.

Olga decided that what Karen Sawdust had been trying to say was:

'Hereisarewardforbeingsokindandgeneroustosome-onewhodoesn'treallydeserveitandIshouldeatitallup-quicklyincasehecomesbackagain!'

So she did just that and she felt much better afterwards.

CHAPTER TEN

The Day the Guinea-pigs
Learnt to Sing

One morning Olga da Polga woke feeling unusually
cold. Overnight there had been a change in the
weather and when she peered through her bedroom
window her breath froze to the glass, making it hard
to see out.

The cold snap seemed to have taken everyone by

surprise. In the distance she could see the vague forms of Fangio and Graham making hasty preparations for their winter homes, and even Noel looked as if he was having second thoughts about taking his morning stroll. He was walking very gingerly indeed along the frost-covered path, placing each back paw neatly into the spots left by his front ones as he picked his way down the garden in order to survey his property.

Although Noel tolerated the other animals in the household – and he could hardly do otherwise – he regarded the Sawdust family's garden as being very much 'his' territory, and he was always most offended if he caught sight of any squirrels or birds daring to make use of it.

The Sawdust family obviously hadn't expected a change in the weather either, for the wooden panel over Olga's front door had been left off. During the winter months Olga always had a panel over her wire mesh at night, and although it made the mornings dark she was very grateful, for it kept out the worst of the bad weather.

Olga couldn't make up her mind whether to stay snuggled up in her warm nest of hay for a while or venture out into the cold dining-room in search of some oats. In the end she decided on some oats. She was a great believer in having plenty of food inside her when the weather turned cold. There was nothing like it for warmth.

But Olga had another surprise coming her way. Having scraped out the last of the bowl, she was backing away in order to chew the oats more thoroughly when she suddenly let out a loud cry.

'WheeeeeeeeeeEEEEEEEEEEEEEEEE!'

She had been so taken up with her breakfast she hadn't noticed her water bowl right behind her. She

sat down in it by mistake and then jumped up again twice as quickly as it was very, very cold.

When she looked round she discovered why. The water was completely frozen over!

Her dignity ruffled, Olga gave a shiver and hurried back into her bedroom, burying herself deep inside the warm hay again, leaving only a tiny peephole so that she could watch the goings-on outside in comfort.

Shortly afterwards Karen Sawdust, dressed in coat and scarf, came out to give Olga's dining-room its morning clean. Olga was pleased to see that when she went off to fetch the breakfast she took the water bowl with her so that she could melt the ice. During the summer Olga was able to get most of the moisture she needed from the grass and other greenstuff she ate, but in winter, when she lived mainly on oats, she relied on her water bowl.

As soon as she was on her own again she hurried out for a drink. The water tasted warm and very pleasant, and it made her feel a lot better.

Some while later, after she'd had her own breakfast, Karen Sawdust reappeared. This time she was carrying a small black case, and in her other hand she had a silver object on the end of a long wire.

She seemed to be talking to it. Olga distinctly heard her as she went past.

'One, two, three,' she said. 'One, two, three . . . testing.'

She went down the garden, still carrying the object in her hand, and Olga watched with interest as she held it towards Noel, almost as if she expected him to eat it. But Noel gave it a very disdainful glance, and after a brief sniff he looked the other way, pretending he was only interested in washing himself.

Next, Karen Sawdust tried pointing it towards some birds sitting up in a nearby tree, safely out of Noel's reach.

For some reason or other this didn't seem to satisfy her either, so she approched Fangio and Graham – but they took even less notice.

'Whatever's going on?' thought Olga, as Karen Sawdust drew near, for she could see she looked most disappointed. 'What *can* she want?'

'Hullo, Olga,' said Karen Sawdust, as she opened the front door and thrust the object towards the bedroom. 'Come on, say something. Whee! Whee! Whee!'

But Olga refused to play. The fact of the matter was that although she trusted Karen Sawdust and

didn't think for one moment that she would do her
any harm, she wasn't all that keen on having things
pointed at her without warning. She gave a sniff, and
she agreed with Noel – it wasn't really worth bother-
ing about. The silver object had a most uninteresting
smell – if it could be called any sort of smell at all, and
she decide she didn't wish to know about it.

'I don't know,' said Karen Sawdust as Mrs Sawdust
came into the garden, 'any other time Olga would
be squeaking her head off, but when you really want
her to say something there isn't as much as a peep.'

'Perhaps you should have disguised the microphone
as a carrot,' said her mother. 'You might have got her
to sing for her breakfast then. Anyway, is it *that*
important?'

'It certainly is,' exclaimed Karen Sawdust. 'It's a school project. I'm supposed to get all these animal voices by the end of the week . . .'

Olga's ears pricked up. 'Animal voices! By the end of the wheeek! Why ever hadn't she said? If I'd known she wanted some *voices* I could have done lots.' And she let out a loud 'Wheeeeeeeeee!' just to show how good she was at it. The noise that came out wasn't quite as piercing as the one she'd done earlier when she sat on the ice, but it was very nearly as loud.

However, it came too late. By then Karen and Mrs Sawdust had gone inside, the kitchen door had closed, and there was no one left to hear her effort.

'What's going on?' asked Noel as he drew near. 'What was that awful screech just now?'

'Awful screech!' exclaimed Olga. '*Awful screech*! I was making a special "voice" for Karen Sawdust.

'It's a project,' she continued knowledgeably. 'A school project.'

'A project?' repeated Noel. 'What's a project?'

'It's when you collect lots of different voices by the end of the week,' said Olga, 'and put them all into a case. You start with the worst first and end up with the best. I expect that's why she saved me until last.'

Noel, who'd been about to disappear through his

pussy-flap, paused and looked back at Olga in disbelief.

'Haven't you ever wondered how guinea-pigs
came to have such lovely voices?' asked Olga innocently.

Noel let the pussy-flap fall back into place. 'No,' he
said, 'I haven't!'

Olga settled back, for she could feel a story coming
on.

'Guinea-pigs,' she said loudly, as she caught sight
of Fangio and Graham coming along the path, 'have
the most lovely singing voices.

'When the world began,' she went on, warming to
her tale as the others gathered round, 'no one could
sing. You see, it had never been thought of. All anyone had done until then was make grunting noises.
Apart from a few cats who could meeow,' she added
grudgingly for Noel's benefit. 'But no one thought
very much of *that* as a sound.

'And then one day a guinea-pig made an important
discovery. He found that if he put his head inside
his feeding bowl and made a noise it sounded deeper
than usual.'

Olga looked round for her own bowl. 'I'll show
you if you like,' she said.

The effect of squeaking into an empty feeding bowl was something Olga had noticed quite early on in her life. She had also learned that squeaking into a full bowl made no difference whatever to her voice, and she suddenly realized she hadn't even touched her breakfast that morning. So instead of saying anything she just stood over her bowl for a moment or two with her eyes closed and her mouth wide open.

The others listened in silence until Olga opened her eyes again.

'Did you like it?' she asked.

'Er, yes,' said Noel grudgingly. 'It wasn't bad.'

'I've heard worse,' agreed Fangio.

'I didn't hear anything,' said Graham bluntly.

'You need very good earsight,' said Olga. 'The deeper the sound the harder it is to hear.

'Anyway, the guinea-pig who first made the discovery told his friends, and soon they were all doing it. They found the bigger the bowl the better it sounded. Then they had an idea. They dug a hole in the ground, making the sides smooth and hard, and when they'd finished they all climbed inside and tried again. This time the noise was so loud and deep it could be heard for miles around. In fact, they found that the deeper they went down into the earth the more the other animals liked it.'

'*That* I can believe,' said Noel.

Olga ignored the remark. 'If you've never heard a massed choir of guinea-pigs singing deep notes,' she said, 'you haven't lived.

'Anyway, the same guinea-pig had yet another idea. Suppose, instead of digging deeper and deeper into the ground, they tried going the other way? Suppose they went up instead of down – what would happen then?

'He gathered all his friends together to explain his plan, and after a lot of discussion they set off towards a distant mountain. Because it was a long way away they had to take lots of things with them for the journey. Some of them carried bundles of dandelion leaves on their backs; others were in charge of the carrots. Some had hay and straw for the bedding at nights; others pushed bowls of water and oats along the ground.

'The news of their great adventure spread, and as they got higher and higher up the mountain all the other animals in the land came to watch. Soon the fields below were full of cows and sheep and cats and dogs and tortoises and hedgehogs.

'In fact,' said Olga, who was beginning to run out of ideas, 'all the animals you could possibly think of.'

'Mountains have snow on them,' said Noel suspiciously. 'I've seen pictures.'

But Olga wasn't to be put off. 'That was the hardest part of all,' she said. 'The higher they went, the snowier it became. So they took it in turns to sit in their bowls. Some sat inside while the others pushed, and when the ones who were doing the pushing got tired they changed over.

'They were very *big* bowls,' she added firmly, before there were any more interruptions, 'because it was a *very* long journey. And because it was a long journey, there was hardly any food left.

'When they reached the top of the mountain they found to their surprise that it was hollow and shaped just like a very large bowl. There was a lake inside the hollow and it had frozen over.

'They rested on the bank for a while and then, when they had got their breath back, they kept it all inside themselves and gathered together in the middle of the lake.

'Then at a signal from the leader they all sat down, opened their mouths, and let out a cry.

'It was the loudest and highest sound that had ever

been heard. It was so loud and high and big it rolled all the way down the mountain, across the valley, up the other side, and then fell off the world.

'You can still hear it sometimes,' said Olga, 'when the wind blows it in the right direction.

'When the guinea-pigs came back down the other animals tried to find out the secret of how they had

managed to sing such high notes, but they wouldn't tell. They kept it a secret and it's been a secret until this very day.

'In fact,' said Olga, putting on one of her superior looks, 'I'm the only one left in the world who knows it!'

Olga's audience looked suitably impressed.

'Come on,' said Noel. 'You can tell *us*.'

Olga hesitated. Like all good storytellers she knew exactly how to keep her listeners on tenterhooks.

'It was all to do with the lake being frozen over,' she said at last. 'When the guinea-pigs sat down it was so cold they all jumped up again and did what anyone else would have done. They went "Wheeeee-eeeeee!" at the tops of their voices.

'I'll show you what I mean, if you like.' Olga backed towards her water bowl. 'But I should put your paws over your ears, because it's very, very loud.'

Closing her eyes again, she took a deep breath and sat down ready to give the loudest squeak she'd ever done in her life.

But all she managed was 'WheeeeeeEEEEuggghhh-hhhhhhhhhhhh!'

'Was that it?' asked Noel in disgust. 'Wheeeeee-EEEEuggghhhhhhhhhhhh!'

'It sounded more like a rusty hinge on a wet day to me,' said Fangio. 'There's one down the bottom of the garden. It sounded just like that.'

'I'm going,' said Graham. He gazed anxiously at the leaden sky. 'Tomorrow's another year and I don't want to get caught without a bed for the winter.'

'Wait for me!' called Fangio.

'Good-bye!' said Noel.

Olga watched the others as they went their separate ways. It had been a good story, one of her very best, right up until the end. But the end had been like a damp squib.

And now that was how her end felt – very damp. For in her excitement she had completely forgotten that Karen Sawdust had changed her water and it was no longer frozen over.

'Wheeeeeuggggghhhhhh!' she said to the world in general. 'Wheeeeeeuggggghhhhhhhh!'

It wasn't a deep squeak, and it certainly wasn't a low one; it was a *damp* squeak, and it summed up her feelings to the full.

Had she been around to hear it, Karen Sawdust might well have wanted to add it to her collection, but she wasn't, and so it was lost for all time.

Olga glanced out at the weather. It looked as she felt – cold, and rather downcast.

Taking a deep breath she gave yet another squeak; but this time it had a much more decided note to it.

'Wheeeeeeeeup!' it went. 'I don't really see why I should be the only one round here to suffer. It's high time I emigrated too!'

With that she disappeared into her bedroom, closed her eyes very firmly, and didn't come out again until she was thoroughly dry and ready for her supper.

By the time that was over and her house had been cleaned out for the night, she felt much, much better. In fact, all in all, she was back to being her normal self again.

Really and truly, she decided, there was nothing like a full stomach and a warm house for making everything seem right in the world – especially when you were a guinea-pig, tired out through telling lots of tales.

Olga Takes Charge

CHAPTER ONE

Olga Gives Advice

Graham was in love. There was no doubt about it. Olga first noticed it one spring morning when he came round the side of the house, crawled slowly past her hutch as if it didn't even exist, and then walked with unseeing eyes slap-bang into the closed door of Mr Sawdust's shed.

If it had been anyone else – Noel, the cat, or even Fangio, the hedgehog – they would have made a quick recovery and gone on their way. But in Graham's case, being a slow mover at the best of times, it took him some while to sort himself out. Having been knocked off course he moved on in the wrong direction and wasn't seen again until after lunch.

Having partaken of several succulent blades of grass, carefully folded in two from the middle so that she would get the most benefit from the least possible effort, Olga was about to retire to her bedroom for an afternoon nap when she heard a rustle in the near-by shrubbery.

This time she was better prepared. 'Watch out!' she squeaked, as Graham drew near. 'Wheeeeee! Wheeeeeeeeee!'

Graham paused and gazed up at her with a vacant expression on his face.

'Aren't you going to have your food?' asked Olga. 'Mrs Sawdust put some out for you specially.'

'Food!' Graham scoffed at the idea. 'That's all you guinea-pigs ever think about. There *are* other things in life, you know.'

Olga drew herself up. 'There won't be if you carry on like that,' she said. 'You won't *have* a life if you carry on like that. You'll be all shell and bones.'

Graham considered the matter for a moment. 'You're quite right,' he said. 'Quite right. I *must* keep up my strength.' And without further ado he moved towards the bowl which was standing outside the kitchen door.

Olga preened herself as a sound of steady lapping filled the air. She gave a sigh. There was no doubt about it. Guinea-pigs *knew* about things. It was something they were born with. How the other animals had managed before she came on the scene, goodness only knew. There was simply no one else to turn to for advice.

She waited for a while and then, during a pause in the lapping, posed the question which was uppermost in her mind.

'What's she like?'

Graham didn't answer for a moment or two. The fact of the matter was, although he wouldn't have admitted it to Olga, hunger had got the better of him and he had a large piece of bread stuck in his throat. Turning his head away, he pretended he was thinking hard. Olga, who thought he was choking with emotion, waited patiently.

'She's big,' admitted Graham at last, 'and . . . er . . . well, I suppose you'd just say . . . she's big. Big for her size, that is . . .'

Olga, her feminine instincts aroused, squeaked impatiently. 'There must be something else about her!' she exclaimed. 'How about her eyes?'

'They're big too,' said Graham. 'She's big all over.'

Olga took a deep breath. 'I mean ... what colour are they?'

Graham busied himself with the bowl of food again. Being in love made you hungry. 'I don't know,' he said at last.

'You don't know! *You don't know!*' Olga could hardly believe her ears. Tortoises! No wonder they had a reputation for being slow.

'You *must* have seen them,' she said.

For some reason or other Graham seemed to find the question slightly embarrassing. 'Well,' he said between mouthfuls. 'Yes, and then again ... no. I mean, I know they're there. They must be. But the thing is, well, she's big, you see, and they're a bit high off the ground.'

Olga gazed at Graham as he stood there looking up at her helplessly, a dribble of milk running down his chin. She didn't like to say anything, but she couldn't help feeling that if she'd been his new friend she might not have wanted to look at him either.

'There must be something else about her!' she exclaimed impatiently. 'What does she talk about? What does she say?'

'Well, er ...' Graham shifted uneasily under

Olga's piercing stare. 'She hasn't actually said anything ... yet.

'But I know she'd like to,' he added hastily. 'It's just that she's very quietly spoken, and being so big her voice is a long way off the ground.'

Olga digested this latest piece of information. Happy though she was in her house with all its 'mod. cons.', as Karen Sawdust called them, there were times when she wished she could get out into the world and see things for herself. Apart from that, Graham's continual harping on the size of his new friend was beginning to irritate her.

'I once knew a giant guinea-pig,' she began, her imagination getting the better of her. 'The largest guinea-pig ever known in the whole world. He was so big I always knew when he was coming to see me because it got dark early. And he had wonderful fur. I mean ... all guinea-pigs' fur is nice compared to other animals', like cats, for instance, but ...'

Olga broke off. Graham had disappeared. Completely and utterly disappeared.

'Wheeeeeeee!' she squeaked in disgust, and

went into her bedroom in a fit of pique. If people wanted her advice about matters the least they could do was to stay and listen. Apart from that, she'd been rather enjoying building up to her story and she spent most of that afternoon busy with her day-dream, storing it up in her memory so that she could bring it out later when she had a better audience.

But gradually, as the day wore on, her thoughts returned more and more to Graham. He'd looked so forlorn as he'd blinked short-sightedly up at her. Something would have to be done about the matter.

Olga reached a decision. She went into her dining-room and gave voice to a loud squeak. The kind of squeak which she reserved for moments of great importance. Moments when she wanted to summon an audience.

'Graham's in love?' repeated Fangio. 'What does that mean?'

Olga sighed. Tortoises were bad enough, but hedgehogs! 'It's something you wouldn't know about on account of your prickles,' she said stiffly, 'but it can be very painful.'

She hesitated, wondering whether to try out

her new story, but thought better of it as Noel came into view.

'What's up now?' he asked sleepily.

Olga told him about her earlier conversation with Graham, embroidering it a little here and there in order to make it as interesting as possible.

'If it's as big as all that,' said Noel hastily, '*I'm* certainly not going down the garden to look for it. It's bad enough having Karen Sawdust and her friends playing war games, without being trampled on by a giant.'

For once Olga rather regretted her vivid imagination.

'Well, perhaps it's not as big as all that,' she admitted grudgingly. But Fangio and Noel had gone.

And then it happened. There was a pounding of feet and suddenly, without warning, a large, round shape loomed up in front of her. Olga gave a shriek of terror and scuttled into her bedroom as fast as her legs would carry her.

'There! I told you to be careful.' Karen Sawdust's voice reached Olga through the hay. 'Now you've frightened her. I expect she wondered what on earth it was.'

'It's only a tin hat,' said her friend defensively.

'It may be only a tin hat to you,' said Karen Sawdust severely, 'but to a guinea-pig it must look like a giant.'

There was another patter of feet, this time in the opposite direction, and then silence.

Olga stirred as the words sank in. 'Tin hat . . . giant . . .'

Suddenly she put two and two together. 'Tin hat . . . giant . . .' Graham had been in love with a tin hat all the time! No wonder he hadn't got anywhere. She couldn't wait to tell the others . . .

And then she paused, her romantic side taking over. Better to have loved a tin hat and lost than never to have loved at all.

Already an ending to her own story was taking shape. That's what she would do. She would tell Graham a story that would be so

good, so exciting, it would take his mind off the problem.

'Wheeee!' Olga gave a sigh of contentment as she snuggled down into her hay again. 'And it'll be so much better for him in the long run!'

CHAPTER TWO

The Day the World Ran Dry

Olga really had intended thinking up a story for Graham. As things turned out, something happened shortly afterwards which not only took her mind off the matter, but while it lasted made even Graham forget his troubles.

It all began when Mr Sawdust did something called 'having a week off in order to take advantage of the fine weather'.

It all sounded very complicated to Olga, and even when she overheard a conversation which had to do with removing Venables, the toad, from the garden pool and taking him to a friend's house down the road, she didn't give it a great deal of thought.

The Sawdust family were always doing strange things and she had no doubt that she would find out all about their latest goings-on sooner or later. She'd long since learnt that if you spent most of your time in a hutch, life had a habit of coming to you in the end, provided, of course, that you were patient – and guinea-pigs were nothing if not patient. There wasn't much that went on in the neighbourhood that didn't get back to her in double quick time, either by way of Noel or via the various other inhabitants of the garden. She was quite content to wait.

Even when Mr Sawdust reappeared carrying a large plastic bucket containing the few gold-fish who normally shared the pool with Ven-ables, she still wasn't over-bothered.

Olga had other, far more important things on her mind – like the state of her grass, for exam-ple. Olga liked her grass to be as moist as possible and normally she had no complaints whatsoever on the matter. The Sawdust family went to a great deal of trouble to make sure she always had an ample supply, and even during the winter they often went miles in their car in search of fresh supplies, making sure it was clean and not taken from ditches too near the road, where it tasted of oil and exhaust fumes. On the whole it was so good that Olga often went for days at a time without having to go near her water bowl, she got all the moisture she needed out of the succulent juices contained in the blades.

But it had been a very dry spring. All the Sawdust family agreed they could hardly remember when it had last rained, and with the lack of rain the grass had grown steadily drier and drier until, really, it was just like eating hay. Not that Olga minded hay, but hay was hay and grass was grass, and she liked a bit of both.

It got so bad that Olga could hardly picture what good grass tasted like. And then, just as the memory was on the tip of her mind, the banging started and drove it clean out again.

Bang! Crash! Wallop! ... Bang! Bang! Crash! Crash! Wallop! Wallop!

Olga was so startled she ran into her bedroom squeaking with fright. Burying her head deep

into the hay, she didn't come out again for the rest of the morning.

The hammering and banging went on until nearly lunchtime and it was followed in turn by the sound of digging and the scraping of a shovel against concrete. What it was Olga neither knew nor cared. All she knew was that the peace of her day had been disturbed.

The story she'd been about to make up for Graham had gone from her mind for ever and any thoughts she may have had about enjoying a quiet nap dreaming of things past was entirely out of the question.

It was late that same afternoon when Olga

woke to the sound of a faint scratching outside her hutch. It was followed by a series of snuffles and snorts. She pricked up her ears and blinked sleepily through her bedroom window.

It was Graham, in all probability returning from a wander in the garden, traces of which were clearly visible on his shell.

'Wheeeee!' she squeaked. Perhaps he would know what had been going on.

Olga hurried out to her dining-room and peered through the wire-netting door at the figure below. She was wide awake now and all agog for the latest news.

'She's gone,' said Graham briefly, as he caught sight of Olga. 'I've looked everywhere. In the bushes. Under the trees. In the strawberry patch. Behind the brussels sprouts. I can't even find any sort of a trail. It's a rum do and no mistake.'

Olga clucked impatiently. For a moment or two she was tempted to tell Graham the truth. Then she thought better of it. She knew Graham from old and in his present mood he was liable to go off again without so much as another word and probably wouldn't be seen again for days. In the nick of time she changed her clucking into a sort of a long-drawn-out sniff. Almost immediately she wished she hadn't, for there was a very strange smell coming from somewhere close at hand. She soon discovered why.

'I've even looked under the compost heap,' continued Graham. 'Just in case – you never know. Took me ages. I got lost and I couldn't find my way out again. Then I looked in the pool. I thought she might have fallen in. But that's empty.'

'Empty?' repeated Olga. 'The pool's *empty*? But it's *never* empty. It's never, ever been empty – not since the day it was made.'

And it was true. Olga could remember it all quite clearly. There had been a great deal of fuss at the time, especially when Mr Sawdust had turned the water on. Everyone had clapped and cheered as it spurted out of the ground at the top of the rockery, and had then run down through a series of small waterfalls into the main pool at the bottom. But all that had been a long time ago – several summers, in fact, until it was now so much a part of the garden that it had long since been taken for granted.

'Well, it's empty now,' said Graham briefly. 'Bone dry. There's a sort of hole in the bottom, but she couldn't have gone down that – it's much too small.' He gazed short-sightedly up at the sky. 'Perhaps she got carried off by a giant bird. That's why there's no trail. I've heard of giant birds,' he added darkly.

But Olga wasn't listening. Her mind was racing in all directions. Suddenly everything was falling into place. The way Mr Sawdust had been rushing around doing things. The removal of the occupants of the pond . . . First Venables, then the goldfish. And now she came to think of it, she distinctly remembered a remark Mrs Sawdust had called through her kitchen door at the height of it all. 'Don't forget there's a water shortage,' she'd said.

Now she knew what had happened Mr Sawdust's reply seemed even more ominous. 'Don't worry,' he'd said. 'I've managed to save most of it. I've pumped it into the old bath down the bottom of the garden.'

Olga felt a chill inside her stomach. Things must have reached a pretty pass if the Sawdust family were reduced to saving their water in an old bath. One of the things which made humans different from guinea-pigs was the way they treated water. They were forever washing things up in it, sitting in it, spraying themselves with it, and, – worst of all, pouring it all away afterwards.

She gave vent to a shrill squeak. 'Wheeeeeeeeee!' she shrieked, as she ran round

her dining-room. 'Wheeeeeeeee! Help! Hellllp! The world's sprung a leak! The world's sprung a leak! Everything's run dry! Help! Hellllp!'

In her haste and excitement she very nearly knocked over her water bowl. Fortunately, it was wide, and had a flat bottom to stop any such thing happening. But it was a close shave, and, as she crouched down on the floor of the hutch waiting for some kind of reaction to her cries for help, she thanked her lucky stars that it had been no worse.

Noel was the first to arrive on the scene, not looking best pleased at having his afternoon nap disturbed. '*Now* what's going on?' he meeowed. 'It sounded as though you'd been trodden on. I was in the middle of a lovely dream about a nest of mice I'd found, too.'

'*Trodden* on?' repeated Olga. She opened her mouth in order to let Noel know exactly what she thought of such a suggestion, and then thought better of it as she caught sight of Fangio approaching slowly from the other direction. Fangio spent a lot of his time in an old box in the garage, so he was often late for meetings, but

Olga felt there was no point in wasting her breath until all her audience had assembled.

As soon as they were settled she repeated all that she'd heard from Graham, plus her own views as to what it meant, adding a little bit here and a little bit there as she went along, to make it all sound more interesting. Olga enjoyed telling a story and by the time she'd finished the others were in the hollow of her paw and hanging on her every word. Noel's jaw had dropped, Fangio's eyes were as large as saucers, and even Graham had quite forgotten about his lost love. It was all very satisfying.

'The thing is,' said Olga, 'what are we going to do about it?'

'*Do about it?*' The thought of doing something about the situation obviously hadn't occurred to the others. They gazed up at Olga in amazement.

'Serves them right if you ask me,' said Noel, glancing darkly towards the house. 'They're always wasting water. It might teach them a lesson. They'll just have to be like cats from now on – use their tongues for washing a bit more.'

Olga gave an impatient squeak. She felt

the others were missing the whole point of her story. 'You'll look a bit silly when your tongue's gone dry,' she said. 'It's rough enough as it is. Just you wait. When all the water's gone it'll be just like concrete.' Olga had once felt Noel's tongue on the end of her nose when he'd been exploring round her garden run, and she hadn't liked the feel of it at all.

'And what about the garden?' she continued. 'There won't be any lettuce leaves or insects. They'll all die and in the end we shall too. You can't live without water.'

The others digested this last remark.

'It's up to you all,' squeaked Olga, striking while the iron was still hot. 'It's up to you all to save the world.'

'It's up to *us*?' repeated Noel suspiciously. Somewhere along the line there seemed to have been a change of direction. 'I thought you said *we* must do something about it.'

'So we shall,' said Olga grandly. 'I shall be in charge and I shall think up a plan. I'd come and help out if I could, but I can't. You've no idea how helpless I feel, living in a hutch and not being able to *do* things.'

'It's no worse than being a tortoise and not being able to run fast,' said Graham.

'Or a cat that's put out in the snow when it doesn't want to go,' agreed Noel.

'Or being a hedgehog and having all your milk run away,' added Fangio.

Olga, who'd been about to defend her position, stopped in mid squeak.

'I don't see what losing your milk's got to do with it,' she said crossly.

'Well, you said all the water has disappeared out of the pond,' said Fangio patiently, 'so I expect it's got a crack in it.

'The same thing happened with my saucer of bread and milk the other evening. Mrs Sawdust put it outside the kitchen door as usual, and I'd just started to eat it as usual, and do you know, the saucer was cracked and all the milk started to run away. And do you know, when I pushed the bread against the crack with my nose, it stopped running away.'

It had been a long speech by Fangio's standards, so long he'd almost forgotten what he'd been going to say, so he paused for breath while he thought the matter over.

'Is that all?' demanded Olga, who was rather fed up at the way Fangio was getting all the attention.

'No, it isn't,' said Fangio firmly. 'Because when I ate the bread all the milk started to run out again.'

Noel was quick, but Olga was quicker. 'That's it,' she squeaked. 'That's it! That's what we'll do with the pool.'

'What do you mean, "That's what *we'll* do with the pool"?' demanded Noel suspiciously. He didn't like the way Olga was looking at him.

Olga gave a deep sigh. She sometimes wished guinea-pigs weren't quite so intelligent compared to other creatures. There was such a wide gap it did make explaining things a little difficult at times. She would simply have to be patient.

'There's the pool,' she began, as slowly and as distinctly as she could manage. 'Now, you all know that. It's just down the garden by the rockery. It's a big hole in the ground and it's usually full of water, only at the moment it isn't ...'

'Oh, *do* get on with it,' hissed Noel.

Olga ignored the unseemly interruption. 'If Mr Sawdust has taken Venables and all the fish out of it and pumped the water into the bath it must mean that it's started to leak and that's why all the water is disappearing. It's probably been doing it for a long time, only no one has noticed it before. Some of us, mentioning no names,' she added meaningly, but staring hard at Noel, 'never notice *anything*.'

'Now, if we can fill the hole with something to stop the water running out – like some old pieces of bread – we shall save the world!'

'But I haven't got any bread,' wailed Fangio. 'I don't get it every day. It's a special treat.'

'I *never* get it,' said Graham. 'Not that I mind. I don't like bread.'

415

'How about bran and oats?' said Noel with a wicked gleam in his eye.

'They would be no good,' said Olga firmly. 'No good at all. If they were you'd be welcome to all I have, but I know they wouldn't be any good. I get the bits in my water bowl sometimes and they just float. No, what we need is something special ... something that goes really hard when it dries, like ...' – she gazed out at the others in search of inspiration and, as her eyes alighted on Noel, it suddenly came to her–' ... like your Pussy's Pleasure.'

'That's a good idea,' said Graham. 'I've heard Mrs Sawdust grumbling sometimes when she's been washing your bowl.'

'Trying to, more like,' agreed Fangio. 'I heard her going on about it the other morning when I went past the kitchen. She said your Pussy's Pleasure had gone as hard as concrete on the sides.'

Graham and Fangio looked up at Olga admiringly. 'I wish I got ideas like that,' said Graham.

'Now, look here ...' began Noel.

'You know you don't like it,' said Fangio. 'It'll be a good chance to get rid of it.'

While the others were talking Olga had a quick nibble from her bowl of bran and oats and then sat back listening. She was tempted to chip in and say that the sooner Noel's Pussy's Pleasure was out of the way the better, but wisely she resisted the temptation. She was content to let Graham and Fangio argue her case for her.

Really, things couldn't have worked out better, and she quite saw what Graham meant when he said he wished he could have ideas like hers. She sometimes wondered where on earth they came from herself.

Noel's Pussy's Pleasure had been a subject for discussion in the Sawdust family's household for several weeks past, ever since it had first been advertised on television as the biggest breakthrough in cat food since frozen fish.

One evening Mr Sawdust had arrived home staggering beneath the weight of a large cardboard box full of tins, having taken advantage of a bargain offer in the local supermarket.

At first Noel, who was very set in his ways

when it came to food and hated any kind of change, had treated the matter with the contempt it deserved. Unlike the cat who appeared in the television commercial, and whose excitement whenever a bowl of Pussy's Pleasure came within sniffing distance was such that it practically had to be put into a strait-jacket, he'd tried to ignore the whole thing. If the Sawdust family wanted to waste their money that was up to them.

But lately, faced with the prospect of either eating it or going without he'd taken to having the occasional snack.

However, the thought of having to get through a whole cardboard box of it filled him with gloom, and even the news that the Sawdust family would be able to send off for a new feeding bowl with his name on the side in return for ten labels from the tins didn't make the taste any better.

'All right,' he said at last. 'You win. At least it'll be better than *eating* the stuff.'

Once he'd made up his mind, Noel lost no time in putting Olga's plan into action and for the next half an hour or so his pussy flap was

put to good use as he hurried back and forth
between the kitchen and the pool.

While Noel was busy doing this, Graham and
Fangio made their way down the garden so that
they could watch the proceedings from the edge
of the pool and give encouragement when
needed.

By squeezing herself against the side of her
dining-room and pressing her nose hard against
the wire netting, Olga was able to get a grand-
stand view of it all and she felt well pleased with
the way things had turned out.

She was just wondering if she might get
another medal to go with the one she'd once
received for saving the Sawdust family's house
from burning down, when she was brought
back to earth by Mr Sawdust's voice. A very

cross Mr Sawdust by the sound of it. He didn't seem at all pleased.

'What on earth's going on?' he cried. 'There's blessed cat food everywhere. Look at it!'

He came outside the kitchen and stared down the garden. 'And what's Noel doing in the pool? Treading all over my wet cement ... I'll show him ... I'll teach him to bury his Pussy's Pleasure all over my new fountain. I haven't even tested it yet. It'll be Pussy's Doom by the time I've finished.'

While he was talking Mr Sawdust picked up the end of a length of hosepipe coiled up on the concrete and disappeared into the kitchen again. A moment later there was a hiss from somewhere inside and the hosepipe began jumping about like a thing possessed.

There was a pause as it settled down again and then, before Olga's astonished gaze, there came a spluttering noise and a column of water shot up from the centre of the pool, carrying all before it. A moment later, as the water died down, there was a soft patter patter as Noel's dinner rained back down to earth. But the sound was short lived, for almost immediately it was drowned by a screech from Noel; a screech of mingled surprise and rage as the truth dawned on him, and it was echoed in part by

Graham and Fangio as they tried to scramble clear.

Olga backed away from her front door as

Noel, looking for all the world like a drowned rat, came stalking back up the garden and paused by her hutch. For once she was glad to be safely behind her wire netting.

'How was I to know Mr Sawdust was putting a fountain in the pool?' she squeaked. 'You're the one who always knows what's going on. It *could* have been a leak in the world.'

'That was my dinner,' hissed Noel. 'My dinner. Blown to smithereens.'

'You'll just have to try catching a few mice for a change,' said Olga primly. 'It'll do you good.'

'Mice!' The look Noel gave Olga as he made for his pussy flap had to be seen to be believed.

A moment later he was back outside again.

'Oh, no you don't,' said a voice. 'You're not coming indoors in that state.'

Noel opened his mouth and then gave a start as something landed on the end of his nose. It could have been some more of his dinner, only it wasn't.

'Rain!' he said bitterly. 'That's all I need.'

Olga hurried to her door. 'That's all any of us

need,' she squeaked. 'Now there'll be some nice green grass again. Wheeeeee!

'Perhaps,' she added brightly, 'your dinner going up into the sky like that started it off. I expect it hasn't rained for so long it's forgotten how. When it saw your dinner going everywhere, it remembered. I'll tell you a story if you like . . .'

'Pah!' said Noel, and he stalked off in search of a sheltering bush.

'Wheeeeee!' said Olga sadly, addressing anyone who happened to be listening. 'Wheeeeeeeeee!'

Really, it was very difficult pleasing her friends all the time – or even some of the time. And with certain of them, mentioning no names but it began with 'N', there was no pleasing them at all!

CHAPTER THREE

Olga and the Sponsored Squeak

Olga was in a jam. In fact, that day she had been in a number of different jams, each worse than the one before, until her mind was in such a whirl she didn't know which way to turn.

Not, she would have been at pains to point out, that she *could* have turned even if she'd wanted to, for at that particular moment she was wedged – there was really no other word for it – *wedged* into the cardboard box normally

424

reserved for her visits to the vet, and en route to goodness knew where.

What made matters worse was that it was all happening without so much as a by-your-leave.

The day had begun in its usual leisurely manner, with a breakfast of bran and oats and a handful of grass, all washed down by some fresh, clear water. Then, because it was 'cleaning-out' day, she'd been put in her run on the lawn for an extra feed.

Olga always liked days out on the lawn. There was nothing quite the same as grass you'd chosen yourself, fresh, juicy and just right for nibbling. Not to mention the possibility of stumbling across the odd dandelion leaf or piece of clover, and after the dry spring Mr Sawdust's lawn once again had an ample supply of both. He'd tried to get rid of them by putting down something called 'weedkiller', but there had been so much protesting on her behalf from the rest of the family he'd never tried it again.

And quite right, too. Olga could never understand humans and the way they carried on, often destroying what was best in the world just because they felt it 'didn't look nice'. Olga remembered the incident well because she hadn't been allowed out for several weeks afterwards; not until the dandelions and clover had all died.

Her mind was full of these and other thoughts when she happened to hear her name mentioned. She pricked up her ears at once.

'I bet Olga could do it,' came Karen Sawdust's voice. 'I bet Olga could do it better than anyone else's guinea-pig.'

Olga nodded approvingly. She had no idea what they were talking about but whatever it was she felt sure Karen was right and she could do it better.

'You should hear the way she goes on sometimes when she's hungry,' continued Karen Sawdust. 'You can hear her for miles.'

'Hear me for miles,' Olga repeated to herself. 'What *can* they be on about?'

And then all was revealed. It seemed that Karen and some friends had got together and were organizing a sponsored squeak for all the guinea-pigs in the neighbourhood. It had to do with something called a charity in aid of other animals who weren't quite so lucky, and as far as Olga could make out people were being asked to guess which guinea-pig would have the longest and loudest squeak.

There was no doubt in her mind as to who that would be. In fact, she was so excited by the idea she let out one of her loudest ever squeaks. It was so loud it brought the others dashing to the side of her run.

'Olga!' cried Karen Sawdust. 'Are you all right?'

'*Am* I all right?' Olga gave another squeak. 'Wheeeeeeeeeeeeeeee! I was only showing you, that's all.'

And with that she settled down to more eating. If she was going in for something special that evening, like a sponsored squeak, she would need all her strength.

OLGA TAKES CHARGE

Olga spent the rest of the day 'conserving her strength'. So much so that when the time came for the Sawdust family to set off she was fast asleep, and her squeals were so loud when she was woken up and put into the cardboard box they threatened to wake the entire neighbourhood.

'If she keeps that up,' said Mr Sawdust, 'we'll be home and dry.'

'The people I feel sorry for,' agreed Mrs Sawdust, 'are those who've put their money on the other guinea-pigs. They won't stand a chance.'

As the memory of where she was going slowly came back to her, Olga sat in the bottom of the box preening herself, only giving vent to a very occasional squeak – just to make sure her voice was still working.

Gradually the warmth and motion of the car brought on a feeling of drowsiness again and she was just settling back in her hay so that she could enjoy the ride when it happened: the first of the jams.

One moment they were driving merrily along, enjoying the evening sunshine; the next moment it went very dark and the car came to a halt.

It had to do with something called a 'rush hour' and according to Mr Sawdust it was a 'blessed nuisance', for it meant they were stuck under a railway bridge.

Olga was just thinking it was yet another example of human strangeness – calling something a 'rush hour' when all you did was sit and wait, when there was a roar from somewhere overhead and the whole ground shook. Worse still, it was followed almost immediately by another clattering roar, this time going in the opposite direction.

'Do you think you ought to see if she's all right?' asked Mr Sawdust.

'There, there.' Karen Sawdust reached down and patted Olga as she cowered in her box. 'Don't worry. It's only a train!'

Olga gazed up at Karen Sawdust as if she could hardly believe her ears, which she couldn't. How *could* she say it? How could she say such a thing when only a few weeks before she'd said quite the opposite.

Olga remembered the occasion very clearly because she'd been on her way to the vet to have her toe-nails cut, something she always hated, when – and it may even have been under the very same bridge – they had been caught in a traffic jam, just as they were now, and a train had passed overhead. At the time it had been so loud and so fearsome Olga had let out a squeal of terror.

Afterwards, Karen had given her a long lecture on the subject, telling her that if you happened to be under a bridge when a train went over it was considered *very* unlucky indeed to say anything at all until someone had asked you a question. Karen had clearly felt very strongly about it, so much so that Olga had spent a sleepless night wondering what was going to happen to her. In the event nothing did, but it had been a narrow escape.

Now, here they were, stuck under a bridge and not one but *two* trains had passed over. Her lips were doubly sealed, which meant she would need to be asked two questions before she could open them again. And all this on a night when she needed her lips to open wider than ever before.

But there was worse to come. In the excitement of the moment Mr Sawdust missed his chance in the traffic and got stuck in the wrong lane. During the long wait that followed Olga counted four more trains passing overhead.

Four! That meant she needed to be asked ... Olga wished she was better at sums and in the end had to resort to counting pieces of hay ... it must mean she had to be asked no less than *six* questions. Then, and only then, could she open her mouth to speak.

And the Sawdust family weren't helping at all, for although they kept asking each other questions they weren't talking to *her*.

'She's looking very strange,' said Mrs Sawdust leaning over the back of her seat to take a closer look. 'Very strange.'

'The sooner we get out of here the better,' said Mr Sawdust. 'Blessed traffic.'

Olga couldn't have agreed more.

'Are you all right, Olga?'

'Phew!' Olga just managed to stifle a squeak of delight as Karen Sawdust bent down to speak to her at long last. One down and five to go.

'She doesn't seem to want to answer,' began Karen Sawdust. 'I do hope she hasn't lost her . . .' The rest of the words were lost as there was a loud rumble overhead.

'Sorry,' called Mr Sawdust as they began to move again at long last. 'I couldn't hear for the noise of that train.'

Olga sank back into the hay, her hopes well and truly dashed. Now she was back to six again!

The rest of the journey was like a nightmare. Although the Sawdust family were plainly worried about her condition, try as she might Olga couldn't get them to ask her about it. She tried jumping about in her box, even climbing up the side pretending she was trying to escape, but it was all in vain. Once or twice, when Mr Sawdust went round a corner, she took advantage of the fact and seized the opportunity to roll over on her side, but that only resulted in Mr Sawdust being told off for driving too fast. The last time she tried it on was as they went over a bump going through some gates to where THE EVENT was due to take place, but in her desperation she overdid it and rolled right over on to her back where she lay with her legs sticking up in the air, looking most undignified.

It was all she could do not to cry out. All the same, it did produce three questions – all in a row.

'Olga!' cried Karen Sawdust anxiously. 'What *are* you doing?

'Look at the state of your fur. How could you at a time like this?

'What *is* the matter with you?'

Olga couldn't answer any of the questions, but at least she was halfway to being able to, *and* there would be no more railway bridges to get stuck under.

Because of the delay they were the last to arrive and, as Olga was lifted out of her box, the air was already full of excited squeaks from the other guinea-pigs. But they only served to make her feel even more miserable. Oh, dear, what *was* she to do?

She brightened slightly as Karen Sawdust chose that moment to ask her exactly the same question. 'Oh dear, Olga,' she said. 'What *are* we going to do?'

Normally Olga would have replied with a very loud squeak indeed, but the nearer the time came for the judging the more determined she was that on no account would she go back on her decision to follow Karen Sawdust's instructions about bridges and trains down to the very

434

last letter. She'd managed to get so far and now wild horses wouldn't have made her change her mind. Olga could be very stubborn when she chose.

'Why not try shaking her?' suggested someone, as they came to see what the matter was. 'Perhaps her squeak's stuck.'

Someone else near by gave voice to what struck Olga as a very coarse laugh indeed. 'Try holding her up by her tail. Tee! Hee! Hee!'

'How *can* they make silly jokes at a time like this?' she thought.

And then she felt rather than saw someone else approaching. Someone important, because everyone else stopped talking. Yes, he had a white coat on. It must be the man in charge. And still she had two more questions to go.

The next moment she felt herself being picked up again, gently but firmly.

'Well, now,' said the man, giving her a poke with his finger. 'And who have we here?'

Olga took a deep breath and thought one of her hardest ever thoughts in the hope that something would happen. 'I'm Olga da Polga,' she thought. 'And I could out-squeak anyone here if only I was allowed to, but I've still got another question to go and now I'm never going to be able to because it's going to be too late and . . .'

And then it happened. Karen Sawdust and the judge both spoke at once.

'You're a funny sort of chap,' said the man, as he went to put her down. 'The strong, silent type.'

And, 'Olga,' groaned Karen Sawdust, 'how *can* you be so difficult?'

Olga's indignation knew no bounds. Relieved from her bonds at long last she raised her head, opened her mouth, and gave vent to the loudest, the most piercing squeak she had ever uttered in the whole of her life.

'Wheeeeeeeeeeeeeeeeeeeeeeeeeeeeeeeeeeeeeeeeeeeeeeeeeeeeeeeeeeeee!' she went. '*Chap! Difficult!* I'm not a *chap*, wheeeeeeeeeeeeeeeee! And as for being *difficult* . . .' She took an even deeper breath and gave another squeak, and then another and another.

'Well,' said the man, when he'd recovered himself. 'We don't have to look any further, do we?'

But this time Olga didn't answer. 'I may,' she decided, 'keep some questions in reserve.' She had a lot to tell the others when she got home. 'And who knows?' she thought. 'I might get stuck under one of those blessed railway bridges again on the way back. Then what would happen?'

CHAPTER FOUR

Olga's Dream House

One evening Olga came to her front door and let out two loud squeaks. The first one was short and sharp. Then she took a deep breath and gave another, much longer one.

To an ordinary passer-by there was nothing remarkable in this. Olga often squeaked. Usually it meant she was hungry.

But another guinea-pig, or any of the other animal inhabitants who happened to be within earshot, would have known at once that something was wrong.

To start with, Olga wasn't making sense,

which was most unusual, for she never wasted her squeaks on trifles. The first one sounded like 'FANGEY' and the second, much longer one, sounded for all the world like 'O'SHIDE-AWAY', and it was said in tones of total and utter disgust.

All was not well with Olga.

The troubles had started several days before and had to do with dogs, or rather with one dog in particular – a fearsome hound called Dag-wood.

Dagwood was staying as a 'house guest' with the family next door. At least, that's what the Sawdust family's neighbours called him. Mr Sawdust called him something else. What it meant Olga wasn't sure, but whatever it was she heartily agreed with the tone in which it was said, for Dagwood was a pest. Neither she nor any of her friends had been given a moment's peace ever since he'd arrived on the scene. As far as she was concerned, '*garden* guest' would have been a much better description – or even 'gar-den *pest*'. Dagwood's heavy breathing and his snorts of frustration as he dashed hither and thither on the other side of the fence trying to

439

find a way through had to be heard to be believed.

Matters had come to a head that afternoon when, unable to contain himself a moment longer, he'd dug a tunnel underneath some boards and into the Sawdust family's garden.

As ill luck would have it Fangio had been passing at the time and he'd received the brunt of the attack, plus a very severe shock into the bargain.

Unlike most hedgehogs, Fangio often came

out for a stroll during the day. He liked a chat, particularly before he began his night's work, but on this occasion he got far more than he'd bargained for.

Fortunately, before Dagwood actually sank his teeth into him, Fangio managed to roll himself up into a ball, but it had been a very nasty moment indeed.

After chasing Noel up a tree, Dagwood turned his attention to Graham. But Graham was more than ready for him. He simply withdrew his head into his shell and pretended he was a passing stone.

More frustrated than ever, Dagwood had then set upon Olga and, as she'd been at pains to tell the others at every opportunity since, it had been a terrifying experience. One moment she'd been enjoying a quiet nibble on the lawn, the next moment there had been a roar and a deafening crash as Dagwood landed on top of her run, barking fit to wake the dead. She could still feel his hot breath on her face as he scrabbled at the grass, trying to force a way under, and she shuddered to think what might have happened had he succeeded.

Fortunately by then the noise had brought
the Sawdust family running and before he had
a chance to do anything of the sort they'd come
to the rescue and he'd been driven off.

The chase had taken him through the middle
of Mr Sawdust's vegetable garden, over the
rockery, through several flower beds, over the
strawberry patch, and finally into the pond. The
crowning insult came as he scrambled out again

and then shook himself dry over everybody. The trail of damage he left behind had taken Mr Sawdust several days' hard work to put right.

All the animals agreed that *something* would have to be done, but none of them knew quite what.

All eyes turned towards Noel. Cats being the traditional enemy of dogs, they felt sure he would have some ideas on the matter. But Noel would have none of it. Although he left the others in no doubt as to what would happen next time he and Dagwood came face to face, he obviously had no intention of seeking out an early meeting.

'I've got much more important things to do,' he announced in superior tones, punctuating his remark with a bang from his pussy flap as he disappeared indoors rather faster than usual.

There the affair was left, and as it happened it was just as well, for the very next day Mr Sawdust himself decided to take over.

Olga had barely finished breakfast when Karen and her father arrived outside the house laden with all sorts of bits and pieces.

They came and went several times, first to the

443

garden shed, then to somewhere called a 'Do-it-Yourself Shop', and after that to the garage. Each time they arrived back they were carrying something new.

Finally, Mr Sawdust went indoors and came out again carrying his toolbox and a large book.

'Right,' he said. 'We'll just check we've got everything, then we can start work.'

Olga sat listening as Mr Sawdust's voice droned on. 'Thirty feet of four by three-quarters – prepared. Fifteen feet of two by one. Polythene sheet. Wire netting. One inch pipe. Elbow. Backnuts. Nails ...'

Each time Mr Sawdust called out an item from his list, Karen Sawdust gave an answering 'yes'.

'Bacon rind ...'

'Mummy said she'd let us have some later,' replied Karen.

'Good. We mustn't forget it.'

'Bacon rind!' Olga, who'd nearly nodded off to sleep, gave a squeak of surprise. What *was* going on? What could they be making?

The thought was hardly out of her mind when the answer came.

'It's going to be a lovely house,' said Karen Sawdust. 'And safe as anything.'

'And air-conditioned,' said Mr Sawdust proudly, as he picked up some of the wood. 'Don't forget that.'

As Mr Sawdust and Karen disappeared round the side of the house in order to do some sawing, Olga sank back into her hay with a look of rapture on her face.

She had no idea what 'air-conditioned' meant, but it sounded very special indeed. Perhaps it had something to do with her fur. Perhaps they'd meant 'fur-conditioned'; not that her fur needed anything done to it. But that was only a minor detail. The important thing was she was going to have a new house. Trust the Sawdust family to make sure she was kept safe and sound and free from attack. There was no doubt about it, ever since she'd been with them she'd been properly looked after. Food, water, hay for her bedroom; she'd never once been left to want.

On the other hand, she *had* been with them for quite a long time. Olga wasn't sure how long. There had certainly been several summers, and winters, too; not to mention the bits in between, and her hutch, nice though it was, hadn't altered in all that time.

She wondered what her new house would look like. Perhaps it would be very grand and have a moat and a drawbridge like the one she had once stayed in with Boris.

Boris ... a dreamy look came over her face as she thought of Boris, and of her family – long since departed.

On the other hand, it would need a very big moat indeed to keep out a dog the size of Dagwood. As it was he'd practically filled the pond. She wasn't too sure about a moat if it was going to be that big, for it would mean she would be a long way away from all that was going on. Far

better to have some special wire with spikes in.
Olga liked to see what was going on, and as if
to prove her point she peered out of her front
door in order to see how her new house was
progressing.

The hammering and sawing had been growing louder all the time and the comings and
goings more frequent.

Mr Sawdust was busying himself with a paint
brush. 'It's some special stuff that preserves the
wood but doesn't smell,' he explained to Karen
Sawdust. 'They hate the smell of creosote.'

Olga nodded her agreement. She knew all
about creosote from when Mr Sawdust had
painted the fence near her hutch one day. The
smell had been so strong it had put her off her
food for several days.

Having finished off the painting, Mr Sawdust
picked up what was obviously one of the most
important parts of the operation – the fitting of
what he called the entrance tunnel.

'There,' he said, as he hammered a long,
square-looking wooden object into place, 'that
should keep any intruders out!'

'Do you think we ought to have taken some

measurements first?' asked Karen Sawdust. 'It wouldn't do for "a certain person" to get stuck.'

'Get stuck! Wheeeeee!' Olga gave an indignant squeak as the words sank in. Fancy suggesting she might get stuck! She was so upset she missed Mr Sawdust's reply, and it was with a mixture of surprise and disappointment that she watched them pick up the new house between them and carry it off down the garden.

It was a very strange looking affair. As far as she could make out there weren't any windows in it at all. It was simply a large square box with the entrance tunnel sticking out at one end like a long neck, and with what looked like a tail made of piping at the other.

She hoped they weren't going to put it too far down the garden. Being kept safe was one thing; being too far away to call for help was quite another matter. Besides, she liked being near the house – it was where everything happened and it was nice to be able to keep a watchful eye on the comings and goings.

All the same, she felt very excited at the trouble that was being taken on her behalf and she couldn't wait to tell the others all about it.

But the others, for reasons best known to themselves, were nowhere to be seen.

Karen Sawdust came back up the garden several times, first for a spade and a wheelbarrow, then for the sheet of black polythene and finally for the mysterious pieces of bacon rind.

'What they can possibly want *that* for, goodness only knows,' thought Olga. Her diet was a strictly vegetarian one and the very thought of eating any form of meat made her feel positively sick.

But when she came out of her bedroom again, having got over the thought, everything had gone quiet. Mr Sawdust and Karen had gone back indoors and even Dagwood was silent for a change.

It was all most disappointing after the earlier excitement. Perhaps they were waiting for the paint to dry properly before letting her see her new house . . . perhaps the bacon rind was meant to keep Dagwood away . . . perhaps . . . Olga closed her eyes and began dreaming about the grand new life she was about to lead. The others would be able to come and visit her from time to time and she would be able to tell them all about it. Perhaps she ought to be thinking up some stories she could tell them to be going on with . . .

It was late that same evening when a bang from Noel's pussy flap brought her awake with a start.

'Wheeee!' she squeaked. 'Wheeeeeeeee! Have you heard? Mr Sawdust and Karen have been building a special house. It's like a castle. It's got a special tunnel and air-conditioning and . . .'

Noel gave a yawn and stretched himself. 'I know. I've heard nothing else all the evening. Plans everywhere. Nowhere to lie down. I've never heard so much fuss. If you ask me there are *some* who are very lucky. The rest of us have got to take pot luck . . .'

'I'll let you come in,' said Olga, knowing full well she would do no such thing when it came down to it. It wasn't that she didn't trust Noel, it was just that . . . well, she didn't *altogether* trust him.

Noel gave her a funny look. '*You'll* let me come and see it?' he repeated. 'Do you know what they're calling it?'

'No, I don't,' said Olga. She was getting rather fed up with the way Noel seemed to know so much more about it all than she did.

'They bought a lot of special letters,' said Noel, 'and they're sorting them out now. Mr Sawdust is going to screw them on to the entrance in the morning. They're calling it FANGEY O'SHIDEAWAY.'

'Fangey O'Shideaway?' repeated Olga. 'I don't think much of that as a name for a house.'

But Noel had gone on his way, anxious to take advantage of the fact that by now Dagwood would be safely locked in for the night.

Olga tried running the words round her tongue again.

'Fan ... geoshide ... away. Fangeyoshide ... away ...' And then it came to her, and as the realization gradually sank in her squeak of indignation knew no bounds. 'Wheeeeeeeee! How could they? How dare they? Wheeeeeeeeee!' She was so upset she could hardly get the words out of her mouth. 'FAN-GIO'S HIDEAWAY!'

Fancy building a house for a hedgehog. The very idea!

And to show just how cross she was, she went straight to bed and didn't speak to anyone again until the morning. By which time, being a guinea-pig, she'd practically forgotten all about the matter.

CHAPTER FIVE

The Battle of Mulberry Hill

Olga often felt that one of the best things about living with the Sawdust family was that they had a particularly nice garden. She'd seen some of the others in the neighbourhood and as far as she was concerned they were nowhere near as good. Mr Sawdust was a keen gardener and apart from the lawn there was a sizeable shrubbery – which Graham and Fangio made much use of (although this was something of a mixed blessing when they were needed in a hurry and couldn't be found). Then there was the pond with its fountain and its waterfalls, and several flower beds, not to mention a vegetable patch which was good for lettuce leaves – especially on days when it was too wet for the Sawdust family to go out in search of grass for her.

But undoubtedly the pride and joy of Mr Sawdust's life was a large mulberry tree which stood on a slight hillock in the middle of the lawn. Olga could never quite see why everyone went on about it so, but go on about it they did. Whenever anyone new came to the house they were always taken out into the garden in order to see it, and if the 'ooh's' and 'aah's' were anything to go by, most of them shared Mr Sawdust's delight.

As far as Olga could make out, it was much more trouble than it was worth. It was large and very old – so much so that some of the heavier branches had to be propped up in case they snapped, and the fruit was so high it could only be picked with the aid of a ladder. Usually, by the time the family got around to doing it most had been 'got at' by the birds. Apart from that, by then the fruit was so heavy – not unlike giant raspberries – that any movement from the ladder made it fall off and burst on hitting the ground, where it left a nasty stain which lasted for days and days.

Olga wouldn't have minded quite so much if it had been nice to eat, but the one time she tried nibbling a mulberry she'd found it so sour it had made her squeak with surprise, and she'd had a nasty pain in her inside for several days afterwards.

However, all this was a seasonal thing which happened once a year in the late summer. For most of the time the mulberry tree just stood there, shedding its leaves or growing new ones, and if Olga thought about it at all it was really only to feel grateful for its shade when she was out on the lawn and the sun was high in the sky, as it was at the moment, or for its shelter when she got caught in a sudden shower of rain.

Little did she dream that one day that very

same tree would turn her into a heroine for a brief period of time, and cause even Noel to look at her with new respect.

Like many of her adventures it came about in a rather strange and unexpected way.

One morning she was outside in her run on the lawn, trying to decide between nibbles of grass whether to carry on for a while or take shelter in the built-in part at the end until someone came out to move her to a fresh patch (there was quite a breeze blowing and it was ruffling her whiskers more than somewhat), when she felt rather than saw something moving close by.

Instinctively she stopped nibbling and sat very still, hardly daring to breathe. Although she knew from past experience that she was reasonably safe in her run, you never knew.

On the far side of the lawn Noel lay stretching out his paws in a luxurious manner as he drank in the warmth of the sun through half closed eyes. Nearer at hand Olga could see the familiar, but equally dormant rounded hump of Graham. She gave a sniff. Fat lot of good either of them would be in time of trouble.

Then, just as she was about to relax it

happened again – only this time it felt even closer.

Suddenly she saw it – a wiggly object, almost as fat as it was long, coming over the brow of the hill at the foot of the mulberry tree. It was so fat it was impossible to see its eyes, or its legs for that matter. But what really made Olga catch her breath was its colour, or rather its lack of colour, for it was a ghastly white from the top of its head to the very uttermost tip of its tail. Even as she watched, the creature was joined by a second one, and together they came down the slope towards her in a series of short hops, looking for all the world like some primeval slugs which had crawled out of the woodwork after

being hidden from the light of day since the world began.

Not that Olga had time to consider the matter. One glance was enough to send her scurrying for the comparative safety of the shelter at the end of her run, letting out squeaks of terror as she went. Once there, she buried her nose in the furthermost corner and lay quaking and shivering as she waited for the worst to happen.

'Wheeeeee! Wheeeeeeeeee!' Her squeaks grew louder still as a shadow darkened the floor of her shelter. Perhaps the creatures expanded when they saw the sun for the first time. 'Wheeeeeeeeee! Perhaps . . .'

'What *is* going on? What's the matter now?' A plaintive meeow from Noel brought Olga back to earth.

'What's the matter?' repeated Olga. '*What's the matter*? Can't you see?'

Taking advantage of Noel's presence she ventured out of her corner and gazed through the wire netting at the lawn beyond, her nose twitching as she tried to catch the scent of the invaders from outer space. For now that her vivid imagination had seized on the problem, that was what she had convinced herself they must be. Invaders from outer space. It was the *only* explanation, for she had never, ever seen anything like them on earth before. She'd sometimes heard Karen Sawdust talking about things from outer space with her friends when she was being cleaned out – usually after they'd been to something called a cinema, but never in her wildest dreams had she expected to come face to face with such beings.

'Wheeeee! Look behind you,' she squeaked, as some more white objects appeared on the brow of the hill.

Noel half turned and then paused, arching his back and stretching out his claws in one continuous movement. For a second or two he remained perfectly motionless; but for a sudden scurry of wind ruffling his fur, he could have been made of stone. Then he pounced on the nearest object. But quick though he was, he wasn't quick enough. Almost before his feet had left the ground his quarry gave a sideways hop and he missed it by a yard.

Olga gave a squeak of fear. Her worst suspicions were confirmed. Anything that could beat Noel to the pounce must be special indeed. As he looked at her sheepishly over his shoulder, pretending he'd only intended to have a wash anyway, she put on one of her 'I told you so' looks. But it was an 'I told you so' look which also said 'I wish I *didn't* have to tell you, and watch out! There's another one right behind you'.

Noel stopped licking himself and took another quick look. Normally the sight of all the white objects jumping hither and thither would have been irresistible. Like most cats, he enjoyed nothing better than a good chase, and the longer it went on and the more difficult it was the better he liked it; but something in the urgent tone of Olga's voice communicated itself to him.

'Don't worry,' he said, as he stood up to go, 'you'll be all right in your run.'

'All right in my run!' Olga's squeak grew higher still as Noel's words sank in. She could hardly believe her ears. He was leaving her to her fate. 'Wheeeee! Wheeeeeeeeeeeeeeeeeeeeee!'

But her cries had quite the wrong effect on Noel. Any hopes she may have had that they would make him change his mind were dashed as he disappeared in the direction of the house. In fact, if anything, they made him quicken his pace and, in his haste, he almost trod on Graham, who was heading in the direction of

Olga's run in order to see what all the fuss was about.

'You could try using Graham as a barricade,' he called, before he finally disappeared. 'They'll never get past *him*.' Noel knew all about these things through watching television in the evenings.

'What's going on?' Graham stopped in his tracks, sticking his head out and craning his neck to and fro as he surveyed the scene.

'Oh, don't just *stand* there,' moaned Olga. 'You heard ... be a barricade.'

'What's a barricade?' asked Graham.

'Oh, wheeee!' squeaked Olga in desperation. 'Of all the times to ask silly questions. For goodness sake! All you have to do is stand there.'

Graham looked even more confused. 'I do wish you'd make up your mind,' he said plaintively. 'First you say *don't* stand here ... then you say *do*.' And he put his head back inside his shell while he thought the problem over.

'I'm coming! I'm coming!' Fangio, his prickles sticking out like a porcupine's, came hurrying across the lawn. Looking neither to the right nor to the left, he went straight past the bottom of Olga's run and disappeared into a flower bed on the other side of the garden.

Olga's moans and groans as she rushed up and down reached fever pitch. By now the lawn was covered in white objects as a never-ending stream fanned out across the top of the hillock. They were everywhere. How *could* the others behave in such a way? Deserting her in her hour of need. It was unbelievable. Wheeeeeeee! It . . .

Olga suddenly stopped dead in her tracks as something landed on her head. Her mouth open wide, a squeak which she'd been about to utter cut off before it had even begun, she felt rather than saw a warm trickle of something sticky run down between her eyes and on to her nose.

But before she had a chance to recover, let alone see what was the cause, there came a patter of running feet and Karen Sawdust burst on the scene.

'Olga! Olga!' she cried. 'What *is* going on? What *have* you done to yourself? You're covered in blood. It's all over your face . . .'

'Blood!' What was left in Olga's veins suddenly went cold. 'Blood? All over my face? Wheeeeugh!' The cry of anguish changed into a gurgle as she felt her run being tipped up and a warm pair of hands took hold of her.

Usually when she was taken out of her run she put up a bit of a struggle. More of a token to show what was what. But for once she was happy to lay back and let things take their course.

She was dimly aware of the jogging motion as Karen Sawdust carried her gently towards the house, past the wide-open eyes of Noel, Fangio and Graham – all of whom had come back to witness the goings on, when she felt all dizzy and everything seemed to go black.

Olga never knew how long it lasted, but when she came round again she found she was back in her own house, all clean and tidy and lying in a rucked up pile of soft hay. The sticky feeling on her nose had gone and although it still felt wet, the strange smell that had accompanied it had gone too.

She looked around to make sure everything was in its proper place – her bowl of water and her bowl of oats, and then she peered out through the front door.

To her surprise she was greeted by a chorus of meeows and squeaks and grunts.

'Are you all right?' For once Noel sounded genuinely worried.

'Wheeeeee!' Olga gave a loud squeak of reassurance. Then, because she liked an audience and had a sense of occasion, she added a sort of groan for good measure. She was really quite pleased with the result.

'It was very brave of you,' said Graham.

'Oh, it was nothing ...' Olga tried hard to remember what had happened and what it was she was supposed to have done.

'All those THINGS,' persisted Graham. 'They were really after you.'

'I've never seen so much blood,' agreed

Fangio. 'Not since Mr Sawdust hit himself with the hammer.'

'*And* he made a lot more fuss,' broke in Graham, anxious not to be outdone. 'He jumped up and down so he nearly trod on me.'

'Oh, it was nothing.' A faraway look came into Olga's eyes as the morning's events gradually came back to her and she felt the beginnings of a story enter her mind. 'I'll tell you all about it if you like.'

She took a deep breath. 'I shall call it the Battle of Mulberry Hill, because it all took place under the mulberry tree. Some of you may want to sit down while you listen,' she added, casting a meaning glance in Noel's direction.

'There's rather a lot of blood in it and you may find it upsetting particularly if you don't happen to be very brave yourself.'

Noel opened his mouth as if he was about to say something, but before he had a chance to the kitchen door opened.

'Good gracious!' Mrs Sawdust took in the scene. 'What *is* going on?'

'It's one of those days,' said Karen Sawdust. 'What with all that plastic packing Daddy's new Hi-Fi came in blowing away . . .' She bent down and picked something up off the ground. 'I wonder if that's what frightened Olga? It's funny stuff. Just like a lot of white worms.'

'It's very light,' agreed Mrs Sawdust. 'No wonder it went everywhere. We'd better pick it up before it gets any worse . . .'

'Poor Olga.' Karen Sawdust poked a finger through Olga's front door. 'Fancy having a mulberry fall on to your head into the bargain. No wonder you were upset. We were too. The way it burst made it look as if you were covered in blood.'

'As I was saying,' continued Olga hastily as Karen Sawdust followed her mother down the

garden, 'I've called this story the Battle of Mulberry Hill ...'

But it was too late, her audience was already
melting away.

'A *mulberry!*' Noel nearly spat the word out
as he leapt up onto a near-by fence and arched
his back in disgust.

Olga turned to the others. 'As I was saying,'
she repeated.

But Graham, showing a surprising turn of
speed, was already on his way, and Fangio was
busying himself with the remains of some bread
and milk he'd found.

Olga gave a sigh and turned her attention to

her bowl of oats. It had promised to be a good story and really, now she came to think of it, one which would probably have been wasted on the others.

Perhaps she would save it to tell to herself some time, but later, after she'd had a good sleep.

'After all,' thought Olga to herself, 'it's so exciting that if I told it to myself now I might *never* get to sleep.' And with that she disappeared into her bedroom and wasn't seen for the rest of the day.

CHAPTER SIX

Who's a Pretty Girl, Then?

'Who's a pretty girl, then? Who's a pretty girl?'

Olga, who as it happened was busy gazing at her own reflection in the water bowl, preened herself as Mrs Sawdust's voice floated out through her kitchen door.

It was a silly question, of course, since the answer was so obvious it was hardly worth asking in the first place. All the same, it gave her a nice warm glow to feel that others were thinking of her.

Clearly, Mrs Sawdust had a friend in for what

was known as 'morning coffee', for almost immediately another, gruffer voice which she didn't recognize, said exactly the same thing.

'Who's a pretty girl, then? Who's a pretty girl?'

'Wheeeeeeee!' said Olga. 'Wheeeeeeeeee! Wheeeeeeeeeee!' There was no harm in letting the others know she was up and about and agreed with everything they were saying.

'Who's a *clever* girl, then? Who's a *clever* girl?'

'Wheeeeeeee!' squeaked Olga. 'Yes, that's true, too.'

'Who's a *clever* girl, then?' Again the same gruff voice repeated what Mrs Sawdust had said.

'How about coming out for a little while?' asked Mrs Sawdust.

'Wheeeeee!' said Olga. 'Thank you very much.'

She took one final glance at her reflection and then stretched herself in readiness. She hadn't expected to go out on the lawn quite so early in the morning; on the other hand it was a nice day and there was really no reason not to.

Mrs Sawdust said something else, but she

couldn't tell what it was for the shrill sound of some dreadful bird screeching, so she contented herself with waiting patiently for someone to come and put her in her run.

There was a bang as Mrs Sawdust closed her kitchen window, and then silence.

After she'd waited for several minutes and still nothing had happened, Olga began to get restive. 'Really,' she thought, 'either people want me to go out on the grass or they don't!' And she was about to let the others know her feelings on the matter when suddenly there was a dreadful commotion inside the kitchen.

There was a series of shrieks and cries and screeches and then Noel's pussy flap popped open and Noel himself shot out as if his very life depended on it; and by the sound of Mrs Sawdust's voice it did just that.

'Wretched cat!' she cried. 'Don't you ever do that again. Poor Josephine!'

Noel landed just a few feet away from Olga's hutch. He sat there for a moment or two and then, sensing that Olga had her beady eyes fixed on him, he had a quick wash as if to pretend that nothing had happened. As he did so a small, blue feather detached itself from his whiskers and floated gently to the ground.

'Just let her wait,' Noel said at last. He paused in his washing and stared at the kitchen door. 'Just let her wait!'

Olga looked most surprised. Although Noel was very independent – or *pretended* he was – Olga sometimes suspected he wasn't quite as independent as he made himself out to be, and

473

it was very unusual for him to have a cross word to say about any of the Sawdust family. Especially Mrs Sawdust, who never let him down when it came to feeding time, or if he was in any kind of trouble.

'Not Mrs Sawdust,' said Noel impatiently, when Olga started questioning him. 'That ... that ... *bird*.' He seemed to have difficulty in getting the word out. 'Fancy having a *bird* in the house. And letting it fly around like that. How was I to know? I thought I was doing them a good turn.'

Noel licked his lips at the memory of it all. 'If it had been any other sort of bird they'd have been pleased if I'd caught it for them. If it had come from outside they would have *asked* me to. Just because it's a budgerigar and it *talks* ...'

'Talks?' Everything began to fall into place. The strange voice in the kitchen. The screeching ... Olga suddenly felt very put out at the thought of there being an addition to the household. A stranger in their midst, without so much as a by-your-leave. One, moreover, that talked ... just like humans.

'What does it say?' she asked, unable to bring

herself to say the word 'she'; half of her was dying to know the answer while the other half felt it would rather not.

'Oh, this and that.' Noel was rapidly losing interest in the subject. He was content to bide his time until the right moment arrived to get his revenge.

Left to her own devices, Olga began to brood on the matter. She viewed the whole affair with very mixed feelings indeed, and when, later that morning, Karen Sawdust came out to 'see to her', she went into her bedroom and didn't utter a word, just to show her displeasure.

When Karen Sawdust went back indoors she heard her telling Mrs Sawdust all about it.

'Olga's in a bad mood this morning,' she said. 'I can't think what's the matter with her. I hope she's not sickening for anything.'

'Perhaps we ought to take her to the vet,' replied Mrs Sawdust. 'Unless, of course, it's jealousy. You never know. Animals are sometimes funny that way.'

'Jealous?' thought Olga. 'Me? *Jealous*? Of a *budgerigar*? How could they?'

As the kitchen door closed she looked around for other ears to unburden herself on.

But if Noel was of little help, the others were even worse.

Talking to Graham was sometimes like talking to a brick wall, particularly if he wasn't interested. At least a brick wall stood still. With Graham, things just bounced off his shell and he went on his way as if nothing had happened.

And just so long as he got his bread and milk occasionally, Fangio couldn't have cared two hoots what went on in the Sawdust family's house. Since he'd got his new house it had taken most of his attention.

'They're still feeding you, aren't they?' he asked.

Olga had to admit they were.

'And cleaning you out?'

Olga nodded.

'Well, then?'

'Well, then,' thought Olga crossly, as Fangio went on his way, 'is all very well, then.'

In the end she had to make do with scraps of information Noel let fall from time to time. That, and an occasional glimpse of Josephine's cage when Mrs Sawdust opened the kitchen window. And as the kitchen window, since Josephine's arrival, was almost always kept tightly shut, and Noel was still biding his time and pretending he had no interest in the matter, it was all very difficult.

Gradually, however, she began to build up a picture of the scene as the pieces of information fell into place like those of a giant jigsaw puzzle.

It seemed that Josephine lived in a cage which hung by a spring from a large stand.

The inside of the cage contained several perches, a ladder, a swing, a mirror, two bells –

which Olga could often hear ringing, and a table-tennis ball.

There was a water bowl for when she was thirsty, and a seed bowl for her food, and when she was tired of that she had a choice of cuttle fish to keep her beak in good condition, things called iodised nibbles to keep her in good health, special grit for the floor of the cage, and millet sprays on Sundays for a special treat.

It made her own list of belongings look very small indeed: two feeding bowls and a twig for her teeth. There was certainly no mirror. She had to make do with her water bowl when she wanted to see her reflection.

Really, it seemed the smaller you were the more you had. Olga remembered Fircone and Raisin, the gerbils; it had been exactly the same with them. Their cage had been full of things.

She felt very disgruntled. 'Really,' she thought, 'it's a wonder she can get inside her cage with all those things.'

And then one morning the inevitable happened. It was almost a repeat of the previous excitement, except that this time the screams

and the shrieks and the screeches were, if anything, even louder.

And when Noel came through his pussy flap
he was accompanied by a small, blue object
which was making most of the noise.

Once outside, the blue object went one way
and Noel went the other, and by the time Mrs
Sawdust got the door open both had disappeared.

The Sawdust family rushed down the garden
calling Josephine's name, but to no avail.

'That's torn it,' said Karen Sawdust, as they
gathered outside the kitchen. 'What are we
going to tell Mrs Holmes?'

'She's due back this afternoon,' said Mrs Sawdust.

'Perhaps we could buy her another one,' said Mr Sawdust hopefully.

'It wouldn't be the same,' said Karen Sawdust. 'Besides, she'd have to teach it to talk all over again.'

'That's the trouble with minding other people's pets,' said Mrs Sawdust, as they went indoors. 'It's such a responsibility.'

Olga suddenly felt quite differently about the matter. If only the Sawdust family had *said* they were only looking after Josephine for a neighbour. She wouldn't have minded a bit.

And another thing: if they had only asked her where Josephine was at that moment she could have told them. Instead of which they had all gone rushing off down the garden like wild things. They'd made so much noise it was a wonder they hadn't driven her away out of sheer fright.

As it was she was still perched on the sill outside Olga's bedroom window, looking rather ruffled, but obviously none the worse for her adventure.

Olga came to a decision. She moved back inside her hutch and then very, very gently, began nuzzling her feeding bowl towards her front door. Bran and oats weren't exactly like bird seed. On the other hand, in her present state Josephine might be glad of anything. From past experience Olga knew there was nothing like the sight of food to set your mind at rest.

Having got her bowl as close to the wire netting as possible she sat very still and waited. Sure enough, after a moment or two, Josephine hopped towards her, easing her way along the ledge until she was able to cling to the edge of Olga's front door.

For a while they both stayed absolutely still,

Olga hardly daring to breathe. Then the ringlet of hearts around Josephine's neck stirred as she opened her beak.

'Who's a pretty girl, then?' she said, staring straight at Olga.

Olga preened herself. 'Well,' she thought. 'Since you ask.'

'Who's a *clever* girl, then?' said Josephine, in a voice as clear as a bell. There was no mistaking the words, or who they were meant for.

Olga was just about to tell her when she stiffened as she saw a familiar black shape appear round the side of the shed.

Her mind raced in all directions. She would have to do something. She recognized from the way Noel had frozen into position that he was almost ready to pounce. And she knew from old that when he did there was no one faster.

She took a deep breath. It was now or never.

Her squeak when it came was exactly right. Even if she'd rehearsed it for days and days she couldn't have done it any better. It was loud enough to reach the Sawdust family's kitchen, yet not so loud that it frightened Josephine, for it started quietly and built up towards the end.

It also had just the right amount of urgency. It said all that needed to be said.

'WheeeeeeeEEEEEEEEEEEEEE!'

'WheeeeeeeEEEEEEEEEEEEEE!' echoed Josephine, intrigued by this new sound.

And 'Thank goodness for that,' said Mrs Sawdust, as she took hold of Josephine and put her back inside her cage.

'Olga,' said Karen Sawdust, 'you're a heroine. You shall have some special groundsel as a treat. I'll go and get some right now.'

'Who'd have believed it?' said Mr Sawdust.

'I wouldn't have for a start,' said Noel, as the Sawdust family went their separate ways

leaving him alone with Olga. 'Fancy doing a thing like that. A *bird*! That could have been my supper.'

'*I* thought she was very nice,' said Olga. 'And *very* intelligent. I could have listened to her all day.

'Which is more,' she added pointedly, staring straight at Noel, 'than I can say for some.'

And with that she pushed her bowl of bran and oats away from the front door and turned her back on the world. Cats were all very well in their way, but they did tend to go on about the same old things all the time. They sometimes couldn't see beyond the next mouse.

Whereas birds – Olga had a whole new outlook on birds. She gazed at her reflection in the water bowl and gave a squeak of approval.

'Wheeeeeeee!' she went. 'Who's a pretty girl, then? Who's a heroine?'

CHAPTER SEVEN

Olga Goes Jogging

One day Olga was slowly coming awake, peering through her bedroom window at the outside world and wondering whether or not it was worth going out into her dining-room before the early morning dew had disappeared, when she had a great shock.

The door leading to the Sawdust family's kitchen suddenly burst open and Mr Sawdust came out, looked about him rather furtively for a moment or two, and then disappeared round the corner of the house in the direction of the road.

In itself, there was nothing unusual about this. Mr Sawdust came out of the very same door practically every day of the year. On weekdays he was usually dressed in a dark suit and carried a small case under his arm. At weekends and during the holidays it was often much later in the morning and he usually wore older clothes, perhaps a sweater or an open-necked shirt.

But Olga couldn't remember ever having seen him coming out so early, and *never* had she seen him dressed in quite such an odd manner. If *dressed* was the right word. *Un*dressed would be more like it, for he was wearing just a thin white singlet and a pair of very short trousers which showed his knees. Olga had never seen Mr Sawdust's knees before and she tried to get a closer look, but instead of moving in his usual dignified manner he kept jumping up and down, and when he disappeared round the corner of the house it was rather as if he was being pursued by some enormous beast of prey.

Olga was so taken aback she sat with her jaw open for quite some time, her eyes large, round and full of wonder.

She couldn't wait to tell the others, especially

Noel, who, because of his privileged position of being able to come and go through his pussy flap, knew everything that was going on in the Sawdust family's house. Or even if he didn't, he pretended to.

Olga felt sure that this time she would have one up on him, for more often than not Noel slept on in the morning on account of having been up late the night before – a rather sore point because Olga's sleep was sometimes disturbed in the early hours by his comings and goings. If Noel was having a 'field night' with mice, the bangs from his pussy flap sounded like machine-gun fire.

This particular morning was no exception, and the sun was high in the sky by the time he made his first appearance of the day. Mr Sawdust had long since returned from whatever it was he'd been doing, changed into his normal clothes, and left for the office.

But at long last the awaited bang from the pussy flap brought Olga running out into her dining-room. She pressed her nose against the wire netting of her front door and gave a squeak as Noel sauntered past looking for a convenient patch of sunshine where he could enjoy his morning wash before going back to sleep again.

He listened to her excited squeaks for a while and then gave a yawn.

'Is *that* all,' he said. 'That's only jogging. I heard them all talking about it last night before I went out. He'll be doing it every morning from now on.'

Stifling her disappointment, Olga considered the matter for a moment or two. 'I don't see much fun in jigging,' she said at last. 'It sounds like a lot of fuss over nothing.'

'It's *jogging*,' said Noel, 'and it isn't meant to be fun. People do it to keep fit and lose weight. They don't keep themselves in good condition like cats because they don't get enough exercise.'

Noel, thoroughly awake now, went into great detail about all he'd heard the night before.

It was Olga's turn to yawn. 'Well, jigging or jogging,' she said, '*I* don't think much of it.' And she buried her head in her bowl of oats to show that as far as she was concerned the discussion was at an end.

Noel looked rather miffed. 'If anyone needs a good jog you do,' he said, 'stuck in that hutch all day. About the only exercise you get is when you eat. It's a wonder you don't seize up. Not,' he added as a parting shot, 'that you'd be able to jog if you tried. You're so fat, if you jumped up in the air you'd go straight through the floor.'

And with that he arched his back, stretched, and before Olga had time to say any more, moved slowly on his way to follow the sunshine.

'Wheeee!' squeaked Olga, when she'd recovered herself. 'Wheelll, really! Cats!'

And she went back into her bedroom in order

to sleep off the nasty taste the whole affair had
left her with.

But as she settled down in her hay she happened to catch sight of her reflection in the
window. She gazed at it for a while. The fact of
the matter was she hadn't taken a good long
look at herself for some while. Looking at her
reflection in her water bowl was one thing.
That was close to. Seen from a distance she had
to admit that there could have been a grain of
truth in Noel's remarks. Only the tiniest grain,
of course, but she had perhaps put on a little
weight here and there. During the summer
months she was often put out in her run on the
lawn and it could be that she'd been eating a
little more grass than usual. It was only natural,
for that was the whole idea – it saved Mr Sawdust mowing it.

But as for being so heavy she'd go through
the floor of her hutch ... 'wheeee!' Olga gave
another squeak of indignation. She'd show him.
The very next time she was out in her run,
where Noel would be able to see her properly,
she'd show him.

As it happened, Olga's chance came sooner

than she'd expected. No sooner had she settled down and closed her eyes than the kitchen door opened once again and this time Karen Sawdust came out.

'Come on, Olga,' she said, as she opened the hutch door and lifted her out. 'It's time you had a bit of sunshine instead of lying in bed all day. It'll be autumn soon and you won't be able to. I should make the most of it.'

Karen Sawdust's remark was like fuel to Olga's fire. If she'd had any doubts about putting her plan into action before then they were now completely gone.

She could hardly wait for the moment when her run was turned over on to its face and she was able to scramble out of the built-up end and on to the open grass.

She gazed around. Luck was with her. Noel hadn't strayed far. He was sitting on a patch of stone near the pool washing himself. Graham was close by, doing something or other – goodness knew what. He was so slow it was hard to tell what he was up to sometimes. Even Fangio was busy catching flies in a corner of the lawn.

Olga waited until she heard the back door

close, then she took a deep breath, closed her eyes, heaved and braced herself for the fall.

After a moment or two, when nothing had happened, she opened her eyes again and found to her surprise that she was in exactly the same spot. She'd fully expected to be on the other side of her run at the very least. 'Perhaps,' she thought, 'I made a very soft landing. Guinea-pigs probably do on account of their silky fur.'

She gave a furtive look round the garden, but nothing had changed. Noel was still busy with his washing. He seemed to have found a particularly difficult patch which demanded all his attention.

Taking a deep breath she tried again, only this time she kept her eyes open. It was most disappointing, but she had to admit, nothing, absolutely nothing, happened.

She tried a third time, then a fourth and a fifth. Still nothing. Panting after her exertions, she was trying to make up her mind whether to try once more or to have a rest for a while, when she felt someone or some*thing* close by staring at her.

'Are you all right?' asked Noel anxiously.

'Am I, huh, huh, hall right?' gasped Olga. 'Of course I'm , huh, huh, hall right. Why shouldn't I be? Wheeeeee! I've just been doing a bit of jogging, that's all.'

'Jogging!' Noel gave her a pitying stare. 'Jogging? You don't call that jogging, do you? You haven't even moved.'

'Wheeeeee! Yes, I have. You haven't been looking, that's your trouble. Too busy washing ... wheeeeee!'

Olga was so incensed she rushed up and down her run, climbed up the side, took a wild bound and before she knew what was happening, felt herself flying through the air. Oblivious of the fact that in landing she'd knocked what was left of her breath right out of herself, she had another go. Now that she'd got the knack her delight knew no bounds. Or rather, it knew lots of bounds, for it felt as though her body had taken on wings.

Then, suddenly, she realized she was no longer alone. Noel let out a screech and disappeared as if his very life depended on it, and faces appeared above her run. Faces and voices. Mrs

Sawdust, Karen Sawdust, and several others she recognized as neighbours.

She felt herself being picked up.

'Olga! Olga! ... dear, oh dear! What's wrong?'

'I've never seen anything like it. Must be some kind of fit.'

'We'd better get her to the vet quickly.' Mrs Sawdust's voice took charge. 'You take her. Someone else find her box. I'll get the car out.'

Olga relaxed. Truth to tell, she felt like a

good lie down after all the rushing about. A drive in the car would be nice. It didn't matter to her if it was a wasted journey. Jogging took it out of you – especially if you weren't used to it. Especially . . . She pricked up her ears. One of the neighbours was talking.

'Perhaps the vet will put her to sleep. It'll be the kindest thing.'

'Put me to sleep? I do wish they'd make up their minds. First they want to take me to the vet. Now they want to put me to bed . . .' Gradually, the remark sank in and as it did so she felt a chill enter her stomach. It started somewhere in the middle and then spread all over her.

'There, there.' Karen Sawdust stroked her gently as she began to tremble. 'The vet'll know what to do for the best.'

'Wheeeeee!' Olga gave a shriek. It wasn't the vet's best that worried her, it was his worst. How could they not understand? How could she possibly begin to explain? If only Mr Sawdust was there – he might have known. 'Wheeeeeeee!' she collapsed into her travelling box in a terrible state.

496

Olga was hardly aware of the journey. Noises that would normally have made her look out with interest passed unheeded.

All she knew for certain was that worried faces kept peering down at her and that even her slightest movement or attempts at squeaking were taken as meaning the very worst.

In the end she gave up and just lay there.

'Hmmmm!' The vet turned her over and gave her stomach a few practised prods. Then he placed something cold and shiny on her chest and appeared to be listening to something.

'A fine time to be listening to the wireless,' thought Olga.

'Hmmm, yes . . . well.' The vet looked puzzled.

Olga lay back where she'd been put waiting for the worst.

'I can't find anything obviously wrong,' said the man.

Olga's hopes rose.

'And then again,' he rubbed his chin and Olga's hopes sank. 'She's probably had a narrow squeak.'

Olga gave a whimper. If her squeak had got narrow that must be a bad sign.

'I think,' he said at last, 'if you ask me, she could do with losing a bit of weight.'

Olga's hopes rose again. 'He knows,' she thought. 'He knows all about my jogging. He's probably going to tell them all about it.'

'Leave her with me,' said the vet briskly. 'I'll keep her under observation for a day or two. *And*,' he added sternly, 'I'll make sure she doesn't eat too much. I shall put her on a very strict diet. Leave her with me and I'll make a new guinea-pig of her.'

The vet was as good as his word. When Olga returned home almost a week later she was indeed a new guinea-pig. Even Noel had to look twice in order to make sure he was seeing aright. Her fur had a shiny glow to it; her eyes were fresh and sparkling; her movements quick and lithe; above all, she was in particularly good voice.

'I've been on a very long jog,' she announced as soon as she was settled into her house, 'and it's done me the world of good. Wheeeeeeee!

'If you're going to do something you may as well do it properly. Wheeeeee! Wheeeeeeee! You should try it sometime.

'I'm a new person. Wheeeeee! Wheeeeeeee! Wheeeeeeeeee! I'll tell you all about if you like.'

But Noel wasn't having any. He looked up at her in disgust. 'I think,' he said, 'I much preferred the old one, thank you very much. At least it was quieter.'

And with that he disappeared into the house letting his pussy flap slam shut behind him.

'Wheeeeee!' said Olga. 'See how much I care.'

And she did a quick jog up and down, just to show she meant what she said.

Then she hesitated as she caught sight of her feeding bowl, full to the brim with luscious fresh oats.

Being fit was one thing, starving yourself was quite another matter. 'If I'm to be a new guinea-pig,' she thought, 'I may as well keep the best of the old.' And soon, save for a steady munching sound, all was quiet, and things were back to normal again. Olga had jogged for the very last time.

CHAPTER EIGHT

Olga's Goodnight Story

Soon after Olga gave up jogging there was a change in the weather. It suddenly grew much colder and Graham and Fangio began making hurried plans to hibernate for the winter, Fangio being torn between his usual hiding-place and his new house at the bottom of the garden, and Graham quite content with wherever the fancy took him at the time.

Even Noel trod more daintily as he came out to survey the estate before doing his daily rounds. No one ever knew quite where Noel went to on his rambles, but they seemed to follow a pattern which he varied from time to time – either to confuse his enemies or simply because he liked a change.

On this particular morning he seemed content to settle down near Olga's house while he watched the comings and goings.

It was while Olga was looking out on it all through her bedroom window that she noticed something very strange. When she put her nose close to the glass and breathed out it became all misty so that she could no longer see through it. She tried it several times and each time added to the first, so that in the end it was just like the special glass the Sawdust family had in their bathroom.

In the end, tiring of this and feeling rather thirsty after all the effort, she went into her dining-room to have a drink, only to discover that her bowl of water had a coating of ice over the top.

'Wheeeeee!' She gave a shrill squeak, which said, in effect, 'isn't it about time I was taken care of?'

The only effect it had on Noel was to make

him stare lazily in her direction as much as to say 'what's wrong now?'

'Wheeeeeeee!' said Olga. 'It's all very well for you. I expect you've had your breakfast, but I haven't. I'm hungry. Wheeeeeeee!'

'You'll be lucky,' grunted Noel. 'It's Sunday. They're all still in bed.'

'In that case,' said Olga, 'I shall give a very loud squeak. I shall squeak so loud it will go into the house, through your pussy flap, through the kitchen, then the hall, up the stairs and into the bedrooms, and it will wake them all up, so there!' And she took a deep, deep breath, just to show what she meant.

'Huh!' said Noel unsympathetically. 'Pigs might fly.'

It was a phrase he'd heard the Sawdust family use several evenings before and he'd been waiting to try it out on Olga, knowing it might upset her – for she hated being called a pig.

Olga paused, let out her breath and stared at Noel. 'Would you mind saying that again?' she demanded.

'Pigs might fly,' said Noel carelessly. 'That means it's never likely to happen.'

503

'Never likely to happen!' repeated Olga. '*Never likely to happen!*' She was so upset her imagination went soaring up into the clouds in an effort to think of something, anything, to wipe the superior look off Noel's face. As it did so her sharp ears caught the sound of an aeroplane high above in the sky. Suddenly an idea came into her mind.

'I'll have you know,' she said, 'that guinea-pigs are some of the best flyers in the world. Much better than birds. They can go much, much higher for a start.'

Noel's jaw dropped. He was used to Olga's extravagant claims and her tall stories, but this one threatened to be the tallest and most extravagant ever. Even Graham and Fangio stopped in their tracks as they passed by on their way down the garden.

Graham, who'd been about to say goodnight for the winter, looked most impressed.

'I never knew that,' he said. 'I hope it doesn't keep me awake. I don't suppose it will.'

Noel gave a disparaging snort. 'I've never seen a pig flying,' he said. 'Nor's anyone else.'

'Not *pigs*,' said Olga. 'They'd be much too heavy. *Guinea*-pigs.

'Guinea-pigs,' she went on, 'are as light as a feather. They're really all fur. The lightest, softest, downiest fur imaginable. Why, they're so light they have to be tied down sometimes to keep them on the ground. A puff of wind and they're away.

'Not like cat's fur. That's very thick and heavy. Now, *there's* something that couldn't possibly fly. Not in a million years.'

Noel's snort was almost as loud as Olga's squeak might have been had she ever made it.

'Show me one,' he said. 'Just show me one.'

Olga glanced up towards the sky again. She was only just in time, for the aeroplane was almost out of sight.

'There's one going over right now,' she said.

Her remark was greeted in silence.

'That's not a guinea-pig,' said Noel at last.

'It is,' said Olga firmly.

'How do you know it is?' said Noel. 'Prove
it.'

'How do you know it *isn't*?' asked Olga, conscious of playing a trump card. 'You prove it
isn't.'

For once Noel was stuck for an answer.

'If you can fly,' he said at last, ' why don't

you? If you're so good at it, show us. You can't even jog, let alone fly.'

'Where are your wings?' piped up Fangio. 'I can't see them.'

'I keep them tucked away,' said Olga primly.

'Anyway,' she turned and stared pityingly at Noel, 'I couldn't possibly fly in here. I'd only bang my head on the roof. Besides, I'm a bit out of practice. That's the trouble with being stuck in a cage all day. It makes you stiff.'

'I wonder where it was going?' said Graham, who'd nearly ricked his neck trying to follow the progress of the plane.

'Probably somewhere warm for the winter,' said Fangio. 'That's what a lot of birds do.'

'Quite likely,' said Olga, glad that at least two members of her audience were on her side at last.

'Well, I still don't believe it,' said Noel. 'You might just as well say that was a tortoise,' he added, as a motor cycle roared past outside.

'If you think *that* you'll think anything,' said Olga. 'Besides, it was going much too fast.

'The thing is,' she continued, 'it all began many, many years ago, long before any of us were born, in the days when guinea-pigs lived in caves.

'That's why we're called "cavies", you know – because we once lived in caves.'

'That's true,' said Graham. 'I've heard that.'

'I live in a garage,' said Fangio, 'but I'm not called a "garages".'

Olga ignored the interruption. It really wasn't worth replying to.

'Some of you,' she went on, looking pointedly towards Noel, '*may* be able to picture what it must have been like all those years ago when they first saw daylight. Picture living in a big cave all your life, in the dark, and then suddenly one day finding the way out into the daylight.

'They were so excited they jumped for joy and to their astonishment they found themselves floating. And because they were so light and because they were already high up, for the cave was at the top of a high mountain, they floated way, way up into the sky.

'That's how they ended up in so many different parts of the world. I expect my ancestors landed in the pet shop down the road and that's how I came to be here.'

Olga settled back, well pleased with her tale.
Once she'd got going it had all fallen into place
very nicely indeed.

As she did so another aeroplane, going very fast this time, and much lower, shot by. Fortunately, it was on the other side of the house and out of sight.

'There goes another one,' she said. 'It sounded as if it was in a hurry to get somewhere. I expect it's going off to do a good deed. Guinea-pigs are always doing good deeds somewhere or other, you know.'

Noel made a choking sound.

'Is something the matter?' asked Olga innocently.

Noel glared up at the sky where a distant drone and a long vapour trail showed where yet another plane was passing overhead. 'You'll be saying next they blow steam out of their noses like those dragons you told us about once.'

'I'm very glad you mentioned that,' said Olga. 'They're what's known as guinea-pig trails. Every time you see them it means there's a guinea-pig going somewhere.

'If you hadn't mentioned it I might have forgotten to tell you. You see, I may not be able to fly myself any more, but that's one thing I *can* still do – make trails.'

And so saying, she hurried into her bedroom, took up her position behind the window, drew in the deepest breath she could manage, and blew out as hard as she could.

'Well I never!' said Graham, as Olga's window went misty. 'Would you believe it?'

'*I* wouldn't have,' said Fangio. 'But I do now.'

Olga hurried out into her dining-room. 'How about you?' she called to Noel. 'Do you believe it now?' But Noel was already disappearing over the fence. He'd seen a squirrel and that was much more interesting.

'Goodnight,' said Graham. 'I shall sleep well after that.'

'Hear! Hear!' agreed Fangio. 'See you next spring.'

'Goodnight,' said Olga. She gazed after the other two as they went on their way. 'If you have any trouble getting to sleep, try counting guinea-pigs,' she called. 'They go over every day. I think I can hear another one coming now.'

'Oh, we shan't,' came a sleepy voice, barely

recognizable as Graham's. 'Not after that. Stories make you sleepy.'

With that remark Olga agreed wholeheartedly. In fact, she went straight back into her bedroom and closed her eyes. Within moments she was fast asleep. But not for the winter, only until it was time for Sunday morning breakfast and another day.